LIES OF MURK

EVA CHASE

BOUND TO THE FAE

1

Sylas

hen I first glance toward the platform by the Heart's pulsing light and notice that Talia is no longer perched on its edge, I don't think much of it. No doubt she's rejoined the dancing or stepped aside to chat with her dressmaker friend from our pack. Astrid will be watching over her, as will Corwin's coterie.

I amble through the crowd of revelers, still in a celebratory mood myself. Just a couple of hours ago, I finally claimed the extraordinary human woman who's won my heart as my official mate—alongside my two cadre-chosen who've earned her affections as well, and with the approval of her Unseelie soul-twined mate. The peace between Corwin's winter realm and ours of summer feels more solid than it's ever been.

I'm far from the only one wanting to celebrate both

those things. It seems as if the whole of the fae world is laughing and whirling on the field around me and in the surrounding forest, moving with the rollicking music. Their eager toasts lace the air with the scent of duskapple wine. And why shouldn't they be as happy as I am?

Whitt draws up beside me, tipping a wine glass of his own to his mouth. My spymaster taps my arm with his elbow and cranes his neck to peer through the crowd. "Where's our mighty mate gotten to?"

"I'm not entirely sure." I scan the revelers myself, my deadened eye adding the occasional after-image, both fleeting and vague, to the scene before me. Talia should be easy to pick out with the vivid pink and purple dye in her hair, a hue few even true-blooded fae could match, but I'm not seeing her.

She could have gone off into the forest, but a twang of uneasiness breaks through the joy inside me. At the same moment, Corwin appears at my side. The winter arch-lord rarely shows much emotion, so the obvious distress on his bronze-brown face puts all my senses on the alert in an instant.

"Have you seen Talia?" he asks in a low, urgent tone, his gaze flicking over the fae around us. "I wasn't focused on our bond, so I'm not sure exactly where she was, but all of a sudden my impression of her vanished completely."

Whitt stiffens. "She's *gone*?"

Before an even deeper horror can grip me, Corwin shakes his head. "She must be alive and clearly not in any conscious distress. The bond is still *there*. I just can't sense her on the other end. It's similar to when she's sleeping and not dreaming, although often I can pick up a bit of her emotional state even then. And she wouldn't have fallen into sleep in a snap like that."

"She was sitting on the platform just a few minutes ago," I say, moving to weave through the crowd. Perhaps we'll find some sign of what became of her there. "Did you notice nothing at all before she disappeared? There was no pain or panic?"

Corwin and Whitt follow me. The raven shifter's mouth twists. "I caught a brief jolt of what felt like confusion and fear, but it was so abrupt I didn't have time to reach out or study it all that carefully. I caught it and immediately focused on her presence, and she'd already gone blank."

"That doesn't bode well." Cold apprehension winds through my body.

At the platform, we find no signs of any kind of scuffle or of where Talia might have gone from here. As we examine the area, August catches up with us. He looked so jovial the last time I saw him just minutes ago, but his frown now shows he's noticed our change in mood.

"What's wrong?" he asks, his substantial muscles flexing across his broad shoulders. "Did something happen to Talia?"

"That's what we're trying to determine," Whitt says in a tense voice so unlike his usual carefree tone that I know he's on the verge of panic himself.

"We need to find Astrid," I say. "She's always kept a

close eye on Talia." As we should have been too. I just hadn't imagined anything could happen to her during this gathering with so many of us who care about her so close by. Guilt congeals in my gut alongside my worries.

Corwin makes a gesture, and within moments, his coterie woman Zelpha is at his side. She takes in our expressions and knits her brow. "Is there a problem?"

"Talia's missing," Corwin says. "She was here by the platform just a little while ago. Did you see where she went from there?"

The brawny woman's eyes widen. "I was glancing over at her now and then, and she seemed fine. But I haven't seen her in... maybe ten minutes? A little scuffle broke out between two men near me who must have had too much wine, and I was busy making sure they didn't come to fatal blows. I'll start searching the woods for her—and check with the rest of the coterie if I cross paths with them."

"We could make an announcement," August says, but he sounds doubtful. We both know that if we make it clear to all the fae celebrating around us that something's happened to the human woman they've begun to revere, the festivities will turn chaotic in an instant.

"Let's see what we can piece together on our own before we cause a mass panic," I say. "Having all of the fae here upset might make it harder to determine what happened rather than easier."

My eyes catch on Astrid's gray hair and wiry form near the opposite end of the platform. I hurry over to the newest of my cadre-chosen, and she heads toward me when she notices me coming. "Is Talia with you?" she asks with obvious hope. "I lost track of her for a moment."

Blast it. I can't give her any relief. "So have we, and from her soul-twined mate's impressions, we have reason to believe she's been incapacitated. Did you see her leaving the platform?"

Astrid's expression darkens with worry. "No. As soon as you went over to the refreshment table, I was keeping her in my line of sight. But then one of the dancers stumbled into me and knocked the feet right out from under me, and a few of us fell in a jumble..." She grimaces, rubbing her elbow where I can already tell a bruise is forming. "By the time I managed to get up, she'd moved. I haven't seen her since."

My apprehension is expanding by the second. I can't shake the growing suspicion that it's unnaturally convenient that our colleagues who would have been watching over Talia were all suddenly diverted shortly after we left her side.

"Make inquiries," I tell her. "Discreetly, but we want to know which way she went and whether anyone was with her."

Astrid nods with a jerk of her head. She heads back into the crowd, stopping to murmur to fae here and there.

Corwin appears to spot something farther away in the crowd. He beckons for us to follow him toward one of his other coterie members, an older man whose name I believe is Verik, who I assume Zelpha brought in on the search. He's standing near Donovan and one of my colleague's cadre-chosen.

Donovan's forehead is furrowed. "You're looking for Talia?" the younger arch-lord says. "Jagan saw her heading into the woods a few minutes ago."

His cadre man nods and motions to the woods to the south. "She was walking with Kyo, one of our pack-kin. I'm sure Kyo wouldn't have meant or done her any harm. She's always spoken highly of Talia and her generosity in healing our curse."

"Then perhaps something befell both of them." I set off in the direction he indicated, knowing the other men will follow me.

As my chief warrior, August pushes a little ahead. At the edge of the forest, he scents the air and then drops into wolf form to lope between the trees. When I follow suit, I catch a slight hint of Talia's sap-sweet smell in the air. It urges me onward.

Whitt's wolf bounds through the woods a few feet to my left. A rustle of feathers tells me Corwin and perhaps his coterie man have taken flight in their raven forms. If Talia's been taken beyond these woods, they'll spot her faster than we Seelie can. But if it's only been a matter of minutes, we may find her just as quickly here on the ground.

Her scent thickens just enough to lead us toward Donovan's pack village. We leave the last of the reveling fae behind, and August stops with a bark of alarm several paces ahead of me. He straightens up into his usual shape and immediately kneels by a crumpled figure.

My pulse stutters with a jolt of alarm. I dash the last short distance to him, but it isn't Talia's smell that fills my nose, though I still catch traces of her essence around. The woman slumped at the base of the tree is old and fae.

As I shift out of my wolf, both Whitt and Donovan come up beside me. August is murmuring with his hand over the woman's forehead. After a moment, her eyelids flutter. She stares up at him and then jerks into a sitting position. "What am I doing here? What happened?"

Donovan crouches down next to August, his tone urgent but full of compassion. "That's what we're hoping to find out, Kyo. One of my cadre-chosen saw you walking this way with Lady Talia. What were the two of you talking about?"

"Lady Talia?" The woman's puzzled expression makes my heart sink. "I—I don't think I've seen her since the ceremony. I went back to my house to fetch a shawl—the night brings a chill to these old bones more often than not —and…" She frowns. "That's the last thing I remember: walking up to my house. Lady Talia certainly wasn't there." Her gaze darts around us, concern flashing across her wrinkled face. "Is she all right?"

I don't sense any hint of pretence in her. She honestly doesn't know.

Restraining a growl, I let loose my wolf once more. I'll be more likely to pick up Talia's trail with my canine nose given full rein.

I prowl through the forest with all my senses on the alert. There are whiffs of her scent here and there in this spot and along the trail she must have walked to reach here—but nothing in any other direction. She didn't touch anything, with her feet or any other part of her, after she arrived in this part of the forest. Which means she was most likely carried off.

By *whom*?

Other than the scents of my companions and the old fae woman, I don't pick up any indication of another presence that passed through. My deadened eye refuses to offer me any glimpses beyond the ordinary, no matter how I urge it to. Clenching my fangs, I dip my nose even lower, drag the air even deeper into my lungs. There *has* to be something. She couldn't utterly disappear.

Whitt and August pad between the trees nearby. Donovan continues talking with his pack-kin in quiet tones, but I can tell he isn't getting anything more useful from her. With a hoarse caw, Corwin's raven alights on a branch near us and cocks his head. He doesn't appear to have any news either.

Then, some distance from the spot where we found Kyo, the faintest hint of something bitter touches my nostrils. I freeze, weaving my head until the smell catches just a little more in my nose. No sniff around that area brings more of it to my awareness, but my fangs are already clenched. I've tasted enough to know what it is.

I spring up onto my feet, every muscle braced. Whitt and August hustle over, shedding their wolves as they come. Corwin drops down to join us, shifting in an instant.

My voice comes out just shy of a snarl. "There was a rat here. It covered its tracks well, but not perfectly. We must find it and whatever other Murk vermin slunk here with it as quickly as possible. Return to the celebration and send off every fae who's able-bodied and still has enough of their wits about them to seek out the mangy rodents."

Whitt's eyes flashed the moment I said "rat." He springs off into the forest, racing toward the field around the Heart with August swiftly overtaking him. As I move to join them, Donovan catches my arm. I'm so furious I nearly snap his nose off.

"Sylas," he says hastily, with a hint of apology, "what would the rats want with Talia?"

That is the question, isn't it?

My thoughts trip over all the minor intrusions of the Murk into our lives over the past few months. Vandalism and a murder at Aerik's castle. The destruction of several homes in the Unseelie's summer fae settlement and a woman who warned of more to come. A plume of toxic, iron-laced smoke, guarded by a man who lunged at Talia when she tried to put it out.

The story I heard from Aerik just a few days ago of how he stumbled on Talia's town in the first place… hunting down a rat.

Have the Murk been sneaking through our lives even more than that without us realizing it? Have they had some interest in Talia all along? I still don't fully understand, but clearly I should have acted on what I did know sooner, more thoroughly.

I should have never given the slightest opportunity for one of those vermin to get anywhere near my mate.

"I don't know," I reply, the rage mixing with my guilt into a searing ache within my chest. "To disrupt our celebration? To send us into a panic? Whatever their reason, it can't be good—for us or her."

Then I hurtle after my cadre, hoping my error won't cost me the woman I love. Because if the rats wrench her beyond the boundaries of the Mists into their haunts in the human world before we find her, we may never find her at all.

2

Talia

As I emerge from sleep, the first thing I register is the smell. Or smells, really, because there are an awful lot of them colliding and clashing, most of which I'd never expect to find in my nose when I wake up.

Sylas's castle smells of warmed wood, and Corwin's carries a faint mineral scent. Both of those mingle together in my bedroom in our new joint castle. Now, I'm assaulted by a mix of bitter metal, acrid smoke, and a thick mildewy odor that has me recoiling before I'm even fully conscious.

My muscles tense, and a twinge runs through my scalp down the back of my head. And inside my head…

Inside my head there's a horrible blank.

The emptiness echoes from behind my forehead down to my gut. I have no sense of Corwin at all, not even the dulled impression of a barrier between us like when he's fully raised his walls against our connection. There've been times he's shut me out before, but this is the first time I've ever felt completely detached from him since the moment our soul-twined bond sprang into existence like a lightning bolt down the center of my being.

My pulse stutters, and my eyes pop open. I shove myself upward, my thoughts spinning. My mind is still blurred with the unnatural sleep I'm shaking off. Staring at the scene around me, I have trouble processing what I'm seeing.

I'm lying on a thin blanket on a tiled floor in a corner of an immense room, larger than even the ballrooms in the fae castles. It's split in three, with the tiled floor I'm sprawled on stretching the full length to the distant wall, falling away into some sort of chasm several feet from me, and then rising into another span of tiles on the other side. At either end of the chasm, an opening to a dark tunnel looms. Pipes, wiring, and metal beams crisscross the dim ceiling high above me.

Scattered across the tiled sections stand little shacks made of a hodgepodge of metal sheets, wooden boards, plastic siding, and all sorts of debris from car tires to tattered scarves. Figures are moving between those buildings, ducking in and out of them, and climbing up and down makeshift ladders along the length of the chasm. Some of them appear to be working, hauling sacks or crates of supplies or fixing materials together into objects I can't identify. Others are simply sprawled in small groups chatting with each other.

Assorted sounds, from rustling to clanking, emanate from all around me. I suspect the smoky smell is drifting from a large, battered steel contraption partway along my side of the room, which whirs and growls with sputterings of sparks. Most of the light streams from flickering panels fixed at seemingly random intervals along the ceiling.

None of the figures are all that close to me. A few of those nearby have glanced my way and then averted their gazes. My voice stays locked in my throat. I'm not sure whether I should call out to them or avoid them.

Where the hell *am* I? What happened to me? I remember—we had the ceremony for me to take Sylas, Whitt, and August officially as my mates. There was music and food and dancing—an old woman from Donovan's pack wanted to give me a gift—a fae man appeared out of nowhere and knocked me out with some kind of magic.

My hand jerks to my waist, instinctively reaching for my knife for protection, but of course I wasn't wearing my usual belt with this lovely dress for the ceremony. In the same instant, the man from my memory steps into my view, so easily he's probably been watching me from just behind me the entire time. My entire body goes rigid, bracing to defend myself.

I still have the bronze bracelet Sylas gave me, smooth against my wrist. If I have to, I might be able to transform it into some kind of blade in time to fend him off… or at least make attacking me a little harder.

The man peers down at me with an air of mild disdain. In the wavering light, I can't tell what color his heavy-lidded eyes are, only that they're dark. Straight, straw-blond hair falls across his pale forehead. It points in a jagged line toward a long nose with a slight bump partway along its length as if it's been broken before.

There's nothing directly threatening in his casual stance, but the human-style collared shirt he's wearing is fitted enough to show the muscular definition in his well-built shoulders and chest. He isn't quite as brawny as Sylas or August, but there's no mistaking the strength he could wield if he chooses to. That he's *already* chosen to wield, against me.

If the magic he used wasn't enough confirmation, the ears with lightly pointed tips that poke from between the mussed strands of his hair confirm my original assumption. Despite his clothing and our surroundings, he's definitely some kind of fae.

"Looking for this?" he asks in the low, faintly hoarse voice that greeted me in the forest before he knocked me out. My gaze falls to his hand. He's dangling a circlet of gold and silver—

My crown. The crown my mates gave me at the end of the ceremony—to celebrate our union, the peace between the summer and winter realms, and everything I've done to help the fae on both sides of the border. I *wasn't* looking for it, hadn't even realized it was missing, but now that I see it in his grasp, my fingers itch to snatch it back.

But I have more important considerations first.

"Who are you?" I say, jerking my attention back to the fae man's face. "Where are we? Why did you bring me here?"

The man flicks the crown in a slow rotation around his

fingers. He ignores all but my last question. "My king felt it was time you met him. I'll bring you to him now."

His *king*? I don't understand any of this. I open my mouth to press for more answers—but a twitching motion by the man's leg catches my eyes, and my voice dies.

A long, slender shape, sinuous and covered with a thin sheen of pale beige fur, grazes his calf and then tucks back behind him. I gape for a second before comprehension dawns on me. Even then, my gaze darts toward the other, more distant figures throughout the room to double check.

Between the distance, the erratic light, and my initial daze, that one detail didn't fully sink into my mind when I scanned the space before. Now that I'm looking for it, my gut twists at how obvious it is. A woman climbing out of the chasm there has a similar but dark shape slanting along her leg to twine around her ankle. A man on the other side has a gray one looped around the leg of the table he's poised at.

Not ropes or cables or any separate tool. With each glimpse, my understanding solidifies.

They all have tails. Long, tapered, lightly furred tails. I've never seen fae with tails before, but if this is their home, why shouldn't this kind flaunt them like the wolf shifters can let out their fangs and claws, like the ravens can unfurl their wings? A fresh wave of panic washes over me.

I've been taken by the Murk. The rat-shifting fae despised by both the Seelie and the Unseelie; the fae best known for playing vicious pranks and taking malicious satisfaction out of hurting both humans and other fae.

I cringe back against the wall instinctively. When I focus on the man in front of me again, there's something hard in his face that wasn't there before. He motions to me with his empty hand. "Let's go. There's no point in delaying it."

My hands press against the cool tiles. "I don't want to go anywhere except home."

"Well, too bad for you that's not in the cards. You can walk, or I can carry you. Either way, we're going *now*."

His voice stays low, but I can tell from the edge that creeps into it that he means it. He's more than half a foot taller than me, and he's got fae strength and magic on his side. There's no way I'm beating him in a struggle, bronze bangle or not. I weigh my options for a few seconds and decide I'd rather go on my own two feet than have him lay one hand on me, if I'm going to end up going either way.

I push myself upright. The silky fabric of the dress my friend Harper made me for the ceremony swishes around me. It's marked with dirt and grease stains now, but I still feel a little elegant in it.

I'm Lady Talia, mate to four of the most powerful fae alive, and I will meet my fate with dignity—and as much defiance as I can manage.

The fae man ushers me to a set of narrow stairs built against the side of the chasm by the nearest tunnel. I walk slowly, catching my balance on my initially wobbly legs. The ache of my recent wound—dealt by one of this man's Murk kin—wakes up in my thigh, and I'd limp anyway because of my warped foot, but I keep my pace as steady as possible.

It isn't much of a drop, no more than five or six feet down. As I pick my way down the steps, I take in the metal bars and slats that run along the concrete floor of the chasm. Recognition clicks in my mind, taking the setting immediately from alien to familiar.

"This is a subway station," I say, the revelation slipping out of me before I can catch it.

"Not anymore," my kidnapper says. "The humans abandoned it, and we reclaimed it."

I guess I should be glad that my situation can't be made even worse by a speeding subway train rumbling down those tracks. It's hard to feel very optimistic as I limp along beside the fae man into the dank, shadowy tunnel.

Small, furry bodies scuttle past us in the darkness, and I can't tell whether they're Murk in rat form or regular rats. Maybe a mix of both. More haphazard structures jut from the walls here and there, little more than vague shapes to my eyes. My escort strides along with an impatient air, navigating the darkness without hesitation.

The mildew smell gets thicker as we walk deeper into the tunnel. Twice, a small light flares in the distance against the thicker blackness. As my eyes adjust, I notice a dull orange glow seeping across the tracks up ahead. It brightens as we near it. A quiver ripples through the air, prickling over my skin with an unsettling erraticness. I can't help rubbing my bare arms.

As we come up on the glowing area, the dissonant

hum of energy intensifies. The wall falls away to reveal a deep alcove about the size of the grand meeting room in the Bastion of the Heart back in the summer realm. Tailed fae stand in a line leading up to a large dais at the far end, which holds a tall throne.

The throne appears to have been constructed out of the rubble of the destroyed section of wall, packed together with clay. The woman at the front of the line is speaking to the man sitting in that high seat. A glowing mass behind him is what's emitting the orange light, which catches off his pale, spiky hair. Three other figures lounge on the dais around him with a vaguely menacing air.

At the sight of my kidnapper, the man waves the woman and the rest of the line away. "Return in an hour," he barks in a tone that manages to sound both terse and flippant.

As the other fae scatter, my escort leads me toward the throne.

Closer, I can see that any color in this man's hair is only reflected from the quaking light behind him, which twitches in time with the erratic energy now trickling right through my flesh. The narrow spikes along his scalp are pure white. But that can't be a reflection of his age, because the face they frame is smooth and sharp-edged without a hint of wrinkles. His yellow eyes track our every step. A white-furred tail swings casually over the arm of the throne.

Like my kidnapper, this man is dressed in human clothes: tight dark jeans and a satiny shirt with a blue-and-maroon pattern, the collar gaping open to show off the wiry muscles and dappling of scars on his lean chest. He's barefoot, his narrow toes tipped with claws like the ones that slashed open my thigh. They gleam on his fingertips too. When we stop in front of him, one more feature captures my attention.

His ears. At first I mistook them for more tufts of his spiky hair. They're pointed as sharply as Whitt's, and Whitt is nearly true-blooded.

From what the other fae have told me about how much the Murk have mingled with humans to bear their children, I didn't think any of the rat shifters had that much fae blood left in them. But then, there are obviously a lot of things the Seelie and Unseelie don't know about their greatest enemies.

The Murk who must be the king my kidnapper mentioned and the... guards? poised around him on the dais watch us silently. My kidnapper dips into a rough bow and nudges me half a step ahead of him. "I brought her to you as soon as she woke up."

"Thank you, Madoc," the king says in the same tone as before, careless and yet brusque. I hold myself stiffly still as he looks me over from head to toes and back again. "Well, they have draped you in a lot of pretty wrapping, haven't they? I hear that you've even won over not just the man your soul was bound to but three others besides—and to the point of them declaring you their mate. You've outdone my expectations. Excellent work."

I blink at him, my stomach balling tighter. "I don't

understand. What are you talking about? Why did you have me brought here?"

He shrugs, a cool glint lighting in his yellow eyes. "Everything important about you came from me. You've served the purpose you were intended for. And now you'll serve me by being here while those idiotic fae of the seasons scramble around in desperation." He grins, revealing a row of crooked teeth.

His words repeat in my head. *Everything important about you came from me.* A thicker chill coils around me. "I've never even met you."

He cackles with apparent glee and stretches out in his throne, tossing one leg over the arm next to his swaying tail. "Oh, little girl, you met me before you met almost anyone. You didn't really think you gained the power to cure curses and win an arch-lord's soul all by yourself, did you?"

My lips part, but no sound comes out. I close my mouth, swallow, and finally stammer, "But how—how could *you*—?"

"I stole you when you weren't even a day old," the king says, his gaze wandering away from me as if the story barely matters to him. "Swapped you out for one of our own infants cloaked in an illusion. Your dimwitted parents never noticed. Then when I'd worked my magic, I swapped you back. You already held the kernel for the rest to sprout. I planted it in your grandmother, urged it on in your mother—these things take time to fully bloom, you know. We've been playing a long game here."

A rush of nausea flips my stomach. Nuldar the sage

said something about that, didn't he? That my grandmother had met a fae who planted the seed… We assumed he meant that my grandfather had fae blood in him, that it'd caused my powers somehow. But it wasn't that—it was this spiteful villain working some kind of magic on my family?

Even as the pieces click together, every cell in my body balks at accepting what he says as truth. I grope for some kind of argument. "But—we went to a pool that shows the past—I asked about when I was born, and when I first met the fae—it showed—"

"Only darkness, right?" The king's gaze focuses on me again, his lips curving into a nasty smirk. "Oh, I know the tricks the fae of the seasons have up their sleeves, and I matched them with my own. I stole you in total darkness, and in total darkness you remained until you were returned home. Nothing for them to unravel with their visions and magic ponds."

Nuldar's creaking voice comes back to me. *She started in darkness. Then she came into the light.*

No. This can't be possible. A tremor courses through me, leaving me shaking despite my best efforts to hold myself steady. "But *why*…"

"I'd have thought that'd be obvious. You have a lot of experience with the viciousness of those fae, don't you? Keeping you half-starved in a cage? Mangling your body? Attacking you at every turn? And you their supposed savior." He shakes his head in mock disbelief. "They've spent millennia trying to crush us Murk, shunning us, savaging us, killing us as often as they can. It was time they got not just a taste but a whole banquet of their own medicine. And you delivered it for me."

One of the fae beside the throne speaks up, his voice cruel in its amusement. "We'll see them all on their knees soon, Orion!"

Orion. Some distant part of my mind files that away as the king's name. The rest is still reeling, but he doesn't wait for me to reply.

"It's all worked out perfectly," he says. "I laid the curse while I placed the seed of the temporary cure in your family line all those decades ago. Drive the wolves wild, freeze the ravens feather by feather—what could be more fitting?"

My jaw goes slack. It shouldn't surprise me after everything he's already said, but still—the enormity— "*You* placed the curse on both of the realms?" The curse that's been afflicting the Seelie and Unseelie for... for decades, like he said.

The curse that's been steadily growing more horrible until I showed up with just the right components to cure it. How else could he have managed that if he wasn't responsible for the curse itself? But I still don't understand *how*.

Orion's lips pull into a mocking sneer. "They never suspected, did they? So sure of themselves and so dismissive of us. Now they've seen our power, and before much longer they'll know who orchestrated their downfall." He chuckles to himself. "The worse the curse got, the more frantic they all got. And then you appeared as if out of nowhere, a beacon of hope. With a little encouragement, we had them all seeing you as their blessed savior, the one figure standing between them and despair. And now I've yanked you away from them."

He has. Away from *all* of them, more completely than I'd ever imagined was possible.

My voice comes out thin. "My—my soul-twined bond. I can't feel—"

Orion snorts. "Oh, we couldn't have you drawing your supposed beloved here, could we? Since my magic created the spark for that connection, I can shield it well enough. He won't reach you while you're within my home."

He isn't saying the bond is gone completely. Maybe there are some limits to what his powers can accomplish.

But that doesn't help me while I'm stuck here.

I swallow thickly. "And what happens next?"

"Oh, I'll let them stew in their misery and panic for a little while, and then we'll sweep in and claim all the Mists for ourselves. I'm sure you'll continue to be a useful tool throughout that mission. And you'll get to watch all those who mistreated you laid low."

Orion speaks as if I should be happy. I wrap my arms around myself, finally getting enough control to stop shaking, but nausea is still clamped around my gut. My thoughts whirl, shying away from accepting anything he's said as the truth.

I thought—I thought the Heart *had* blessed me, to push back the curse, to bring the realms together.

The Murk are known for mischief, for playing tricks on people. Maybe he's just trying to make me believe all this so he can manipulate me somehow, or simply for his own amusement. I don't have to accept his story at face value.

None of it really makes sense, after all. The Murk are supposed to be the weakest of all the fae by a huge margin, living so far from the Heart, constantly breaking its laws. How could they have managed to orchestrate a curse so massive it affects every one of those he calls the "fae of the seasons," controlling their behavior, even killing them?

"I don't believe you," I say, raising my chin. "You couldn't do even half of that when you can barely draw on the Heart's power at all."

Orion laughs again, but for the first time true hostility darkens his expression even as his eyes gleam brighter. "Oh, I don't have any need for the Heart of the Mists, little girl. I made my own." He swings his arm toward the stuttering mass of orange light that fills the space at the back of the platform.

I stare at it and then at him again. "You *what?*"

His lips peel back over his uneven teeth. "I made my own Heart. A Heart for the Murk, to fuel our powers by our own rules. With every bit of confusion and agony we provoke, it grows stronger, fiercer. Just in the past few hours I can feel it beating even more furiously. And that's all thanks to you."

3

Madoc

The woman hasn't touched the plate of food one of Orion's servants brought her. The scraps scavenged from the homes and eateries above us probably don't compare to the elaborate feasts she enjoyed in the castles of the Mists, so maybe she thinks she's too good to bother with the stuff.

Orion follows my gaze and pops a grape into his mouth. "If she wants to starve herself, she can give it her best shot. I doubt she'll keep it up for very long."

Having watched Talia from afar many times over the past several months, I'm not so sure about that. The memory comes to me of seeing her poised within one of those floating carriages, her knife at her own throat, holding herself hostage to ensure she wasn't taken captive. She meant it. I could taste her resolve even at a distance.

But I keep my mouth shut on the matter. There's no

point in arguing with the king unless you're sure it's something worth pissing him off over.

Something about the way she's sitting hunched in the corner of the throne room, the skirt of her fancy but tarnished dress tucked around her slim legs, niggles at me. Her usually vibrant hair droops around her face. She hasn't let any tears fall, but there's a burning in her gaze that suggests a deep anguish.

Which is to be expected. *I* expected it. It shouldn't bother me.

It might be just that the pose reminds me a little too much of the one glimpse I was able to get of her in that summer fae Aerik's cage. As if *we've* caged her, even though there's nothing holding her in that spot.

"She doesn't seem particularly enthusiastic about the plan," I say, keeping my tone carefully mild—and quiet, even though there's little chance her human ears could pick up our conversation from over there near the tracks.

"It's shock," Orion says. "Humans have such fragile constitutions, don't they? She'll get over it, and then she'll realize that I've given her a great gift. She's been instrumental in bringing down all those haughty bastards in the Mists. From what you and my other spies reported, most of them have been horrible to her. It'll just take a little time for the deeper understanding to sink in."

"Of course." I roll the tension out of my shoulders and consider the other fae lounging in our king's company. One of the men meets my gaze with narrowed eyes. The woman who's most frequently been warming Orion's bed these days shoots me a lascivious grin I'm sure is intended as a taunt rather than an invitation.

Even if she were inviting me, I know better than to lay my hands on anything my king has claimed as his own.

Most of Orion's closest colleagues are several decades if not centuries older than me. They established themselves at his side when I was still a young man proving my worth. Some of them had a hand in the tests of my loyalty and determination. I'm never quite sure whether they're happy I passed those tests or annoyed to have one more fae sharing access to the king's ear. Who knows what they say to him during the long stretches when I'm away overseeing his plans in the Mists?

But if they've snarked about me, it hasn't seemed to affect Orion's opinion. I've shown how far I'm willing to go for him. Every time he's called for support, I've stepped up first. He knows he can count on me.

And the others don't like each other any more than they like me or I like them. Whatever sort of court our Murk king has, it's a cutthroat one. But it needs to be if we're going to carve our way through those we hate even more to bring our people to the home they deserve.

My gaze slides back to Talia. She's pushed her hair back from her face and is tentatively scanning the room, her eyes warily alert.

"Should I assign guards to monitor her movements?" I ask. "Or will we be limiting the parts of the Refuge she has access to?"

Orion shrugs, his tail flicking in the air. "All the entrances are well-sealed. Not even a fae could get past them easily without knowing the right tricks, let alone a human. I see no need to waste our energy keeping that close an eye on her. We'll give her plenty of rope and see what she does with it."

The hint of a smirk that touches his lips makes the hairs on the back of my neck rise, but I tamp down my apprehension. Talia will learn quickly enough not to cross any of the fae here, especially Orion. She *has* to learn that. This is her life now, and she'd better get used to it.

We're giving her more freedom than those bastards in the Mists did, despite all the rhetoric they've spewed at her that I can tell she's bought into. The horror on her face when she noticed my tail…

I shake that memory off too. "Would you have me return to the Mists and observe how the fae of the seasons are reacting to losing her?"

Orion shakes his head. "Oh, no, Madoc. I have a much more important task for you." He tips his head toward the woman. "I may not be concerned about her escaping, but it will be much more fun digging in the knife if we can decimate those puffed-up pricks with their savior on our side. And she's been so close with their leaders, I'm sure she knows plenty of things we'd want to know too."

My trepidation returns. I smooth it out of my tone. "What would you have me do, then?"

"I have to spell it out?" My king rolls his eyes. "You've watched her more than anyone else here. You know her well enough. Cozy up to her, win her over, and coax whatever information you can about the workings of the arch-lords' courts out of her. If you can lure her into your bed as well, so much the better."

A twinge shoots through my abdomen down to my groin. "You want me to seduce her."

"Wouldn't that be the perfect cherry on the sundae?" Orion says, idly tossing another grape. "Transfer her loyalty from those she calls her mates to you. I can't imagine it'd be that hard, considering how many of the idiots she gave herself over to. And it shouldn't be any great trial for you. She's easy enough on the eyes."

None of the other men she's welcomed into her heart and her bedroom have been reviled rat shifters, though. Her distrust of the ravens was only overcome by the soul-twined bond Orion manufactured. I don't have any benefit of that—not that I'd want her poking around in my head.

But he isn't wrong that she's pretty enough. I've studied that face from afar enough times to know it becomes outright stunning when lit up with a full smile. She just isn't likely to aim any of those smiles at me.

"I'm the one who took her," I point out. "She has enough animosity against the Murk in general—no doubt right now she hates me even more than the rest."

Orion waves off my subtle objection. "Then consider it a challenge to grow your skills. She feels alone and frightened. She'll be eager for an excuse to cling on to someone. Make yourself that someone."

He turns away to speak to Grigor at his other side about something to do with the scavenging runs. It's a clear dismissal. A prickle runs down my spine with the sense that he expects me to show I'm up to the task immediately. If I hesitate, he'll question why.

It would be awfully satisfying to know we've conquered the fae of the seasons by turning the woman they've celebrated so much against them, wouldn't it?

I step off the dais and amble over to Talia, leaving a few feet of distance when I stop. Her gaze darts up over me, and her whole body tenses, her jaw clenching. She automatically assumes I'm here to hurt her somehow, when I brought her all this way without a single injury other than a few stains on her elaborate dress.

She bought into the other fae's accusations about the Murk so easily. I'll happily start by tearing down as many of those lies as I can. What can I offer her that'll upend her misconceptions about us?

I crouch down so I'm level with her. I need to at least get her talking with me first. This won't be something I can rush, no matter how easy Orion thinks it'll be.

"Not hungry?" I ask with a motion toward her plate.

Talia glances down at the food and then at me. "I don't trust that I'll feel better rather than worse after I eat whatever you've given me."

She's sharp enough to have learned at least that much about faerie food. I let out a light chuckle. "There's nothing enchanted there. This is all pure mortal food. We don't often indulge in faerie delicacies down here."

"And why should I believe you?"

"Why would we want to get you drunk or high?" I ask. "If Orion wanted you not in your right mind, he could arrange that much more quickly with his magic. He doesn't, though. You're one of us now. You've helped us more than most of the fae around me. He might not show it all that well, but he appreciates your contribution. I certainly do."

Talia's shoulders stiffen even more. "I didn't make that 'contribution' on purpose."

"And that isn't your fault. There's no way you could have known. You didn't betray anyone, if that's what's bothering you."

She slowly unfolds her pose, settling her legs on the ground and drawing her back up straighter. I can't suppress the flicker of admiration both at the admittedly appealing curves hugged by the fabric of her dress and the studied defensiveness in her stance.

Before, she was mindlessly shielding herself. Now she's prepared for some kind of battle.

A battle with me. I haven't made any progress yet.

"I don't want to be here," she says. "I want to go home. But obviously you're not going to let me do that. You can't expect me to be happy about it."

"That's fair." I will my voice to soften, to shed any irritation I might feel at her devotion to the fae of the seasons, as if *they're* the victims in the grand scheme of things. "Orion's said that you can roam anywhere you'd like in the King's Refuge here. You might not be happy, but I could help you find a spot where you'd be more comfortable. We could even construct you a house of your own."

She studies me for a long moment, still wary but

taking in my words. "I don't think there's anywhere here I'll be comfortable."

"You haven't seen much of the place yet, or given it much of a chance." I hold up my hands. "I realize you're probably not ready to hear this yet, so I'll just lay it out there and you can make of it what you will. The stories you've heard about the Murk are just that—stories. Told by those who've always wanted to keep us beneath them, who need excuses to justify how they've pushed us aside. We have craftspeople. We have artists. We bleed and love and sometimes even cry more than any of the fae currently living in the Mists can bring themselves to do. No one here intends to harm you. I'll be patient with you, but whenever you're ready, there's so much I can show you."

Talia's expression has shuttered. She's definitely not ready now. "No, thank you," she says firmly. "I just want you to leave me alone."

"I can do that too. But I'll be easy to find if you need any help later on."

I back away, returning to the edge of the dais. She might not be won over, but at least I planted a few seeds of my own—doubt about the overblown tales the bastards of the seasons have filled her head with, curiosity about everything the Murk truly are.

It's a start. Orion took several decades growing his seeds that've come into fruition in her. He can allow me a week or two.

And I've scored one minor victory already. I don't watch her overtly, but from the corner of my eye, I see her reach toward her plate and bring a grape to her lips.

4

Talia

D own in the subway tunnel, it's impossible to tell what time of day it is—or whether it's even day at all. The only light comes from the flickering panels and the erratically pulsing glow of what Orion called the Murk's Heart.

So I'm not sure how many hours I've been hunched in the corner at the far end of the huge alcove from Orion's throne and his Heart, gathering myself. My breaths ebb and stutter, sometimes so shallow I start to feel dizzy. My heart skips beats, racing now and then sluggish and then skittering again, as uneven as the dissonant energy that's washing over me.

I want to get away from that unnatural thing, but where would I go? Would the Murk even let me wander around, like my kidnapper—Madoc—suggested, or are they just looking for an excuse to punish me even more?

Except they don't really seem to think they're punishing me in the first place. Their king talked as if I'd been part of some grand mission. The way he sneered when he talked about the fae of the seasons, maybe it's hard for him to imagine why anyone would want to go back to them.

No one has paid much attention to me since he stopped talking to me, other than the woman who brought me a plate of food with barely a glance my way. I forced myself to eat as much as I could stomach, knowing I have to keep my energy up, and nothing horrible has happened to me. Someone else snatched up the plate with my leftovers before I'd quite decided whether I could swallow more.

That was what feels like ages ago. My stomach is still knotted with tension, but one of those knots now aches of hunger. My throat has gone scratchy with thirst.

I don't see any obvious place to get a drink here, though, and I have to admit I'm scared to ask. Madoc left the throne room a little while ago. The only person still in this immense hollow that I've spoken to is the king himself, and the thought of going up to Orion again, of pleading for anything from him, makes my skin crawl.

Plenty of others are approaching him. A steady trickle of fae slink in and out of the throne room, all of them with the long, twitching tails that mark them as rats. Some bring small trinkets that he motions for them to add to a pile at the back of the dais. Some crouch low and make requests I can't hear from where I'm sitting. Others appear to be reporting to him about whatever activities they've been carrying out.

I should probably creep closer so I can overhear what they're saying, so I have a better idea what the Murk are up to and what I might do about it. But then I'd risk drawing Orion's attention again—and I'd be absorbing even more of that unsettling, erratic energy.

My gaze moves behind the king to the orange glow of the Murk's Heart. A tremor runs through my body, and my pulse starts thumping hard all over again. Can it be true that Orion managed to conjure a force that rivals the Heart of the Mists?

But then, how else could he have cast such a huge curse on all the summer and winter fae? From what my mates told me, it started out with only a mild effect: an hour of wolfish savagery, ravens falling ill but not dying. But as their distress grew, their pain fueled that awful thing and allowed Orion in turn to strengthen the curse so it got worse and worse... A horrible vicious cycle.

A cycle I'm a part of. *I* was one of the Murk's tricks, getting the Seelie's and Unseelie's hopes invested in me and then yanking me away from them. All the panic they must be feeling over my disappearance is only making the Murk more powerful.

I had no idea about any of this, but that fact doesn't lighten the guilt clamped around my lungs.

I only ever wanted to help the other fae, and instead I've set them up for even greater misery than they were facing before. And who knows what else, if Orion sees through his awful plans.

Gradually, through my horror and hunger, resolve gathers deep in my gut. I've been used as some sort of weapon against the place I've taken as my home, against the men I love more than anything, but there has to be a way I can undo some of the damage. I should find out everything I can about this place and what happens here, about Orion's sadistic plans and what else the Murk are up to. And then I have to find a way out of here so I can warn the fae back home.

I'm just stirring, stretching my limbs before I attempt to stand up and slip out into the tunnel, when Madoc strides back into the throne room. A couple of other Murk carrying large platters of food come in behind him. The spread they've brought looks like more of a meal than the collection of scraps I was given earlier. The creamy, buttery scent that reaches my nose makes my stomach gurgle. I tuck my arm around my belly as if I can hold in the sound.

Maybe Orion heard it from across the room—rat ears must be keen too—because he flicks his hand toward me. "Bring her. I'd dine with my human accomplice."

Madoc steps toward me and motions for me to follow. I straighten up tentatively, studying him.

He tried to reassure me when he spoke to me earlier, but I'm not sure why. He was pretty cold to me when I first woke up in this place. And he's the one who dragged me here to begin with.

If I've learned anything about the Murk, it's that you can't trust any of them, no matter how they appear.

I did want to find out more about what's happening

here, though, and who better to hear it from than the king and one of his right-hand men? As much as my instincts might be urging me to cringe away and huddle in a ball until the world rights itself, I know that's not going to get me anywhere.

I've faced all kinds of horrors before. Maybe none of them were quite as gut-wrenching as this one, but that doesn't mean I can't find my way through this too.

Keeping a careful distance from Madoc, I limp up to the dais. Orion eases off his throne to lean against its base with his legs sprawled out. His tail coils next to him. One of the servants sets the largest platter, which holds several plates, by his side. The other brings around plates to the fae who've lingered on the dais around him, who I'm guessing are among his inner circle.

Do Murk have cadres or coteries? Do they even have lords? I have no idea what the hierarchy here is other than Orion clearly rules over them all.

"Sit," he tells me briskly when I reach the dais. I sink onto the low platform with its scarred wooden slats where I can reach the platter without getting too close to him or any of the other fae. Madoc sits across from me. He waits until Orion grabs a handful of the fettucine that's giving off the creamy scent before reaching for what looks like a spring roll on one of the other plates.

Orion slops the pasta down on one of the empty plates the servants brought, licks the sauce off his hand without any hint of concern, and then picks up a fork to dig into the noodles. I watch Madoc take a bite of his spring roll and decide those must be decently safe. As delicious as the fettucine smells, I don't want to eat anything Orion's fingers have been in.

"Well," Orion says, peering at me, "you've been tucked away taking everything in for quite a while. What do you make of my kingdom?"

I take a bite of the spring roll to give me a chance to think while I'm chewing. A mix of pork and vegetable juices with a tang of spice washes over my tongue, and it's all I can do not to stuff the rest in my mouth all at once. It's not August-level cooking, but after the day I've had, it might as well be.

I clear my throat, and Madoc sets a bottle of water near me in offering. I guess it's not too hard to figure out that I'd be thirsty at this point. Orion takes a swig from a bottle of wine with a company label on it, obviously human made.

One thing I'll say for the Murk: they don't seem to be as disdainful of anything human as the other fae are. Maybe it's possible to end this war before it goes any further. I've managed to talk down fae who hated me and what I stood for before, managed to help negotiate a peace treaty between summer and winter when both wanted to strike out at the other.

If Orion's even a little more willing to take my thoughts into account than the fae of the seasons, I might have a chance at swaying him. I just need to know what he wants.

"You obviously have a lot of subjects working to carry out your plans," I say, measuring my words and keeping a close eye on his reactions. "It's amazing that you were able to create a Heart of your own. I can see why they'd follow you."

Orion grins, but there's a bit of a cruel edge to it. "You have some brains, then. Good. I doubt the fae of the seasons gave you much chance to use them."

My mates and at least a few of the others did, but I bite back a protest. I need to get on his good side if he's going to listen to me. "As a human among the fae, I've needed to use every skill I do have to survive."

He hums to himself and gulps down another forkful of pasta. "I suppose I didn't equip you as well as I could have. The cure and the mate bond—more unusualness than that and it might have become too suspicious. It does seem to have been enough to keep you alive."

"Yes," I say, hiding my surprise as well as I can. The cure and the mate bond aren't the only things unusual about me.

Does he not know about the fact that I can use true-name magic to some small extent? It doesn't sound like it. Could that talent have been an unintended and unknown side effect from the magic he worked on me?

If that's the case... I catch myself before my hand reaches for the bronze bracelet Sylas gave me. I have a secret weapon—in more than just the cuff I could transform into a blade. I can manipulate air and light a little bit too.

And I have Whitt's true name. I can't reach out to Corwin—the hollow of the muted bond digs into my chest—but I might be able to talk to another of my mates.

Tell him where I am, as much as I can determine that. Warn him.

I can't let that hope show on my face while Orion is watching me. I reach for what looks like a flaky yellow pastry that turns out to be filled with spiced ground beef and take a couple of bites before speaking again. "What are you going to do next, now that you've taken me back? You said you want to win the Mists for yourself?"

Orion nods with a careless wave of his hand. "Leave the scheming to us, little girl. It's our specialty, after all. If you want to stick it to the fae who treated you like dung, you're welcome to come along for the ride."

"What are you going to do to the summer and winter fae?" I venture. He can't mean to *kill* every one of them, can he?

"They'll meet the fate they deserve." The king peers at me more intently. "You're concerned about the ones you made your mates, aren't you? Don't bother yourself about them. You never mattered to them for more than what you could do for their people. You'll find much better companionship here, and none of *my* people will shun their own for associating with a human."

That last point might be true, but my throat closes up with a swell of emotion. I grasp the water bottle and take a swig from it just to have something to do with my hands.

I know my mates care about me far more than Orion believes. The ache of missing them brings a burn to the back of my eyes that I don't want the Murk king to see.

When I feel like I've gotten a better grip on myself, I let myself speak again. "I'm glad to hear that. But why do you want the Mists anyway? It seems like you've made yourself really at home here, and you have access to everything the human world offers." I motion to the food.

Orion snorts. "The Mists belong to the fae—they should belong to *all* the fae. They're where we truly belong. Oh, we'd still make our visits to this world when we wanted to, but we've been driven to the shadowy corners of our true home for too long. It's time those tables were turned and we claimed what should have been ours all along."

He throws back more wine and sets the bottle down with a thump. "Less about that subject while we're eating. It's giving me indigestion thinking about the bastards who've rooted us out."

"You seem to have accomplished a lot already," I say meekly, feeling awkward and like I'm going to swallow my tongue at the sort-of praise I'm offering this man. I'm not going to say I approve of his campaign against the fae of the seasons. I just want him to get the sense that I'm trying to understand. But it sounds like I've gotten as far as I can with him right now.

I finish my bottle of water and several more tidbits off the platters. The pangs of thirst and hunger fade away.

Orion lifts his chin toward me. "Don't feel you need to keep to this room. You're with us now—almost one of us. Don't disturb any of my people at work, but they shouldn't hassle you either."

"Okay," I say, wondering how true that actually is. A pinching low in my belly alerts me to a more pressing concern than exploration. "Um, are there some kind of bathrooms down here?"

Orion throws back his head with a laugh and motions to Madoc. "We aren't *animals*. Show her to the facilities."

Madoc gets up without a word. I follow him out of the throne room. As we walk along the dark subway tunnel to the next station over, I find myself trying not to stare at the bobbing of his tail with his steps. The question itches at me too much to keep it in, though.

"Why does everyone have their tails out all the time down here?" I ask. I haven't seen any of the Murk really *using* their tails, other than occasionally nudging items closer or holding them steady. "I know you don't have to." The Murk who attacked me by the burning patch that let off that awful iron smoke didn't have a tail, and I don't think Madoc did when I ran into him in the woods by the Heart.

"Orion likes us to embrace our full nature," Madoc says. "Too many of us have spent our whole lives hiding what we are so that we can get by without a backlash. He's trying to change that."

I sympathize with that reasoning more than I want to. I suppose, no matter how villainous many of the Murk have been, there are probably at least a few who don't have much interest in playing pranks or hurting anyone, who don't deserve the treatment they'd get as soon as anyone discovers what they are. I shouldn't assume they're all the same any more than it was fair for the summer and winter fae to assume the worst of each other.

I don't agree with Orion's intentions or the way he's

used me, but his people have raised him up as a king and supported his campaign for a reason.

That thought sticks with me as I duck through the doorway at one end of the station platform that Madoc points me to. Inside, I find a row of urinals on one side and stalls on the other.

My nose wrinkles at the faint smell of urine, but it's not as bad as I'd have expected if these aren't working at all. The toilet I use flushes. The fae must have managed to reconnect them to the sewer system, or else the people who abandoned this stretch of subway forgot to disconnect them in the first place.

I gaze at my reflection in the dingy mirror for a few seconds. My hair is rumpled, my face even paler than usual. I look almost as frail as I did right after Sylas rescued me from Aerik's cage.

How much of the pain I've been through did Orion plan, and how much was simply chance?

Madoc is waiting for me on the platform when I emerge. This station looks a lot like the one where I woke up, with structures that I guess are houses scattered all along the platforms and fae moving around them and across the tracks.

He answered my last question. I might as well try him with another. "How many stations do you have in the— what did you call this place?"

"The King's Refuge," Madoc says, and glances toward the next tunnel entrance. "There are five stations all connected and a maintenance area as well. It's the biggest Murk colony I'm aware of."

From the number of houses and fae that I've seen, it's probably bigger than any of the fae villages in the Mists.

"Would you like to see more of it?" Madoc asks in a cautious tone. "I could show you around."

Does he really want to act as my tour guide? I scrutinize him, and he gazes steadily back at me. Maybe he doesn't have any real animosity toward me, only the fae I've associated with. As if that's much better.

Either way, when I do my exploring, I don't want company for it.

At my hesitation, he goes on, offering a small, slanted smile. "I know this can't be easy for you, finding out so much about your life that you had no idea of, losing the home and the people you'd gotten used to. Of course you'll need time to adjust. And if you want to talk about any of it—I may not be fond of the fae you left behind, but I can still listen."

I don't know how to believe his apparent kindness. I swipe my hand across my mouth, and the niggling inside me deepens. "The Murk have been paying attention to what's happened to me in the Mists, haven't they? Orion would have wanted to know how his plan was progressing."

Madoc nods. "We have many people keeping an eye on the realms there. I've visited often myself."

Without the other fae realizing it. With the magic of the Murk's Heart, they must have developed spells for better concealing their scent and other signs of their presence.

I wet my lips. "But it wasn't only watching. There were

Murk who destroyed part of the Unseelie village in the summer realm. And one who started a fire with iron in the smoke. What was all that about?"

Madoc pauses before he answers. His eyes, which I can now tell are gray, momentarily turn even darker. "Sometimes we just meant to keep them on their toes. But Orion wanted to be sure the fae on both sides of their border cared about you as much as we could encourage them to. The ravens were all but worshipping you with just a little nudge here and there, remarks we let them overhear, but the wolves had taken your blood for granted. With the iron-laced fire, we arranged a bit of a spectacle where you could show what a hero you were to them too."

The whole problem with the smoke had been a setup —specifically that only a human could stop. And the Murk who'd sprang at me…

My hand drops to my thigh where the lingering wound still aches a little. Unlike the fae of the seasons, the Murk can end their own lives. They're too separate from the Heart of the Mist's power for it to stop them the way it has other desperate fae like Corwin's mother.

"The man who attacked me," I say slowly, "I didn't do anything to him at all. He had a spell on him to make it look like I'd killed him, but really he did it to himself."

The corner of Madoc's mouth twitches. I can't tell if it was heading toward a greater smile or a frown. "You catch on quickly. Orion is bringing us out of the darkness we've dwelled in for so long. Many of us are happy to give our lives for that cause."

My arms come up to wrap around my chest. I look

out over the fae moving through the subway station again, my heart sinking.

An enemy that committed to destroying my home will be awfully hard to defeat. But will I really be able to convince Orion that there's another way before it comes to full-out war?

5

Talia

The second time I wake up in the Murk colony they call the King's Refuge, I'm alone in the little house of corrugated steel Madoc arranged for me, which is about the size of a large tent. He assured me that I could have something larger prepared if I wanted it, but all I wanted was somewhere to sleep without so many rat shifter eyes on me.

I'm far enough away from the Murk's Heart that it isn't rattling my nerves anymore, but I catch a faint, erratic quiver of my skin as I rub my eyes. Is there anywhere in this network of tunnels where I'd be able to escape it completely?

Maybe not, but I need to attempt a bigger escape. Which means I have to get a better idea of what and who I'm dealing with out there.

I tug at my new clothes—a long-sleeved tee and

sweatpants Madoc had one of the other fae bring me so I could change out of my dress—and glance at the silky bundle I've left carefully folded in the corner. I'm glad for the change because I don't want the other Murk paying particular attention to me when I'm wandering around, and the dress definitely stands out here. But other than my bracelet, it's the only thing I have that connects me to the home I left behind.

I will get back there. And I can get started on making that happen now.

Cautiously, I clamber out of the hovel. The same unpleasant mix of smells reaches my nose, and there's a faint metallic tapping sound carrying from farther down the subway station. The rat shifters must be at work there.

My head still feels muggy. I didn't exactly sleep *well* in the nest of blankets Madoc left for me, with everything I've discovered in the past day buzzing around in my mind.

I go over to the bathroom and splash some water onto my face at the sinks, which thankfully work, although I'm not sure I'd want to attempt drinking the water their faucets spew out. Madoc pointed out the cases of bottled water that stand in one corner of every station and that the Murk must replenish regularly. If they don't trust the tap water, I certainly don't.

My stomach grumbles. I make my way along the platform to where a long table is set up. A couple of Murk are laying out an odd variety of food across it: bagels and a huge tub of cream cheese, a large tray of fried meat patties that appear to have cooled, various boxes of cereal with no bowls or milk to use with them, all sorts of fruit from bananas to mangos that look a bit bruised but otherwise all right, and more.

I pick up a muffin and a pear, biting into one and then the other tentatively. Fae brush past me to take their own meals from the table. Other than a few evaluating glances, which give me the sense that they know who I am, they ignore me. I guess that's better than overt hostility. Madoc at least didn't lie that his people wouldn't hurt me.

As one of the rat shifters who laid out the spread steps away, wiping her hands together, I venture a question. "Where did you get all the food from?"

She studies me with sharp eyes and gives me a tight smile. "We take whatever we can find and make off with what doesn't put us at too much risk. It should all be fine for you."

So they steal it from the humans above. Although from the looks of some of the items, they might have already been discarded before the Murk took them. The rat shifters can't have much choice, living the way they do. Where would they grow or hunt for their own food like the fae of the seasons do?

"Thank you," I say, because even though I don't trust any of the fae around me, she was at least patient enough to answer.

"Take anything you want," she adds, with a tip of her head toward the table. "We bring more throughout the day. You're Orion's—no one will fight you over it."

Do the Murk sometimes fight each other over the best

scavenged morsels? But what really sends a shiver through me is her casual reference to Orion, as if I *belong* to him.

In his subjects' eyes, I probably do.

I thank her again and wander on along the subway platform, scanning the activity on both sides of the tracks and down in their chasm. A lot of the Murk don't appear to be doing much of anything other than lounging around and talking. But maybe the ones here are those who don't currently have any work to do. I spot others vanishing into the tunnels and emerging from them. One man heaves a large box onto the platform just a few feet from me.

"What's in there?" I ask, feeling a little more confident that he's not going to snap at me for daring to talk to him.

He scrambles onto the platform next to his cargo, his tail swishing to help him balance. "Lead bars," he says. "Bringing them to the crafting workshop."

Because presumably it's easier for the Murk to work with materials they've already gathered rather than summoning them out of the earth, just like I need a bronze object in my hands before I can shape it. I motion to the box. "What are you going to craft with them?"

A sly smile flashes across his face. "Whatever our king asks of us to further our plans."

I'm not sure I like the sound of that, but he's carting the supplies away before I can pry any further.

I continue exploring, picking my way carefully through the dark subway tunnels, where only occasional magically-charged lanterns provide a faint illumination, and making my way through two more stations. The last tunnel leads to a larger sort-of cavern filled with unfamiliar machines and other tools. This must be the maintenance area Madoc mentioned.

No fae are in that space now. I move along the walls, checking all the equipment over in case I spot something that might be useful, and notice a square opening on the back wall, a few feet over my head. A cover of interlaced steel bars is fixed over it.

I can't reach it right away, but I manage to shove one of larger machines up to the wall beneath it and climb up on top to reach the opening. The square space is just large enough that I'm sure I could fit inside it.

A faint, cool draft washes over me when I bring my face close. It's got to be an air vent of some sort. I think I catch a hint of car exhaust. Does it lead all the way outside?

It doesn't appear to be an entrance the Murk use. I can't see any way to open or close the cover. The steel panel is held in place by several heavy bolts, dappled with rust that's starting to meld them into the cover itself.

I look down at my bracelet, hope flickering up in my chest. Maybe it isn't a blade I'll need most to defend myself—maybe it's a wrench. I could shape the metal into one if I concentrated, couldn't I? It shouldn't be all that much harder than making a knife.

I'll remember this spot for later. I don't want to use up any of my meager magical energy on that right now. I might need all the strength I can summon to reach out to Whitt.

My mates need to know that I'm all right and that the Murk are trying to destroy them.

I slide down off the machine and crouch next to it, leaning against its solid metal side. No footsteps or rustlings of a rat's passing reach my ears for several minutes. Can I trust that I'm actually alone?

Orion didn't seem all that concerned that I might leave. Maybe he's convinced that's impossible anyway. I didn't notice any Murk following me as I explored.

I bite my lip, waiting a little longer just to be sure. Then I cup my hands around my mouth to muffle as much of the sound as possible, close my eyes, and picture Whitt's handsome face: his sun-kissed brown hair, his sparking ocean-blue eyes, his typical crooked grin.

Homesickness wrenches at me so hard it brings a flood of tears to the back of my eyes. My breath turns ragged.

I'll get back to him—him and my other three mates and the home we've made. I *have* to.

"*Wye-con-ell*," I murmur under my breath, putting all the concentration I can into reaching out to him across the vast distance between our worlds. "*Wye-con-ell*. I need to talk to you. Hear me. Let me hear your answers."

My voice gets more urgent with each word. A fizzing sort of static rushes through my mind.

Then, all at once, a hint of my mate's warm sandy scent grazes my nose. I have a vague impression of him, somewhere out there—far more ephemeral than when I tried out using his true name after he first gave it to me, but definitely something apart from the dark, dank room I'm hidden away in.

Talia? Whitt's voice says in my mind, as if carried on

the wind across miles, so faint I can barely make it out. *Talia, where are you?*

I squeeze my eyes tighter shut and train all my attention on my sense of him far away in the fae world. An ache spreads over my scalp with the effort. *The Murk took me. I'm in the human world. Some kind of—*

A more jabbing pain splits through my focus. I press my hand to my forehead as if I can force the discomfort back. How much of a message do I have the strength to convey to him before I lose this connection completely?

Whitt's voice fades in and out as the magic between us wavers. *Have they hurt you? Where… you? We've been… we can.*

I struggle to decide on the most important information I need to pass on to him. I don't think I know enough for my mates to figure out where this Murk colony is and come for me, not yet. And… I'm not sure I'd want them to anyway. Will they be able to overpower Orion and his people on their own ground, with their Heart so close and the Heart of the Mists so far away? They have no idea—they won't be prepared.

It's bad enough being torn away from them. I won't lead them to their doom.

My hands clench in my lap. I put every shred of energy I have into the few words I can send him. *I'm all right. Working to find a way back to you. Watch out for the Murk. They mean to invade the Mists.*

The ache digs deeper. A sweat breaks out on my back, and I gasp in a breath. I can't tell whether all of that reached Whitt. His voice and my impressions of him are fragmenting even more. *We'll... soon... if they... in there... love you.*

I love you too, I think back at him with a pang through my heart, but in the same moment, the tenuous connection snaps.

I rock backward, banging my shoulders on the machine I'm sitting against. The headache has expanded all through my skull. When I turn my head, pinpricks of pain stab at the backs of my eyeballs.

I'm obviously not going to be holding extended conversations with Whitt any time soon. But at least he knows I'm alive and reasonably okay. Hopefully he heard enough of my warning to tell everyone to be even more on guard against the Murk.

Gripping a bar that protrudes from the machine, I haul myself to my feet. My head spins, the pain turning blaring for several seconds before it retreats just a little. I take shallow breaths in and out.

Am I even going to be able to make it back to the nearest station?

Holding my head as still as I can, I take careful steps toward the tracks, setting my hands against the machines for balance. I manage to find a slow but steady pace that doesn't provoke the throbbing in my skull too badly.

When I reach the tracks, I focus on the gravel path between the rails. One step, then another, with a rasp of my boots over the gritty stones. After all my wandering, my ankle is starting to hurt too, a duller throb echoing up my leg.

It feels like years later that the starker glow of the

station touches the edges of my vision. I take my next steps faster and immediately regret it.

Agony whirls up behind my temples. I sway to the side, the toe of my boot catching on one of the rails. I tumble forward toward the sharp gravel—

—and firm hands grasp me just as my knees brush the ground with a faint sting.

"Steady there," Madoc says, easing me into a sitting position. As I wince and press my palms to my temples, he cocks his head at me. "What's happened to you?"

"I—" I can hardly find my words amid the pain. "My head hurts."

He peers closely into my eyes, so near that his scent washes over me, cool and faintly electric like the atmosphere just before a thunderstorm. Is he actually worried about me?

"Maybe the sudden, jarring change in environment is affecting you," he says, lowering his voice even more as if he's guessed hearing any sound at all sets off fresh sparks of pain. "Let me do what I can, and then I'll get you back to your house and bring one of our healers to you."

He touches his knuckles to my forehead and murmurs a few words. A welcome chill floods through my skull, dulling the pain. It's still *there*, but the throbbing has become more distant. My thoughts seem to fade in volume at the same time.

"Better?" Madoc asks, and I manage to nod. "Wait right here. I'll get you a cart so you don't need to walk."

In my dulled state, a mumbled plea slips out of me. "I want to go home."

Madoc obviously knows I don't mean the hovel I slept in. He brings his hand to my cheek with unexpected gentleness. "You'll find a good home here among us. We'll *make* it a good one for you. I promise."

He strides off, leaving me puzzling over the raw emotion that crept into those words, as if he meant them more than I'd ever have expected.

6

Corwin

"You and your companions can make use of these rooms for as long as you need them," I say to the man I've just ushered into one of the larger guest apartments in the palace of Heart's Cadence. My gaze slides past him to the cursed woman—his mate—hunched on the bed, and my stomach clenches with the knowledge that they will only need the space here until she passes.

At the moment, I'm starkly aware of the horror of losing one's mate. At least I can take some small measure of hope from the fact that based on the message Talia managed to convey to Whitt, she's nowhere near death. That still doesn't get us any closer to retrieving her from the wretched Murk that wrenched her away from me.

And with her gone, anyone the curse touches among my people have no hope at all.

A punch of tangled anger and grief hits me in the chest. I set my jaw and steady myself as well as I can. My guests are watching me.

"Let me know if there's anything we can do to make you more comfortable," I say. "My staff will be ready to see to your requests or summon me if necessary."

"Thank you, arch-lord," the man says with a dip of his head and a tight smile, and I feel I can finally step away from them.

It's unlikely they'll be the last to require my hospitality. Since Talia's disappearance three days ago, they're already the second travelers to arrive seeking her cure. My colleagues and I explained the situation in as calm a way as we could and sent the larger entourage of folk-flock who'd joined the curse victims back home. Terisse has taken the other victim and her family into her palace.

Being helpless to do anything to hold back the curse on my own only multiplies my anguish. And I can imagine how torn up Talia would be to think of the people who may die in her absence. The Murk have dealt us a harder blow than they may even realize.

Or maybe this is exactly why they've stolen my mate— to strike out at us in ways not just personal but with consequences for our entire realm and the summer realm besides. It's by far the most immense gambit they've ever pulled off.

How were they able to sneak past so many sentries to reach Talia? To bewitch the Seelie woman before that and force her to draw Talia away from the celebration to the forest where she was more vulnerable? It's beyond anything we've ever seen or heard of the Murk before, and that leaves uneasiness twisted all through my gut.

I've only made it partway down the hall from the guest quarters when one of my staff hurries over to me. My heart sinks with the thought that yet another curse victim has arrived, but what he actually says doesn't make me feel much better.

"Arch-Lord Laoni is waiting in the terrace room, my lord," he says. "She wishes to speak to you."

I grit my teeth and set off to see what my most hostile colleague wants now.

It doesn't surprise me to discover that Laoni hasn't even bothered to sit down. She's standing between the scattered chairs, gazing out the tall windows that look over the terrace and the sweeping landscape beyond. As if to remind me that she doesn't jump to my bidding, she stays there for a moment after I've entered the room before deigning to turn to face me.

"Corwin," she says, studying my face. "You look frazzled."

Her tone gives the observation an implied criticism, as if I should be totally at peace even with my soul-twined mate in the hands of our greatest enemies. I bite back the cutting remark that leaps onto my tongue, pulling together the appearance of professionalism. "I'd imagine that's not surprising, considering the circumstances. It hasn't affected my duties."

Her eyes narrow, and I suppose she's thinking about my mother—about how completely *she* fell apart when she lost her own soul-twined mate with my father's death. The other arch-lords have always questioned my fitness for the position based on their fears about my familial "instability." Even after Talia cured Laoni and kept her curse secret as Laoni wished, she's still out to pick at me every way she can.

"What progress have you made toward finding your mate?" she demands, as if the only reason we haven't retrieved Talia yet is some failing on my part.

"I have sentries and soldiers, including three of my coterie members, scouring every inch of the realm for any trace of Murk presence," I say tightly. "Arch-Lord Sylas is doing the same on the summer side."

"And yet they've turned up nothing."

No doubt she's only concerned because of what fate *she'll* meet if we don't rescue Talia within the next few weeks, before the curse returns to her. I fold my arms over my chest. "If you wish to see faster proceedings, you're welcome to add more of your own flock to the search."

Laoni's chin comes up. "I've sent several on that quest already. I can't leave my domain completely undefended if the filthy rats decide to strike out in some other way."

"Well, I'm doing everything I can," I say, my patience fraying too much for me to keep the irritation out of my voice. "It is *my* soul-twined mate they have, and I won't rest until she's back by my side. If you have a suggestion that might actually help, by all means, share it. Otherwise, as far as I can tell you're only here to harass me."

Laoni's expression twitches, and her gaze hardens. A flash of shame rushes through me. I've worked so hard on keeping a controlled front, especially with my colleagues. My fears for Talia *are* unraveling me.

"I'll leave you to your work, then," Laoni says stiffly, and marches off to the terrace to fly to her own domain.

After she's soared off, I remain in the room for several minutes, gripping the back of one of the armchairs. My pulse thuds in a heavy rhythm. With every beat, the emptiness where my connection to Talia should be reverberates through me, digging the pain of her absence deeper.

I can't let my distress shatter me completely. I'll have no chance of fighting for Talia then, and I'll fail my flock and all the other people I rule over as well. But how can I center myself when such a huge piece of my soul is missing?

My gaze rises to the ceiling. There *is* someone in this palace who has an idea of what I'm experiencing. I don't know if she'll be at all coherent, but maybe talking to her will help me sort through the turmoil inside me at least a little.

I move through the halls swiftly, not wanting to be interrupted while I'm so unsettled. As I climb up the staircase that leads to my mother's quarters, I consider casting the usual calming spell to soothe her nerves before I enter. But perhaps she deserves the respect of being faced in her genuine state, with all the anguish she's dealing with that I rarely see these days.

I wish there was a better way to keep her from harming herself without locking her up. But the memories of the horrific scenes that resulted from her past attempts at ending her life, always in vain but not without gore and bloodshed, make the thought of offering her the freedom she deserves impossible.

"Mother, it's me," I call through the locked door. "I'm coming in."

When I open it, I find her crouched near the stairs that lead up to her bedroom. She takes a leap forward as if to spring for the open entrance, but I close the door and quickly lock it.

Mother's shoulders slump. She darts over to the table she's upended yet again and then hunches there, swaying slightly.

"Hello, Mother," I say quietly, my heart wrenching all over again. I can't imagine being reduced to the near-feral state she's in, but I can understand the agony she's gone through better than I ever could before.

I walk across the room and sit on the floor against the built-in shelves, across from her current refuge. She mutters under her breath and then adds in a voice that's almost a whimper, "Let me out. Let me end it."

I swallow hard. "You know you can't, no matter where you go or what you do. The Heart won't let you destroy the life it's given you."

Her chest heaves with a strangled sob. She drops her head into her hands.

"You feel like that life has already been destroyed, don't you?" I murmur. "Part of your soul ripped away from you. I—I may have to face the same thing."

Mother twitches, and then lifts her gaze to take me in. "Your mate..."

"You might remember Talia? She's come to see you before. She… The Murk have taken her. They've interrupted our soul-twined bond somehow. I can't sense her at all."

Another surge of emotion rolls over me with the admission, even though it isn't new. I bring my hand to my mouth as if I'm in danger of sobbing myself.

Coming here might have been misguided. Am I only making myself feel worse?

But before I can decide to leave, Mother eases forward. Haltingly, she crosses the room until she's squatting right in front of me. Her head cocks as if she's trying to make out who I am.

Then she reaches and, for the first time since her grief overwhelmed everything else, takes my hand.

"My son," she says in a small, thin voice.

I squeeze her fingers, a bittersweet ache forming in my chest at the gesture. "I'll—I'll make it through. I have to. But I just wanted to see you. You're the only one I know who's been through it and won't judge me for my pain."

She stares at me for a long moment. Something clears in her eyes, just briefly. "If I could have shielded you from the horror of it," she says, and lapses back into silence.

"I know you couldn't have, any more than I could have protected you. I still can't really help you, as much as I'd like to. But… you're not alone."

Mother sways back and forth as if to some imaginary song and then swipes her forearm past her reddened eyes. "I am, but I'm not. I—" She focuses in on me again, gripping my hand. "It's the deepest pain for the deepest bond. But for all the pain, I wouldn't have given it up. We are lucky to have ever been so blessed—to have gotten what time we had—" She inhales raggedly and drops her head again, a tremor running through her. "If I could only follow that bond to its end…"

"I know," I say, my own voice raw, but something inside me has steadied.

Disturbed as she is, there's truth in what she said. I'm lucky to have been twined so closely with a woman like Talia for as even as short a time as I was. I need to focus on that and not the loss of it—on what I'll *still* have, when we defeat the Murk, not on anticipating an even greater loss.

"Thank you," I say. "For hearing me. For your words. Is there anything I can bring you—"

The wildness is already returning to her eyes. She flings her arm toward the door. "To go out—to find a blade or a cliff—"

My throat constricts. "It won't work. But maybe, if we can finally end this curse, you'll find at least as much peace as you just gave me."

7

Talia

The last thing I actually *want* to do is spend more time in Orion's unpredictable presence with the glow of that horrific Heart pulsing over us. But when my searing headache has finally faded enough that I can think coherently, I know I have to try.

I'm obviously not going to be able to construct any kind of complex plan with Whitt or rally the fae in the Mists when I can barely get across two sentences over the distance without incapacitating myself. My only real hope of helping stop the war Orion is intent on waging is to change his mind. If that task seems impossible, well, I've just got to take it one step at a time.

I limp through the station toward his throne room. It looks as if the Murk are just rousing for the day—if it is day. The lights that had been dimmer when I first emerged are glimmering brighter now.

When I reach the immense alcove, the Murk king is standing beside his regal seat, stretching his arms with a small yawn. A servant hustles over to bring him a steaming mug. I catch a whiff of coffee as she passes me.

His usual companions aren't with him right now—the dais around him is empty. I guess they must go back to their own houses to sleep.

Where does Orion spend his nights? I glance around, but nothing in the throne room looks like the kinds of houses the rest of the Murk have. Does he just lie there on the platform basking in his Heart's erratic light?

A shiver travels down my spine at the thought, but at the same moment the Murk king takes notice of me. He gives me a grin as jagged as his spiky white hair and motions me over. "Decided to join me for another breakfast, have you?"

With the first breakfast being just yesterday, was it? I think I only lost the better part of a day to that headache. Does that mean I've been gone from the Mists for nearly three full days now? I'm not sure how long they kept me unconscious after Madoc grabbed me in the forest.

I could have been missing for over a week for all I know.

All the Unseelie fae who'll have been struck by the curse since then—all the efforts my mates must be going to trying to find me—

I can't do anything about that until I find a way out of here.

Pushing the uncomfortable thoughts aside, I make my unsteady way over to the dais and sit on the edge. Orion appears to have forgotten about me as quickly as he noticed me. He paces along the dais, giving orders in a low mutter to the various underlings who are now gathering in the throne room.

Just as he's sent the last of them off, a couple more servants stride in carrying platters of food like yesterday. The king drops into the same spot at the base of his throne to consider their offerings.

"Do you want coffee?" he asks, and it takes me a second to realize he's talking to me, since he didn't even look up.

I wouldn't mind being perked up with caffeine, but the bitter scent trailing from his mug makes my tongue recoil. I'm not sure I'd be able to get down the kind of stuff he's drinking. "No, thank you."

"Well, eat. We won't be starving you here." He snatches up a chicken wing and pulls a strip of meat off it with his teeth. His gaze lingers on my boots, and I suspect he's thinking of the other mistreatment I suffered at the hands of the Seelie. A pang runs through the arch of my foot at the memory of Aerik's cadre man snapping the bones.

"I wondered if you've had any news from the Mists," I venture, taking a small roll dusted with dried coconut. "About how they're doing with me gone?"

He makes an amused sound and peers into my eyes for the first time. The predatory gleam in his yellow ones makes the hair on the back of my neck stand on end. "You're worried about the pricks you left behind."

I tuck my feet closer to me. "They weren't all awful to

me. Some might have hurt me, but others did a lot to help me heal. I don't think you should see them all as horrible."

"I have many more centuries of experience with the other fae kinds than you do," he says in a tone that makes me wonder just how old he is despite his smooth face. "But yes, I have people monitoring the Mists. Everything is proceeding well."

He doesn't elaborate on that, although I've heard enough from him before to assume that "well" by his standards is "badly" by mine. His gaze slides away from me, and he raises his hand in greeting. Madoc has just appeared at the entrance to the throne room.

"I've already eaten," the other fae man says when Orion gestures to his spread, but he sits down on the dais across from me anyway and considers me. "Feeling better now, Talia?"

I nod, my hand instinctively moving to my forehead. "It's completely gone."

"You shouldn't strain yourself," Orion declares. I assume Madoc told him about the state he found me in. "If I feel I need you to pitch in, I won't hesitate to tell you. Otherwise you're at your leisure."

Does he suspect that I was doing something he wouldn't like? I fumble for words. "I—I think it was just the stress of… everything."

He hums to himself. I can't read him at all.

I've got to put out some kind of feelers. "If the fae of the Mists are upset with me gone—you could use that without even needing to attack them, couldn't you? Negotiate with them. There's lots of unclaimed land in both realms. I'm sure there's room for all the Murk to live there as well."

Orion snorts. "And make ourselves subject to their arch-lords and rules, for however little time until they find some loophole to kick us out again? Didn't you learn anything about them in your time there?"

I'm not going to get very far if I'm too argumentative. I can already tell he doesn't like having *his* authority challenged either. "You might be right about that," I say. "But—wouldn't it be better for your own people to try to find some kind of compromise instead of battling to take over all of the Mists? If there's fighting, some of the Murk will die too."

"My people are willing to make the necessary sacrifices to bring us to a better place for the rest of eternity." Orion takes a big gulp of his coffee and blows out a puff of steam. "The Seelie and Unseelie will never meet us as equals. As far as they're concerned, we're dirt under their boots."

"But you have me now. That gives you leverage. You could even ask for a chunk of the Mist lands to be given completely to the Murk. They'd have to live with displacing a bunch of lords, but oh well. You *should* have a place there. You're fae too."

I must manage to sound reasonably convincing, because Orion pauses for a second as if he's thinking my statement over. But then he shakes his head. "I can't risk avoiding a smaller slaughter in the beginning only to lead us to a much larger one later on. To be sure of getting what we deserve, we have to take it by force—all of it. The fae of the seasons have owned the entirety of the Mists for millennia; it's our turn now. Besides, they deserve some bloodshed of their own after stomping us down for so long."

"The ones who first cast you out won't even be alive anymore, will they?" I have to point out.

"I'm sure a few of those pricks have held in there. And their heirs haven't been any kinder."

I bite back the urge to point out that the Murk haven't done anything to warrant kindness from the other fae recently. Does he really expect the summer and winter realms to extend an olive branch when his people are causing all the havoc they can both there and here in the human world?

I'm not sure what else I can say, so I take a handful of raspberries and pop them into my mouth to cover my uncertainty. At least I know more than I did before about what's driving Orion, what matters to him. There has to be *some* way I can present a compromise that'll appeal to him. Even if it only gets him face to face with the fae of the Mists to talk—so that they can get the upper hand and end this war before it really starts.

A couple more of the men from Orion's inner circle amble into the throne room. Orion grabs a drumstick to take with him and walks over to consult with them by the far end of the dais. I swallow the berries, their juice turning sour in the back of my mouth.

"You're worrying too much," Madoc says. "You'll give yourself another headache." He gets up and beckons me.

"Come. I'll show you part of the Refuge you won't have seen yet. Maybe it'll even reassure you about the future."

I can't imagine what in this place could accomplish that, but I get up anyway. Orion seems to trust Madoc quite a bit. Maybe Madoc will listen to me more than his king has and be able to translate my arguments into a version Orion will accept.

He leads me in the opposite direction from the way I went exploring yesterday, through one station and another. The other fae are getting to work throughout the Refuge, more supplies coming and going, more sounds of construction echoing off the ceilings. My skin prickles with apprehension.

Just how long do I have before Orion decides to launch the next phase of his attack? What is he waiting to see in the Mists before he decides to go ahead?

Even if he's planning on waiting months, I have to get out of here before then. The Unseelie's curse will be gripping more and more of them, taking their lives without me there to banish it. And how bad will the summer curse be if I haven't returned by the next full moon? Orion may have ramped up the strength of the curses even more now that he's taken me away from them.

I can't express any of those worries to my companion. Madoc clearly doesn't see anything wrong with his king's approach. I don't know where to begin with him.

Thankfully, he starts up the conversation first. "The way we run things here is pretty different from what you got used to in the courts of the Mists, isn't it?"

A cool draft tickles over my skin in the dark tunnel. I

rub my arms as I consider my answer. "I guess. The way everyone supports Orion, it isn't that different from how things work between a lord or lady and their pack or flock."

"We're all united, though," Madoc says. "Every Murk is happy to follow Orion's guidance. The fae of the Mists are constantly arguing between themselves, from what I've seen. Even the arch-lords. The ones you weren't tied to picked on you plenty of times, didn't they?"

I can't deny that. Maybe I shouldn't want to if I'm trying to get into his good graces. "They did. There are definitely plenty of them who were… less than kind." Not that I could call any of the Murk I've met exactly "kind" so far either.

Madoc nods. "It must have been hard, being thrust into a situation like that and needing to find your footing with them while showing powers none of them understood. As much as it benefitted us, I'm sorry you had to deal with them on our behalf, unknowingly."

I blink, peering at him through the shadows. Is he really sorry? His tone has stayed soft, with that hoarse note it always seems to have as if he's never quite cleared his throat enough.

It's hard to believe his sympathy isn't just more Murk trickery.

"What are you showing me?" I ask, wanting to change the subject.

A mysterious smile plays with his lips. "You'll see. It's a spot I set up for myself for when I need to think beyond what's right in front of me." He glances sideways at me.

"When we do go to the Mists, we won't treat every fae the same, of course. If there's anyone who particularly deserves to be crushed, or any you think we should go easier on, we could take your suggestions into account with whatever guidance you can offer."

My chest constricts. I don't want them crushing anyone at all, not even the vicious fae like Aerik and Tristan who barely see me as worthy of having a life. But that definitely isn't what he wants to hear.

"I'll think about it," I say instead.

He seems to accept my answer. I study what I can see of his profile in the darkness. "It doesn't bother you at all, the thought of all that violence? It's not really the Murk way to get into direct combat, is it?"

Madoc lets out a dry chuckle. "That much might be true. But some fighting will be worth it to claw our way back to the position and the home owed to us. And I'm sure we'll find ways of bringing our own approach to the battles that lie ahead."

He touches my arm, just a brief graze of his fingers over the skin above my elbow that makes the muscle there jump, guiding me with him into a narrow passage I hadn't noticed in the tunnel wall. It's a stairwell, the steep concrete steps leading up to a narrow landing and then another. After the first couple of flights, a faint ache wakes up in my warped foot. I wonder how far under the ground we are here.

At the third landing, Madoc pushes open a door with a creak of its hinges and moves to usher me into the room on the other side. My legs balk automatically. It's just starting to sink in how far we are from the other Murk now… not that I could expect any of them to leap to my aid if Madoc wanted to hurt me in front of them. But being in an enclosed space with him sets my nerves jangling.

Madoc watches me, maybe guessing at the reasons for my hesitation. "If you don't want to see it after all, we could leave," he says without a trace of judgment.

His lack of urgency and my desire to earn his trust win out over my worries. In his eyes, I belong to his king, don't I? He wouldn't want to damage his ruler's belongings.

I shake my head and limp past him into the room.

It's a small space, windowless like every other part of the Refuge I've seen, with a few cushions along one side and a box that holds an assortment of human snacks—chip bags and prepackaged brownies and that sort of thing—by the other. Papers tacked to the walls show a speckling of penciled dots, some with lines sketched between them. But what draws my gaze is the telescope set up at the far end of the room, pointed at the spot where the wall meets the ceiling.

"I know it looks ridiculous," Madoc says, going to it, "but it's enchanted. Not easy to get a good look at the stars when slinking through the human world. When our Heart grew strong enough that I had enough power, I tied this telescope magically to one in a science lab up above. Its view of the universe is projected to this lens."

He runs his fingers over the device, and in that moment I can tell I'm seeing genuine appreciation.

Whatever else he cares about, that telescope matters to him.

"Why do you want to see the universe?" I ask.

Madoc shrugs, dropping his hand with an abruptly sheepish air. "I've always found the stars fascinating. All that energy and light, so far out of reach. And there's something both wonderful and awful about the thought of how much more there is beyond the worlds we can visit here." He makes an awkward gesture as if he thinks he's said too much and tips his head toward the drawings on the walls. "There's also an art to it, a sort of soothsaying you can perform looking at the constellations. I've been developing my skill at that."

I take a closer look at the patterns of dots and lines. "And what have you found out from them?"

"As I imagine you've realized, any kind of fortune-telling magic is never very exact." He considers the drawings as I do. "But I believe they show a better, less confined future for the Murk. What I do outside this room is to make sure as many of us reach that future as can. Hope shouldn't be as distant as the stars."

Something in those words resonates straight through my chest and brings a lump to my throat. "You know," I say, quietly but with total honesty, "I hope you get that better future, all of you." I just don't want it to happen through the deaths of everyone I care about back in the Mists.

Madoc's gaze jerks to me. In that instant, he looks startled. But then his expression relaxes with another smile, and he motions me over to the telescope. "Here, get a glimpse of the universe and see if it doesn't put everything in some perspective."

He pushes one of the cushions over so I can kneel at it by the telescope's eyepiece. I bring my face to it tentatively.

As I peer through the device, closing my other eye, my whole vision fills with a dark sky dotted with blazing stars, closer than I've ever seen them when gazing up at the sky on my own.

I thought it was morning, but it's actually night outside, at least in whatever part of the human world we're near. I guess it isn't surprising that the Murk have their schedules upside down, sleeping through the day instead.

And now, after hearing the way Madoc talked, I can't help wondering if there's more to him than I've realized as well. I can't believe he's only looking to "sow spite," no matter what the old rhyme says.

But if his goal is still to see the fae of the summer and winter realms fall, does that really make a difference? I'm not any closer to stopping that destruction.

He's right about one thing. Staring up into the heavens makes me feel very, very small.

8

Talia

The disturbance starts with a few shouts that echo into the station from the nearest tunnel. There's a strange quality to them, both exhilarated and vicious, that makes my head snap around where I was sitting near the scavenged food table eating a hasty dinner.

Several of the fae around me leave off their conversations or work to glance in the same direction. When more voices join the chorus, they slip off the platform onto the tracks and head for the tunnel.

The commotion is coming from the direction of Orion's throne room. Uneasiness coils around my stomach as I follow the fae. I'm not sure I *want* to find out what's going on, but I know I need to. I can't afford to stay ignorant of anything that's going on with my captors, no matter how horrible.

Maybe especially the horrible things.

In the tunnel, the orange glow of the Murk's Heart wavers even more than usual over the many figures streaming into the throne room. I manage to slip inside among them and find a crate by the wall that I can scramble onto for a view over their heads. Keeping my balance with a hand against the cool concrete beside me, I peer over the crowd.

Orion is standing in front of his throne, his head cocked to one side with an expression I can only call cruel amusement. The lash of his tail from side to side suggests he's not actually all that *happy*, though. A few of his close hangers-on have gathered around him, looking a little more alert than usual.

I don't see Madoc among them. Stupidly, his absence sends a flash of worry through me, as if I should be concerned about whether something's happened to him.

He's the one who stole me from my home and my mates. But… he's also the only one of the Murk who's shown much concern for my well-being. I can't help suspecting I'd be even worse off here without him.

The swarm of fae have left a small open space in front of the dais. Just a couple of Murk stand there, one with scars dappling every plane of his hardened face and another with her hair cut into a broad, bristly mohawk. A slim fae man with floppy black hair and umber skin crouches on the floor between them. I can't see his face, but his posture is taut with terror.

"We found him crying in one of the store rooms," the bristly woman says, her voice harsh as sandpaper.

"*Sniveling* like an infant, when he was supposed to be bringing materials to the forges."

Forges? I haven't come across those yet. Is that what those lead bricks were for too?

I don't know what they're making, but the first place my mind goes is *weapons*. My muscles tense. I strain my ears to hear better over the murmuring of the crowd.

Orion steps right to the edge of the dais, looming over the three of them. His tail sweeps back and forth like the snap of a whip. "You swore to stand strong in my service, Bren. I have no need for whimperers and cowards."

"I'm not a coward," the floppy-haired man says in a determined youthful voice that makes me think he might not even be an adult yet by fae standards. "I—I only took a moment. Evie—she and I—we were going to be mates, but she hasn't come back from her last scouting trip, and it's been weeks, and I— It seems like she isn't coming back. I won't let it affect my work for you again!"

Orion's lips curl with skepticism. "If it's happened once, it can happen again. We suffer all kinds of losses under the heels of the fae of the seasons. That's why we have to stay focused on overturning them. How can I count on you if you behave so feebly when we're not even in the thick of a battle?"

I wince inwardly. The poor boy—he's lost his intended mate, probably to some violent end, and he isn't allowed to show his grief without being berated for it?

"I'll conquer it and come out stronger," the young man insists. "I swear it. I want to destroy every one of those bastards from the Mists."

Orion hums to himself. "You've aspired to stand right beside me, Bren. I don't think a few words are enough to convince me I should still consider you for that honor." Even from across the room, I can see the feral gleam in his yellow eyes. "Action means so much more than words. Let's see that strength in action now. I need to know just how dedicated you are to this war."

Bren's shoulders twitch, but he shoves himself to his feet. "Of course. Whatever you want, my king."

Orion's gaze skims over the gathered figures and lands on someone in the crowd. He raises his hand with a beckoning gesture. "Colby, you've been begging for more recognition lately. This is your chance to prove yourself too. Let's see which of you is actually prepared to do whatever it takes for your people."

An icy shiver runs down my back. What's he talking about?

The crowd parts to allow another young man to squeeze through to the clear area in front of the dais, this one a little shorter and stouter than Bren. I can't tell how much of that stoutness is muscle and how much fat. Bren eyes him, his hands balling into fists at his sides, and Colby juts out his jaw in defiance.

The two older fae who brought Bren in front of Orion pull back to the edge of the crowd. I catch the woman's satisfied grin.

The other Murk gathered in the throne room start to whoop and cheer as if egging the two men on. Orion folds his arms over his chest and glowers down at Bren and Colby. "You know how it works. Only one of you can stay.

You decide which that is. Or if you aren't willing to face the challenge, you can turn tail and scamper off now."

Bren shakes his head, though his wide eyes look panicked. Colby draws himself up taller. They start to circle each other, staring each other down. Another shiver crawls across my spine to shudder through my gut.

All at once, Colby lunges at Bren. He knocks him to the ground, punching him in the face and clawing at his neck. Bren flails at him with fists and knees, managing to roll away with blood streaking from a row of scratches across his throat. He smacks his tail into Colby's ankles and flings himself at the other man's legs when he wobbles.

As they roll around, clawing at and grappling with each other, the cheers of the crowd rise. Orion watches with a pleased smirk stretching across his face.

My stomach lurches queasily. My own hands clench with the urge to slap that look right off his smug face.

The two young men wrestle with each other with increasing fervor. Bren gets in a slash with his claws that rips through Colby's shirt and spills blood down the side of his torso. Colby batters Bren's nose hard enough for it to spurt more blood across them both. Torn hair flies up; grunts and groans echo off the high ceiling. They're both panting raggedly between each blow. I stand rigid on the edge of the crate, my heart thudding.

Colby scrapes his claws across Bren's cheeks and forehead deeply enough that the other man shrieks and I flinch. But then Bren whips his arms around Colby's knee and wrenches with a wild heave and a slap of his tail against the ground. The cracking of breaking bone carries through the raucous encouragement of their audience.

Colby topples onto his back with a cry. In an instant, Bren is on him. With his face twisted into an expression that looks more beastly than human, he digs his fingers into Colby's hair, claws splitting the scalp, and slams his opponent's head against the hard floor. And again. And again. Blood starts to splatter the pale concrete. Colby goes limp, but Bren snarls and rams his head down even harder.

He's going to kill him, smash his skull right in two. It's over—can't they see that? Isn't this enough?

A noise of protest breaks from my throat, but it's swallowed by the eager clamoring of the audience. Before I've even though about what I'm doing, I jump off the crate and throw myself into the crowd toward the fighters. If I can just get there in time, if I can make them stop—

An errant elbow clocks me in the temple. I reel to the side and push myself forward again—and firm arms catch me from behind.

Madoc's hoarse voice reaches me, his breath warm against my ear. "You can't do anything about it. Charging in there will only make things worse—for you and them."

I squirm against his hold, but he pulls me right against his solid chest, his arms wrapping tighter around me. A sputter of denial escapes me. "I have to— If I just—"

"It's already over." He nods toward the dais. Over the heads of the crowd, I can just see Bren's floppy hair, damp with blood, where he's straightened up. "What's one more dead Murk anyway?"

Madoc asks the question flippantly, but I sense a hint of bitterness in his tone. Does he really think I see things that way?

"I've never wanted *anyone* to die like that," I say. "Colby didn't have to. They could have ended the fight when he passed out. They could have found some other way to decide that wasn't fighting!"

Madoc's grip loosens just a little. He eases around enough to study my face. "It really matters that much to you?"

I glare at him. "Yes. I wouldn't want to see even *actual* rats forced to tear each other to bits. I might not agree with everything the Murk have done, but I can still think you deserve better than that." I fling my hand toward the dais.

Madoc doesn't seem to know how to respond to that declaration. And then my attention is drawn back to the platform—to Orion, who's bringing his hands together in a slow, emphatic clap of approval. He applauds Bren's performance with so much enthusiasm I feel sick all over again. Then he motions the young man up beside him.

Blood is streaking down Bren's face, and not all of it is his own. But he smiles fiercely at his king, who claps him on the back.

"You've shown what you're made of," Orion declares. "Someone fetch Nami to patch up my new knight. And get rid of the trash on the floor, will you?" He lifts his chin disdainfully toward the spot where Colby's battered corpse is lying.

A cold wave of certainty washes over me. I swallow

hard, my stance loosening enough that Madoc lets go of me completely.

There's going to be no reasoning with Orion. He clearly doesn't operate on reason in the first place. He *enjoys* violence and pain, like the worst stories told about the Murk.

It's because of fae like him that the others hate the Murk so much. He even enjoys turning his bloodlust on his own people, fae who are desperate to serve him and please him—the fae he claims to care so much about bringing to a better world.

I can't think of a single thing I could say to him that I'd have any hope of getting through.

My shoulders square of their own accord. Why should I even bother *trying* to get through to him?

I've spent so much of the past several months wrapping my head around different points of view and working toward compromises with people who hate me… and I'm done. This is my limit. I'll play along to Orion's tune as much as I have to in order to survive and get back to the people who care about me, but I won't waste one more particle of energy on considering his warped point of view.

I deserve more than that.

I'll find out whatever I can about the Murk's Heart and Orion's plans while working toward my escape, and then I've got to get the hell out of this place to warn all the people he means to slaughter.

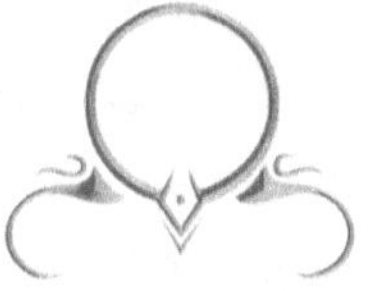

9

Whitt

I know I've spent too long staring at ink on parchment when the words begin to blur together on the page in front of me. I lean away from my desk and tip my head against the back of my chair, closing my eyes.

Scrawled handwriting continues to taunt me on the insides of my eyelids. I let out a sound of frustration that's half growl, half groan.

There's nothing in all the historical records I've accumulated that suggests the Murk should have had the ability to accomplish anything close to the kidnapping of our mate. We had guards all around the celebration area. That woman from Donovan's pack should have scented trouble the second the man who charmed her stepped anywhere near her, well before he had a chance to addle her mind. Whoever he was and whoever might have been working with him, he should have left so much more of a trail.

But somehow the Murk have learned to disguise all sign of their presence so well that our wolfish noses can completely miss it. Not only that, but they've been able to dull the soul-twined bond between Talia and Corwin so thoroughly he's sensed nothing at all from her these past few days. I don't know whether they've stifled her talent with true names or she's simply so distant it's a struggle for her to reach me, but she barely managed to convey any message to me at all either.

The worst part is, there were warning signs before this. The blasted buildings in the Unseelie's summer settlement. The iron-laced smoke it appeared the Murk created at the edge of the arch-lords' domains. We *knew* they were showing more skill and strength than we'd believed could be possible.

But we still never considered they might be able to pull off a crime this immense.

We shouldn't have left Talia's side for even a second that night. We should have ensured one of us or a trusted guard was within hand's reach of her any time she left our shared castle. Maybe even within the castle—can the Murk eschew the Heart's vow when entering the border territory?

I have no idea. The weight of all the things I don't know presses in on my skull.

I rub my forehead as if I can alleviate the pressure that way. I'm the strategist and spymaster. It's my blasted *job* to have all the information we need and the understanding to make use of it. And yet I missed whatever clues might have allowed us to be better prepared, and in all my searching, I've come up with nothing that's been able to bring Talia back to us.

The mite is counting on me, and I couldn't even promise her we'd get her back soon.

There's a soft rap on my door. I open my eyes and straighten up in my chair, catching my lord's scent. "Come in."

Sylas steps inside, his expression as grim as it's looked since we first discovered Talia's disappearance. I'd swear his deadened eye gleams an even starker and more deathly white than it did before. He looks around my study, at the books and scrolls scattered across the shelves where I haven't bothered to reorganize them properly, at more of the same heaped on my desk, and at my own expression. His mouth twists with a trace of sympathy.

"Still nothing?" he asks.

I shake my head, knowing it's the same for him. If he or any of our people scouring the realms for Talia had picked up any hint of her location, he'd have led with that news.

Sylas sighs and then draws his head up into a more authoritative stance. I've never seen as much anguish in him as he's let show over the past few days, but he's still an arch-lord, and he knows he has to act like one regardless of his personal concerns. He fixes his gaze on me. "Has she managed to reach out to you again?"

I offer another shake of my head and an apologetic gesture. "I got the impression it was very difficult for her even the first time, and what she was able to pass on to me was fragmented. It might be better that she's not attempting it again if she isn't sure she can inform us yet of anything that would actually bring us to her, so she can conserve her strength."

Or she may have been caught and prevented from trying again, or be otherwise incapacitated. I don't want to voice those possibilities.

At least we know she's alive. Corwin may not be able to make use of their bond, but it hasn't broken for him either. I saw how the loss of Isleen, even after her many betrayals, hit Sylas. The pain of a shattered soul-twined bond is impossible to ignore.

"Yes," Sylas says. He doesn't remind me to tell him as soon as she does make any sort of contact, because he trusts that I will regardless. He walks restlessly to the other end of the room and then back before meeting my gaze again. "I'm concerned about Corwin."

My mind snaps to sharper alertness. I haven't seen much of our Unseelie counterpart since our initial discussions about Talia's capture—he's been busy organizing his own people's efforts. "In what way?" I ask.

"When I've spoken to him recently, I've had the sense that he's withdrawing. He's brushed off all my offers of help and kept our conversations unusually brief even by his typical standards. Her loss is a blow to all of us, but to him, with the bond gone silent… I think it may be taking a much graver toll than he wants to let show."

I frown. "Can't you get him to open up a little about it? You have your own experience along those lines."

Sylas makes a hopeless gesture. "I'm also his equal in standing, and I suspect he feels even more that he needs to keep up a professional front with a fellow arch-lord. I thought… You're adept at reading people, and you have some idea of what that deep a bond is like. Perhaps you'd be able to get through to him or at least make sure he isn't faltering too badly. It might be good for you to step away from the books as well."

I can't argue with him there. I glance down at my desk and rub my aching eyes. "I'm not sure how fond of me Lord Bird is, but I can certainly give it a shot."

Sylas manages a brusque chuckle. "I expect he'll be more fond if you refrain from calling him 'Lord Bird' to his face."

"You asked for my help. Don't question my methods," I retort in an attempt at light-hearted teasing that I can tell doesn't quite hit the mark. Exhaling raggedly, I stand up and shake the tension out of my limbs. "I'm sorry. I'll see what I can do. Is he off in that diamond fortress of his?"

"I heard from the last guard change that he entered the border castle not too long ago," Sylas says. "I'd start there."

I nod and head out.

Stepping into our shared castle from the summer side and gazing around the grand entrance hall makes my throat constrict. We built this place specifically to give Talia a home where she could fulfill all her responsibilities and spend time with all her mates without needing to constantly travel back and forth between the realms. It feels *wrong* for the place to be standing without her in it or anywhere nearby.

We'll get her back, I think at the walls, as if they need the reassurance as much as I do. *The Murk will not win in the end.*

I walk through the rooms on the first floor to where the wooden construction blends into the diamond of the winter side. Down one of the halls, Corwin's scent reaches my nose. I follow it up the stairs and toward the castle's private chambers, but it doesn't lead me to his own bedroom. I find myself standing outside Talia's, right in the center of the castle.

After a moment's hesitation, I knock on the door. "Corwin?"

There's a faint rustling that suggests he's getting off the bed. He opens the door a moment later, dressed as impeccably as usual in his Unseelie arch-lord finery but with a slightly sheepish expression on his face that softens any snarky thoughts I might have had.

Our interloping raven cares a lot about formalities and appearances, but he isn't made of ice underneath. I've seen outright fire in him when it comes to defending Talia.

"I was about to head out and rally another search party," he says, with a flick of his gaze back toward the room. "I— The covers still smell of her. It helps bolster my spirits."

I hold up my hands. "I won't judge." I pause and then decide it's safe to add, "I understand why you'd want to seek out any semblance of a connection to her that you can."

Corwin opens his mouth, closes it again, and ducks his head just for a second. "Well, I should go on to speak to my flock. Unless there's news?"

"No. I only thought I'd see how you're coping. I could join in the search—perhaps the cold air will sharpen my senses."

But the raven shifter is already shaking his head. "That's all right. This is my realm, and it's my duty to ensure the security of all its people. I'm sure you have plenty to attend to on the summer side."

He's trying to brush me off like Sylas mentioned. Only I'm much less polite than my lord is. I grasp his arm before he can literally brush past me. "Just a moment."

Corwin levels his dark gaze at me. "What?" he says with a hint of irritation, but the gleam shimmering in those eyes speaks of a whole heap of other emotion he's holding in, most of it painful.

I grope for the right words to get across what I think I need to say. "When I first noticed how lovely Talia is, I thought I couldn't have her. There were… circumstances in my past that made me feel ill-equipped to be a good mate to anyone. So I pushed her away through no fault of her own, because I didn't want her to discover those failings."

Corwin's forehead furrows. "Why are you telling me this?"

"Because I was wrong. Because it was better to have the subjects that were gnawing at me aired out than to hide them away. I wish I'd trusted her sooner. There's a strength in standing with someone over standing alone, as I'd imagine you've discovered too."

He inclines his head, still looking uncertain. "But I can't stand with her now. That's why I have to do everything in my power to find her."

"Of course. But that principle doesn't only apply to her." I tap my chest. "We're in this together. You know that Sylas, August, and I will fight just as hard to bring her back. Your pain isn't the same as ours because your bond is different, but we're not going to judge you for that either. So I hope you won't push *us* away to try to stop us from noticing it. We'll be stronger searching for her if we collaborate, just as we have been in so much else."

Corwin's shoulders come down just a little, releasing a subtle tension I might not have noticed if I hadn't been watching for it. He glances away with an audible swallow and then meets my eyes again. "You're right. I shouldn't turn away help that's offered, and I should recognize that you're all just as entwined in her loss as I am, even if it's in different ways. I haven't meant—"

I wave off his apology before he can do more than begin it. "It wasn't my intention to chide you, only to knock a little more sense into that already sensible bird brain of yours." I smile to offset the hint of mockery in my words. "Before you go rushing off on another search, perhaps we should try putting our brains together? None of the past searches have turned up anything, have they?"

Corwin grimaces. "No. But we can't stop trying."

"Of course not. My point is just that it's becoming increasingly clear that however the Murk stole Talia away, they have enough magical power to both cover their tracks and mute her bond with you."

He nods slowly. "I suppose that's true. But how could those vermin—"

I cut him off with a gesture. "We can't know how, so there's no point in worrying about it. Let's just focus on what is. The rat shifters have a substantial amount of magical power, far more than we'd ever have guessed. Perhaps enough to rival our own kind."

"Now there's a horrifying thought," Corwin mutters, sardonically enough that I like him more.

"Indeed. So…" I cock my head. "If *you* were going to use magic to erase all sign of your presence and passage through various types of terrain, what sort of spells would you turn to?"

I consider the same question as Corwin falls into silent pondering. I hadn't let myself really accept the idea of the Murk being on the same level as us before. But if they were—if they could pull off the same kinds of careful yet potent spellwork…

"They might rely on the wind, to some extent," Corwin suggests. "Strong gusts to disperse their scent."

I snap my fingers. "Yes. And perhaps they've made use of some sort of carriages of their own that don't need to touch the ground."

"They would need to include visual illusions as well, so that they're not seen. Especially when they're on the winter side where the terrain is generally more open."

I'm not used to dealing with ice and snow. "What sorts of illusion would work best for that?"

Corwin rubs his jaw. "If *I* were attempting an effect like that, I might make use of light and reflections. Replicate the glare of sunlight on frozen surfaces so it seems completely natural."

A smile springs to my lips. "*That* sort of magic would leave some traces behind, at least in the short term. What do you say we conduct a quick search just the two of us, tracking any traces of warped light on and around your plateau here?"

Corwin doesn't look fully convinced, but a little more energy has come into his tone. "What did you have in mind?"

I motion toward the winter-side doorway. "We make a circuit of the plateau and then drop to the lands below if necessary. Cast periodic seeking spells for that specific type of magic. I'll prowl the treed areas in wolf form, and you scan the open areas as a raven. We'll see if either of us come upon anything questionable—and signal the other as soon as we do."

Corwin draws in a slow breath. "That sounds reasonable," he says, which from him I know is significant praise. "Shall we see to it immediately?"

I grin. "No time like the present."

It does feel good to be out in the real world *doing* something other than digging through records, even when the real world I'm currently in has bitingly cold air and rather a lot of that quite natural, glaring reflected sunlight Corwin mentioned. My spirits stir eagerly as I intone a spell I send off to the north, through the rest of Corwin's domain. He adds his voice to mine to strengthen the seeking spell. Then we leap forward into our animal forms.

The ice prickles under my wolfish paws, but my fur fends off the worst of the chill. I stalk through the sparse forest, my nerves on edge to catch any quiver of alert from the spell we cast. When I emerge, Corwin circles overhead with a low caw that seems to voice his own lack of results.

Gradually, we make our way through the other arch-lords' domains, thankfully avoiding the rulers of those domains so far. I've nearly reached the edge of a strip of forest to the southeast when a tingling races over my skin.

I let out a forceful bark and spring forward. The tingling intensifies as I narrow in on the spot. Right at the edge of the woods, where the needled branches would hide the view from above but anyone lurking here could keep an eye on both the nearest palace and the flock village by it, a faint magical glimmer remains embedded in the snow.

I dart out from under the tree cover to show Corwin the spot and wheel back, shifting upright as I do. Corwin lands beside me mere seconds later.

He notes the same glimmer I did. "It's relatively recent," he says with an edge in his voice, kneeling by it. "I'd guess it was conjured in the past day."

"But no scent of the rats," I point out. "No prints or other marks of their presence. It's possible it wasn't them. Would there be any reason for your own people to be casting those illusions here?"

"I doubt it." Corwin stands and frowns down at the trace of magic. Then he looks at me. "They're slipping past even all the guards and sentries we've called to the task—they're still spying on us. Are they just enjoying seeing our distress over Talia's loss? Or..."

My gut clenches, the momentary lifting of my spirits fading. I fill in the question he couldn't quite voice. "Or are they planning something even worse?"

10

Talia

I wait until the Murk around me have settled into their homes to sleep, during what I guess must be daytime in the world outside the Refuge. I hear a few still roaming past my little hovel, probably patrolling. When I poke my head out, the overhead lights have dimmed enough that I have to squint to make out any shape more than a few feet away.

Orion always appears to be up when the rest of his people are. I assume he has to sleep sometime. I gaze into the dark stillness for a while longer before gathering the boldness to slip over the edge of the platform and creep along the tracks.

The tunnel swallows me in an even deeper black, but only for a few breaths. As I feel my way along across the gravel between the rails, the glow of the Murk's Heart comes into view up ahead, seeping out over the tunnel walls with its sporadic flickering. I fix my gaze on it to guide me, even though the sight of it makes my pulse skitter.

When I reach the entrance to the throne room, I peer inside carefully. The dais stands empty, no figures lounging on its well-worn surface or in the king's chair. There's no sign right now of the king himself. The entire room is empty other than the jittering glow and the erratic jolt of the Heart's energy over my skin.

Setting my feet as silently as I can, I limp across the rough cement floor to the glowing orange mass. With so little other light, its erratic energy niggles at me even more than usual, sending a crawling sensation through my body in waves. I shudder, hugging myself, and force my feet to carry me all the way onto the low platform.

I skirt the throne and walk right up to the Murk's Heart. Bracing myself against the spurts of energy that waft over me, I scan the ground beneath it and the wall around and behind it for any clues to its full nature.

Is it drawing on any kind of fuel here? Has Orion used some kind of magical artifact to help power it? Is there anything at all I could disrupt to damage the Murk's source of magic—to weaken them enough that I could reach Corwin again, that the fae of the seasons could challenge the rat shifters on their own turf and win?

Or even just to prevent the war Orion's planning. I'd settle for that, regardless of what happens to me.

But I can't see anything except the immense patch of condensed energy, which stands a few feet taller than me and equally wide. Not as big as the Heart of the Mists, but still formidable. Still potent enough that the roots of my hair are starting to prickle the longer I'm standing so close.

I wave my hand into the midst of the glow, and a searing pain stabs through my fingers. I yank them away so quickly I almost stumble backward. My skin doesn't look damaged as far as I can tell in the orange light, but it takes several seconds before the sharp ache starts to fade.

Okay, that definitely didn't get me anywhere.

I shuffle to one side and the other to see if I can make out any other clues from a different angle, but nothing that looks at all useful presents itself. Sucking a frustrated breath through my teeth, I wander around the rest of the dais, prodding the surface with my toes, testing the assortment of concrete chunks that make up the throne, checking the walls on either side for supplies or other items that might be important to Orion.

I find a few newspapers from the past few weeks tucked away on one ledge, but they don't give me any clue about my location. Either Orion has his people raiding newsstands with international subscriptions, or they leap through the portals to visit cities all over the world. The paper that's in English is from Sydney, Australia. There's another written in what I think is Spanish, and two others in letters I can't even read to guess what countries they're from.

Can Orion read all these languages, or did he want them for some other purpose?

I'd like to take them with me in case they'll prove useful, but when they're the only thing left around here other than a few scraps of food waste, it'll be too obvious they're missing. I worry my lip under my teeth and then set the newspapers back in their nook.

I slink back toward the entrance staying close to the wall, searching for other alcoves. There's one narrow opening I hadn't noticed before because of the angle of its entrance, which falls away into a passage of total darkness. I can't tell how deep it is, and there's nothing in view in the area the Heart's glow touches.

When I lean close, a rasp that sounds like an exhaled breath reaches my ears. I stiffen and cautiously retreat.

I think someone's sleeping down there. Orion or someone else?

Whoever it is, I doubt they'll be all that friendly to someone sneaking into what's essentially their bedroom.

Disheartened, I limp the rest of the way to the tunnel. I should probably get some sleep. Tomorrow I'll slip away to the maintenance room again and see if I can loosen up the bolts on that vent cover. If I can't find anything here in the Refuge that'll help me stop the war, then the best thing I can do is get the hell out of here to let the other fae know exactly what they're up against.

I've only just stepped over the nearer rail when the rattle of gravel farther down the tunnel freezes me in place. My heart thumping, I glance over my shoulder. It takes a few moments for enough light to catch on the approaching figure for me to recognize him, and even then, I don't totally relax.

Madoc comes to a stop a few feet from me and raises his eyebrows. "What were you doing in there at this hour?" he asks, his voice quiet.

"I thought of something I wanted to ask Orion," I say, spitting out the first excuse that pops into my head. "I figured he might still be up." I shrug as if to say, *oh well.*

Madoc gives me a penetrating look that sends a quiver of apprehension through me, but he doesn't question my story. "I'd imagine he'll hear your question tomorrow. Do you need help finding your way back to your house?"

"I made it here; I'm sure I can find my way back."

He motions for me to walk alongside him. "I was heading this way anyway. Had a desire I couldn't shake for a middle of the night snack. Not that it's actually night in many places above us."

"A noon snack?" I can't help suggesting.

The corners of his lips twitch upward. "Something like that. You're obviously feeling a bit restless yourself if you're seeking out answers when everyone else is sleeping. Maybe you could do with a snack too."

My first instinct is to refuse, to avoid his company— but I second-guess that impulse before the words work their way up my throat. Orion's not worth trying to convince, but Madoc... Madoc didn't seem exactly *happy* about what happened earlier with the two young Murk men, even if he saw their skirmish as unpreventable.

He's close to Orion. He must know more about his king's strategies and magic than just about anyone else here. I might as well take whatever opportunity presents itself to see what I can get out of him. At least he can talk, unlike their Heart.

"Thank you," I say. "That would be nice. Is there much food around at this time?"

He chuckles lightly. "I keep my own stash."

I remember the box of human snacks I noticed in his telescope room. Unsurprisingly, that's where he leads me —past the station with my house and through another into a farther tunnel, then up the stairs. On the way up, he murmurs a string of syllables I immediately recognize as the true name for light—*sole-un-straw*—and a gleaming white sphere appears at the top of the stairs to guide our way.

In the small room, I settle onto one of the pillows. Madoc paws through his box of snacks, his tail curling around his feet, and asks, "Do you prefer sweet or salty?"

It's been so long since I've had human-made junk food that I'm not sure how to answer. When it comes to August's cooking, the answer would definitely be "Sweet," so that's what I say.

Madoc tosses me a crinkly package that holds what looks like a chunk of chocolate cake in the shape of a half moon. I manage to tear the plastic open and take a bite.

The pastry is weirdly fluffy and yet sticky in my mouth, the white icing adding an extra punch of sugar. A memory wavers up—Mom didn't like us having junk food much, but I think I had one of these at a friend's house way back when…

Madoc has taken a cake of his own. He watches me as he eats his in quick but neat bites. "Not to your liking?" he asks in a tone I can't totally read.

"It's fine," I say. "I just—it's making me think of a long time ago, when my life was normal." It's hard to say whether the nostalgic sensation is good or bad. Maybe a bittersweet mix of both.

"Your life was never normal," Madoc says. "You were meant for this from before you were born. You just didn't know it until recently."

I grimace at him. "It's pretty much the same thing." I pause. "Am I the only human Orion used that way?"

Madoc eyes me again, and I suspect he's deciding how much it's safe to say to me. "You're obviously the only one he's sent into the Mists to win over the fae of the seasons," he says. "Which is for your good too, even if you didn't get asked permission first."

"Because I'm going to be in such a great position after he finishes his plans and conquers the entire fae world?" I say, reining in the sarcasm that wants to seep into my voice.

"You will be," Madoc says, ignoring whatever he picked up from my tone. "You'll have more freedom than you ever did under those fae, whatever favors the few who catered to you might have promised, and you'll be respected as an instrumental part in seeing through our plans. But you'll still get to be a part of a magic most humans never get close to."

Does he really believe all that? I tip my head to one side, studying him in turn. "I saw today just how well Orion treats his own people who're only trying to help with his plans. If that's the kind of respect I can expect, I'm not sure I'm better off with it."

Madoc's gaze flickers. "Anyone who wants to join the fight right at Orion's side has to be tested to make sure they won't crumble under the real pressure. You've already accomplished everything he'll ask of you."

I'm not so sure about that. "So why do you stand with him?" I ask, partly out of real curiosity and partly in the hopes of unraveling a little more of his king's plans. "Are you expecting some kind of great reward once the fae world is his? Assuming you even survive the battle, of course."

"We'll survive," Madoc says darkly. "The Seelie and Unseelie are hardly prepared for what they're going to face when we're ready to launch our full attack. And I don't care about any reward."

My eyebrows arch. "Nothing at all?"

He gazes evenly back at me. "Nothing other than seeing all the other Murk like me throw off the bullies who've been treating us like dirt for so long. Every fae in this place and all the other colonies deserves to regularly breathe air that isn't filtered through miles of subways system, to stay out in the sun rather than having to cringe in the shadows. They deserve to *live*—the centuries upon centuries most of the other fae get but we rarely see."

Passion rings through his voice. I think he really means everything he's just said. I can't quite wrap my head around those words in combination with his support for Orion, though.

My defiance tumbles out before I can catch it. "You want to save your people. As far as I can tell, Orion is more interested in hurting fae—and not just the fae of the seasons. I saw how excited he was watching the fight. He's insane."

Madoc's expression shutters. His voice comes out stiff. "If he is, then it's the kind of insanity that allowed him to do what no Murk before ever has—to create our Heart, to bring us all together ready to take what's ours. We'd have no chance at all without him." He stands up abruptly. "I think you'd better be getting to bed now."

The last of the packaged cake turns chalky in my mouth. I get up and follow him down the stairs, still puzzling over how a man who could profess such honorable goals so genuinely could also accept so much sadistic cruelty from the king he serves.

Was I wrong, and Madoc didn't really mean the rest after all? He could be just as bad as Orion underneath, only better at hiding it.

I can't count on either of them shifting their views, that's for sure.

11

Talia

I meander around the outer portion of the maintenance room for several minutes, acting as if I'm just exploring, listening hard for any sign that I'm not alone. I didn't pass any fae during the last part of my walk here. I can't hear anything but the thumping of my pulse.

Of course, the rat shifters have been able to hide their presence from all the other fae in the past, so I can't assume my senses will be enough to notice them.

Madoc seems to turn up pretty often when I'm around. Is that just coincidence, or has he been following me? I try a little experiment, letting my warped foot snag on a pipe and toppling onto the ground. I suck in my breath and swear, gripping my knee as if it's badly hurt, though I only banged it a little.

No one leaps from the shadows to come to my aid.

The room around me remains silent. After a few more minutes, I feel confident enough to stand up and weave through the machines to the one beneath the air vent.

I'm going to have to risk this move eventually. I'll never be totally sure that I'm alone. If they catch me at this, well, can they really blame me for wanting to get out?

I focus on the thought of sucking fresh air into my lungs, hearing Corwin's voice through our bond, seeing the blue sky again. But once I'm settled into a secure position on the knobby top of the machine with the vent at shoulder height, I have to let the uneasy images of what Orion and his followers might do to me for my disobedience rise up.

It's fear and defiance that fuel my ability to manipulate bronze.

Unfortunately, I'm not exactly an expert on tools. I can't remember if I've ever held a wrench before—I watched Dad use one doing minor repairs around the house now and then, but my impressions of how exactly it's shaped are vague.

I study the bolts, picturing how I'll need the tool to grip their heads, and hold that image in my mind as I grip the bracelet Sylas gave me. "*Fee-doom-ace-own*," I murmur as quietly but forcefully as I can, willing the metal to shift to match the imagined tool.

The bracelet releases my wrist and straightens into the approximate shape, a long handle with a rounded head. The opening that's meant to wrap around the bolts proves to be too small the first time—I can't get it around them at all. When I encourage it wider, it slips right over them.

Gritting my teeth, I repeat the true name once more, nudging it just a tiny bit smaller again and ignoring the splinter of a headache that's just starting to pierce my forehead.

This time, the tool catches on the bolt head and holds there. But that wasn't even the hardest part.

I wrap both sets of fingers around the handle and yank —then yank harder. It takes so much effort the muscles in my arms burn before I feel the bolt budge just a bit. I catch my breath and haul on it again.

It takes a long time before I've loosened that first bolt enough that I could remove it from the vent cover. I've stopped every few minutes to rest and listen for any approaching figures, but those breaks haven't reduced the strain by much. When I finally feel the bolt totally give, my shoulders and biceps are throbbing. I'm not sure I could have kept it up much longer anyway.

I tug the bolt out just to confirm that I can and then slip it back into the hole so that it's not obvious I've loosened it. Then, with the ache of the workout radiating through my body, I contemplate the other seven bolts holding the vent in place.

I don't think I can tackle more than one a day. So, I'm spending one more week here at the very least, and that's assuming I'm able to come and work on them every day uninterrupted. I swallow thickly.

How long is left until the next full moon? How many more Unseelie will freeze to death in the curse's grasp before then?

What if Orion launches the next part of his war before I can get out of here?

There's nothing I can do about that. I'll just keep coming back when I can and giving it my best shot.

I push back the nagging reminder in the back of my head that I don't even know if this air vent will give me a clear passage to the outside world. It's the only chance I have.

My skull prickles with a renewed headache when I transform the wrench back into a bracelet—one that hopefully looks almost identical to the one I was wearing before—but it fades quickly as I limp along the tracks. Which is good, because I've only just emerged into the nearest station when one of the Murk comes hustling over to me.

Not just any of them. It's Bren, his eye socket still mottled purple and brown with bruising, scabs mottling his cheeks from Colby's scratches. When he opens his mouth, I realize he must have lost a tooth in the fight. There's an obvious gap.

And the king he fought so hard for hasn't let the Refuge's healer fix any of that. Maybe Orion wanted to leave the superficial wounds as a testament to the kind of devotion he expects.

"Orion wants you to attend to him," Bren says, a little breathlessly. "You should hurry—it took me a while to find you."

There's a hint of irritation and a question in that statement, but I pretend I don't hear the latter part. "Of course," I say, the battered face in front of me also a stark reminder of just how careful I have to be around the Murk's king. "Is he in the throne room like usual?"

Bren bobs his head and trails behind me as I hobble on through the station and into the tunnel behind. I'd point out to him that I can't walk any faster and he's welcome to carry me if he's so impatient, but I'm a little worried he'd take me up on that suggestion, and I don't actually want his hands on me.

I guess I can't blame him for wanting to be sure he's completely fulfilled his orders. He's even more aware of his king's temperament than I am.

"I saw your fight with Colby," I venture, keeping my tone mild. "Are you all right?"

"I'm proud that I proved I can stand with my king," the young fae man says brusquely.

Something about the boyish smoothness of his face and the determination in his tone reminds me of Jamie. I'm not sure Bren is any older than my little brother in fae terms. My hand drifts to my bracelet, thinking of the spell August cast on it to connect me to my brother. Does the fact that it hasn't alerted me mean Jamie's still safer than I am right now, or has Orion's magic disrupted that spell like my bond with Corwin?

I glance down at my hands, and my heart stutters. My fingertips are stained dark with dirt and grease from clambering over the machines and working away at the old bolt. Bren doesn't appear to have noticed, but I doubt Orion's sharp eyes will miss that detail.

"I, um—I have to use the bathroom," I say quickly.

"I'll go see Orion right after. But you can wait if you want to make sure."

Bren frowns, but he walks with me to the nearest bathroom and only sighs once while he stands by the doorway. I use the toilet just so he can hear the flush and then scrub my hands as quickly as I can at the sink.

When I'm done, the tips are ruddy, but I've managed to wash off most traces of my work. Any lingering smudges I can attribute to feeling my way along the walls in the shadowy tunnels.

When we finally reach the throne room, Orion doesn't look particularly concerned about the delay. He glances over with a nonchalant wave and goes back to talking with two fae women who keep bobbing their heads beseechingly as they speak to him. But after I've sat down a short distance from the throne and Bren has vanished, the Murk king cocks his head at me. "It took you some time getting here."

I shrug as if I assume it isn't any big deal. "I was wandering around the Refuge, getting to know this place —since it's my new home, for now at least. It's pretty big."

"It is. I've put a lot of work into making this colony a city in itself." Orion smiles and waves off the women. Sitting down in his throne, he beckons me closer so I'm practically sitting at his feet. His tail flicks in the air just inches from my arm.

I don't enjoy having to gaze up at him like some kind of pet, but I suspect he wouldn't take it well if I insist on standing and putting myself on his level.

"How long will we be staying in the Refuge?" I ask,

wondering if I can get more information out of him if I come at it from a different angle. "It's impressive, but I can't pretend I wouldn't like to be back in the open air in the Mists. That's the goal, right?"

"It is." Orion folds his hands in his lap and stretches out his legs. "But there's no rushing a revolution. We'll know when the time is best to strike."

It sounds like even *he* doesn't know when he plans to attack. Hopefully that means it won't be incredibly soon.

I want to know as soon as he makes any decisions about that. I weigh my words and then say, "Is there any way I could help? There are a lot of fae in the Mists who've treated me badly. I feel like I should be there, standing up to them."

Orion's expression doesn't appear to change, but a shiver runs over my skin as if his attention has become more penetrating. "Starting to come around, are you?" he says casually.

I motion to the room around me. "It's easy to see that the Murk are more than I was led to believe, and obviously you have some legitimate issues with the other fae. You've got just as much a right to the Mists as they do. I spent too long in their world locked away, not able to contribute much… I don't want it to be that way again."

"You know I can't let you leave the Refuge until there's no chance that raven you're bound to could sense anything through you that would damage our efforts." Orion considers me as if evaluating whether leaving this place was my intended goal.

It's easy to nod as if it doesn't matter to me, because I

never expected he'd let me wander around in the human world right now anyway. "I understand. I'm thinking more about the preparations down here, and being ready to step up once you set off for the Mists."

"Hmm." He taps his lips. "Interesting when that's nearly the reason I called you here. I'd like to rub some salt into the wound—only figuratively, for now. I'm sending a letter into the Mists to remind the fae there how much they've lost. I'd like to add a little of your blood to it so they can be sure we do actually have you. Will you volunteer it?"

Is it really voluntary when his authority and brutality are hanging over me? I don't feel like I have much more choice than the two men who fought to the death yesterday must have.

You don't need to do that, I want to say. *They already know I'm with the Murk.* But then I'd have to reveal how I communicated with Whitt.

And besides, Orion would probably want to taunt them with my blood regardless of whether they already know.

"Of course," I say, with more confidence than I feel. "You've offered me so much here; it's the least I can do in return. Should I do it now?"

He gets up and motions for me to follow him. There's a sheet of paper sitting in one of the little alcoves that I found empty last night. I was hoping that I'd be able to read some of the message he's sending, but it's in the same odd lettering as many of Whitt's books, which wakes up my headache when I look at it for more than a few seconds.

Is there any way I can pass on a message of my own with this act? What message should I even pass on?

Orion doesn't give me much time to think about it. He produces a small pocket knife and reaches for my hand. I let him take it and prick my forefinger.

He keeps his fingers around my wrist as he brings my hand to the paper. I press down, leaving a slight smear, pushing just a little harder one, two, three, four times. I'm not sure it'll say much to my men, but I want them to know I'm thinking of the four mates I left behind, that I'm still enough in my right mind to do so. That I'm figuring out a way back to them.

Orion intones a few syllables to close my finger. He studies the bloody mark at the bottom of the page for long enough that my skin starts to creep. But when he turns back to me, he's smiling.

"Very good. I clearly made you well. If you want to be useful, I'm sure I can find a few more jobs for you. Let's get you started right now."

12

August

The forest along the border in Donovan's domain is the stillest I've found it in the past few days since the Murk stole Talia from this spot. Everyone else has finally gone off to search farther afield. I've joined those efforts, but I keep getting drawn back here.

The last place we know for sure she was. The place that's offered so few clues. But what if there's something we're missing?

I have to keep looking. Have to keep going over every inch of ground with my wolfish nose to the dirt, dragging in every trace of scent. Have to scour every twig for scraps of hair or fabric. Just one little thing could lead us to our missing mate.

I'm not sure how many hours I've been at it when I sit

back on my haunches and gaze around me with now-bleary eyes. I haven't turned up any evidence at all.

Another wolf trots over to me through the trees. I recognize Astrid by her pale fur and wiry limbs. Unable to suppress the tiny flicker of hope that maybe she's come with good news, I straighten into man form as she shifts too.

Her expression offers the opposite of hope. "The party we sent through the portal to Talia's brother's town just returned. Jamie is fine, but there's no sign that Talia's been there any time recently."

I nod in acknowledgment, my stomach sinking. I'm glad the Murk haven't threatened her brother as well, but if they had, it'd at least have given us one more avenue to locating them. And we have so little.

I shouldn't wish that a teenaged boy was kidnapped to make my own job easier, I chide myself. I shouldn't have failed in the first place.

Rubbing my hand over my face, I consider what to say. "Our pack-kin had a long trip. Tell them to rest and eat and whatever else they need to do for a couple of hours. Then I want them to take up the patrol west of Copperweld. And we should send another contingent to the fringes to check the other portals."

Astrid dips her head. Technically we're equals in authority now that she's part of Sylas's cadre, and she has several centuries of experience on me, but she defers to my orders when it comes to the defense of our pack. That's supposed to be my strength. And yet—

"If I may, August?" she says, in a patient voice.

Her hesitation sends a prickle of shame through me. She shouldn't need my permission to speak her mind to me. "Say whatever you need to. I'll hear it."

She motions to the forest around us. "*None* of us were prepared for the Murk to pull off anything like this. It isn't your fault that you weren't either. I have every intention of finding Lady Talia and tearing apart every Murk that tries to stand between us and her, but tearing *yourself* up isn't going to help her."

My embarrassment grows with a rush of heat over my face. "It was my duty more than anyone else's to make sure she was safe. On the very night when I swore to be there for her in every possible way, I let her out of my sight—I let those mangy rats—"

"No," Astrid says, more firmly now. "You didn't 'let' them do anything. They had a very clever scheme that slipped past all of us. All that matters now is unraveling that scheme so we can get her back."

"Of course," I say. "I appreciate your honesty." I know she's right. But my gut stays knotted as she lopes off to pass on my instructions to our warriors.

It isn't just the fact that I didn't catch onto the Murk's plan ahead of time that's gnawing at me. From the very first moment I started falling for my mate, I was haunted by the thought of how easily my affection could end up hurting her. I allowed myself to set those worries aside… but maybe I was wrong to. By taking Talia as our partner, we drew even more attention to her than she'd have had otherwise.

I don't know what I'd have done differently, but I can't shake the sense that I've let both her and myself down.

There's no point in continuing this search over well-trodden ground, though. I can admit that to myself—I'm not going to find anything new. Inhaling the warm, piney air, I let loose my wolf and trot across the terrain, debating where to turn my focus next.

I've spent a lot of recent days telling squads of our pack-kin and other volunteers to go one place or another. Whitt said that he and Corwin came across signs that the Murk are monitoring our efforts regardless. While so many of our people are searching farther abroad, maybe I should give our own lands a closer inspection.

I pause at the castle for a goblet of water and a bite to eat to refresh my senses, and then I slink off into the woods that cover our side of the hill around the Heart. Our domain stretches all the way down and a few miles farther, most of that area forested. It'd give the rats plenty of shelter if they wanted to spy on us in our distress.

The thought makes me draw my lips back from my fangs. I allow myself a moment to dream of ripping into those vermin.

I make a steady sweep of my patrol, back and forth from one end of our domain to the other, lower down the hill with each pass. No hint of ratty scent reaches my nose. No odd glimmers of light catch my eyes. Maybe they use different strategies in the shadows, though. I pause once or twice to cast out a spell to detect magically conjured shadows or other sorts of deflective illusions.

My efforts turn up nothing, but on my next pass through the woods, a different unexpected smell tickles into my nose. It's wolf, and vaguely familiar, but not any I recognize as our pack-kin.

Of course, there's a cacophony of wolfish scents all around. It could be from any of the other Seelie coming and going to report on the search. But this one caught my notice because it's particularly thick in this spot, as if the person stayed here for some time.

I don't see anything around to explain why they'd have lingered here. And something about the vague familiarity sends a wave of uneasiness through my chest.

Frowning inwardly, I sniff around and pick up the trail a little farther down the hill. As I follow it, a twinge of recognition wavers up from my memory.

Jax. The dark-haired woman from Lord Tristan's cadre —the one who once threatened Talia. It's her scent; I'm sure of it.

Why would she have been hanging around in the woods in our domain? I don't remember seeing her among the various search parties we assembled, although to be fair I haven't been able to oversee even half of them myself. Tristan's domain is only about an hour's carriage ride from the Heart, so it wouldn't be unexpected for him to send manpower to help with the search.

Something about it just itches at me in a way I can't explain. So I prowl onward, tracking her scent.

It isn't easy. So many other wolves have passed through this forest that once I leave the spot where she lingered behind, the distinct aspects of her smell mingle with dozens more until there's no longer a clear trail. But I continue in the same direction and pick up a faint whiff of it at close enough intervals to stay on course.

My investigation leads me out of the woods to a short span of fields. My back prickles with the new openness and the knowledge that I'd be easily spotted. I can't see any sign of my fellow fae in the fields.

I hesitate there for a minute and then decide to circle around the open ground, keeping to the shelter of the trees and tasting the air for any sign of where Jax went after she crossed them.

I'm a little more than halfway through my circling when a different odor reaches my nose—a whiff of smoke, seeping from deeper into the woods near me, just beyond the official border of Hearth-by-the-Heart. The breeze has me downwind, so I slink into it, knowing whoever might be up ahead shouldn't be able to sense my arrival.

The leaves rustle overhead. I set my paws quietly, barely disturbing a twig. Subterfuge might be Whitt's domain, but any skilled warrior needs the ability to be stealthy when necessary.

I've crossed maybe half a mile when the faintest murmur of voices reaches my ears. I can't make out the words yet, but I catch another hint of Jax's scent mixed with the smoke from the fire. The breeze shifts, and I ease to the side so I can stay downwind as I creep closer.

When I'm near enough that the voices form audible words, I stop and crouch low to the ground. I can just pick up the flicker of the fire in the distance through the trees.

A figure moves past it—not Jax, but a taller, bulkier man I've also seen among Tristan's close pack-kin. The wavering light dances across a wooden structure behind them. They've conjured at least one building to set up a temporary campsite here.

There's nothing forbidding them from doing so. This unclaimed strip of land lies between a few different domains, not officially belonging to any of them—and even if it did, we Seelie are generally tolerant of temporary visitors as long as they don't bother our packs. But why have they settled in here when they could be home in an hour?

The first part of the conversation doesn't offer much enlightenment.

"I thought the hare would be better if we cooked it, but it hasn't helped much," the bulky man mutters.

I recognize the reply as Jax's voice. "No one's stopping you from hunting down something else."

The man grunts and digs into his meal with the sound of torn flesh. There's a faint thump as if something heavy has been moved. They talk briefly about the state of the game in these woods and how much better the hunting was when Tristan's cousin Ambrose oversaw this area as arch-lord. My hackles rise in annoyance, but their remarks are nowhere close to treason.

I wait, debating how much longer I should stay in the hopes of overhearing something useful, risking another shift in the wind that might alert them to my presence. I'd like to have something more to report back to Sylas than I do so far.

I *could* simply walk up to them and ask them what their business here is, but somehow I doubt I'd get a true answer.

Then the man says, "Do you think the delivery tomorrow will be enough?"

"Maybe we'll want another," Jax says. "We'll see how it goes."

He chuckles to himself with a dark note I don't like at all. "Weapons to protect *Lady Talia* and destroy the Murk. Ha."

I don't like the sneer in his voice when he refers to Talia either. And he sounds as if he's mocking the idea that they'd be protecting her. Is he saying they're bringing weapons for some other reason?

"May as well destroy them, the filthy vermin," Jax says, which reassures me for just a moment before she adds, "They did offer an excellent opening, though, I'll give them that."

My body stiffens. An opening to do *what?*

I strain my ears harder, but the man simply lets out one more chuckle and goes back to his meal. Jax shifts something with another thump. The next time they exchange words, it's to debate who'll keep the first watch. I don't hear anything else that sounds odd.

The wind starts to shift, and I reluctantly retreat. I don't have much, but I need to tell Sylas what I *have* heard.

As if he needs to be dealing with worries over Tristan's pack-kin on top of Talia's loss.

My heart thumps heavy in my chest as I lope up the hill toward the castle. I didn't keep close enough watch over Talia—have I missed even more, a threat to our entire pack, as well?

13

Talia

The iron bars drag at my hands and leave a faintly gritty residue on my skin. My nose has filled with a smell that's far too close to the stink of dried blood. But I can't deny that Orion found the perfect job for a human in the midst of his fae subjects.

The Murk who are working alongside me, using a large machine to melt down the bars and then pour the liquid metal into molds, have to switch off regularly as their faces pale and sweat breaks out on their skin. The Murk's Heart doesn't have the same aversion to iron as the Heart of the Mists does, and its power helps the fae drawing on it resist the usual ill effects they'd experience from being close to the metal they find toxic, which must be how they were able to create that iron-laced smoke in the summer realm. But being near the substance still wears on them after a while.

It doesn't affect me at all, at least not physically. So here I am, feeding the bars into the furnace, knowing that all this work is going toward tools that'll help the Murk attack the other fae.

At least I'm getting a close look at their tactics. When the first batch of molds have set, one of the Murk women working in this alcove calls me over. "Could you move them from the original molds into these?" she says, pointing to another row of contraptions on a table along the concrete wall.

I'd appreciate the fact that she asked rather than ordered more if it wasn't obvious now what I'm making. The Murk are creating cuffs and collars like the one Arch-Lord Celia once subdued Corwin's magic with—constructed with other metals they can handle without harming themselves on the outside around an iron core to turn any fae they lock those bindings around helpless. I wonder if the collar Celia found in Ambrose's things was originally Murk-made too.

I lift the iron cores out of the smaller molds and set them in the center of the larger rings, weighing my next words. "You'd have to get pretty close to someone to get one of these things on them," I say to the fae who are readying the lead they're going to pour around the iron. "How are we going to manage that?" Celia was only able to get the collar around Corwin's neck by taking him by surprise and overwhelming him before he knew what was happening. That won't work on a larger scale.

What else does Orion have planned? The whole reason

I'm pretending to want to join their invasion is so I can find that out.

One of the men gives me a fierce-looking smile. "We've got many other uses for the iron, and Orion is working on spells to let us repel the effects more easily and for longer. We'll have smoke and arrows and darts."

The other rubs his hands together. "I look forward to seeing them suffer a tiny bit as much as they've hurt our kind."

"You've had bad run-ins with the fae of the seasons?" I ask.

The first one nods. "Haven't we all? I lost my mother to them."

"My cousin," the second one mutters with a twitch of his tail.

And what were those fae doing when they were "lost"? Somehow I suspect they were causing trouble, and the other fae were only defending themselves. But I can't expect these ones to open up to me more if I point that out.

"You'll still need to get pretty close even for smoke and projectiles to reach them," I say instead, running my thumb over my mouth as if contemplating the problem. "It's a long way from the fringes to any of the important domains." The other fae would have to notice a huge force of Murk heading their way with all this equipment long before the Murk got anywhere near the Heart of the Mists —unless they have some secret strategy.

"Oh, they'll never see us coming," says the woman who beckoned me over, letting out a harsh chuckle. "Soon we'll have full 'carriages' of our own, and we're only getting more adept at hiding ourselves. All we'll need—"

A voice from behind me interrupts, light but firm. "I think Orion would appreciate more work and a little less talking."

My pulse stutters. I glance over to see that Madoc has come into the workshop alcove. His heavy-lidded eyes linger on me for a moment longer than the others, studying me. Does he suspect that I'm here specifically to hear their talk and not because I really want to be making weapons?

I'm itching to ask what exactly the Murk will "need" to hide a mass of carriages, but it feels too risky to push the subject with Orion's close associate looking on. I set the last iron core in its new mold and go back to the furnace where more of the bars need to be added to the melting vat.

Madoc follows, dismissing the man who was pouring the melted metal into the molds and taking over that job himself. Despite his position with the Murk king, he obviously doesn't mind getting his hands dirty.

Does Orion himself ever come and help with the work? Or does he just give orders and dispense judgment while lounging around his throne?

"So, you decided to take up the cause, did you?" Madoc says to me, his expression tightening only slightly as he sets his hands close to the liquid iron to adjust the angle of the spout.

I wonder what his aversion to the metal feels like, just how much the Murk's Heart is able to shield them. Would these collars work against their makers if we found a way to turn the tables on them?

I'm not sure how much Orion might have told him about the conversation that led to me taking this job. The last time I talked to Madoc, I was criticizing his king's methods.

"I think all fae have a right to the Mists," I say, which is reasonably true. "And maybe the ones who'd have liked to see me locked up deserve some of the same treatment themselves."

The woman near me snorts. "That'd be all of them. If you don't meet their standards, they want you dead or enslaved to them—and we'd never agree to the latter."

"The humans trapped in the Mists don't get much choice," Madoc remarks. "They can't fight back. We'll see them freed too."

My gut twists, thinking of how I'd just started to fight for the rights of the other humans in the summer and winter realms before I was stolen away. I want to see them get their free will back, but not by having all the other fae slaughtered or enchained instead.

One of the men by the lead vat harrumphs. "We don't have any need for mortal servants running around doing our own work for us." He halts and glances at me. "Not that we'd turn away your voluntary help, of course."

His hasty clarification doesn't erase the disdain I heard in his voice. I'm not actually surprised that at least some of the Murk look down on humans just like their Seelie and Unseelie counterparts do. I guess it'd be hard for them not to when we are so much less powerful and so short-lived.

But Orion and Madoc have liked to paint a picture of me being treated as an equal here.

I'm probably respected only for how I inadvertently supported their war. How would they talk to me if I wasn't their king's creation?

The thought of Orion's meddling with my body and spirit sends a shudder through me I can't quite suppress. Madoc's gaze latches onto me again. "Are you all right?"

I can't tell whether he's concerned or suspicious. Maybe both.

I chuck another iron bar into the furnace. "I don't like remembering how those fae treated me in the Mists. It's bad enough that they've damaged my body permanently. They shouldn't get to hold onto my mind too."

The man Madoc took over from, who's hung back in the doorway, lets out a sound of agreement. "Orion says they've infected us all with a sense of inadequacy and failure. That we'd have accomplished so much more if not for all those millennia of being shoved to the fringes and treated like vermin. Many of us they've outright killed or hobbled, but they've marred all our souls. Our new Heart is only just starting to heal them."

No wonder they hate the fae of the seasons so much when Orion is spouting proclamations like that. No responsibility taken for the way the Murk have treated the other fae all this time. How many of the Murk here have really dealt with the Seelie or Unseelie face-to-face in good faith to know what they're actually like?

"It's good that you're finally getting a chance to overcome their bullying," I say, seeing a chance to subtly get at the information I want. "And incredibly impressive that you've come up with so many strategies to put them in their place. The fae I was with had no idea how often you were coming into the Mists. It must be a very clever trick to disguise your presence so completely."

I'm hoping that my praise will encourage some bragging, but all I get are a few chuckles. "That it is," says one of the men.

"The pack and flock you call yours must have stepped up protections after the incidents we arranged with the Unseelie village, the smoke, and the rest," Madoc says in a casual tone I don't totally believe. "What did they think would manage to stop us?"

He's talking as if he's only looking for an amusing conversation, mocking the other fae's efforts, but he's also trying to get at *their* strategy, whether purposefully or not. I nibble at my lower lip nervously, but the truth is I don't know much I could tell him anyway.

"I think it was mostly just a matter of more," I say with a light laugh as if I'm buying into the idea that we're just poking fun at them. "More guards, more sentries. Obviously that wasn't enough, or I wouldn't be here."

Too bad for me.

"And we're all glad for that," Madoc says, shooting me another smile. "The many crimes of the fae of the seasons will soon be repaid in full."

Another waft of the iron scent fills my nose, and suddenly I can't bear to keep up this façade any longer. A burn tickles the back of my eyes, threatening to spill over into tears.

I don't want to be here. I don't want to have to worry about seeing the men I love destroyed by these people—to be helping prepare the tools to do it. I've been hanging in there, keeping up the best front I can, but inside I can feel my strength starting to crumble.

I can't show my true feelings in front of the Murk around me, though. Hefting another iron bar, I let my arms wobble, not totally for show. After I toss that one in, I rub my biceps. "I'm not sure I can keep this up for much longer. My muscles aren't used to this much physical labor."

"Of course," Madoc says. "There are plenty who can take over. We appreciate your help. If you'd like me to bring you to the healer to have the soreness addressed—"

I shake my head quickly. "No, that's all right. I think it's better if my body adjusts without any supernatural intervention. I'll just go take a nap."

I stop in the bathroom to wash as much of the metallic stink off my hands as I can. It remains on my clothes after I leave, little whiffs reaching my nose at random intervals, but one of the Murk took the other outfit they've given me this morning to clean it and I don't have anything to change into right now.

Ignoring the smell as well as I can, I head toward my hovel, but then wander on past it as if I've changed my mind and want to stretch my legs some more. I keep a careful eye on the tracks around me as I drift through the tunnels toward the maintenance area.

No one appears to pay me much mind. My show of

helping with the war preparations might at least have earned me a little more trust from my captors.

I still wait in the maintenance area for several minutes, faking an injury to test for unseen watchers, before I risk using the true name to reshape my bracelet.

This time, it only takes two tries to get the conjured wrench to the right size. But it turns out I wasn't totally lying about my arms being tired. I yank and strain at the second bolt I've picked for what feels like an hour, sweat trickling down my back, and by the end of all that effort I'm not sure I've budged it more than one full rotation.

I lower the wrench, a dull but deep ache radiating through my arms into my shoulders and back. I don't think I can make any more progress today—I barely made any as it is.

My free hand clenches with the urge to slam it into the vent cover in frustration, but that won't give me anything but bruised knuckles. I let out a breath in a ragged sigh.

I thought I might be able to arrange my escape in a week. What if it takes so much longer?

What if the strengths I have aren't enough to get me out of here at all?

There has to be another way I can find a chance to escape.

14

Talia

The first several times I've encountered Madoc, he came up on me out of nowhere. Now I find myself trying to turn the same trick on him.

I've meandered along the passage by the stairs to his telescope room several times before my strategy works out. From far away, I see the station lights catch on his pale hair just before he strides into the darker space of the tunnel. I limp toward him, attempting to keep a casual pace as if I just happened to be walking this way while still approaching fast enough that I'll catch him before he heads up to his private room.

When I'm a little closer, I pretend to just have noticed him. "Madoc?" I call out, raising my hand to catch his attention.

He pauses and then ambles over to me. His mouth forms an offhand smile that today looks a little stiff to me.

Alarm prickles through me. Did he realize I lied about where I was going after my work in the weapons workshop this morning?

He doesn't say anything accusing, though, only nods to me. "Talia. Did you need something?"

"I—" I bite my lip as if I'm nervous about what I'm going to ask, which doesn't require any acting. I'm just nervous for different reasons than I want to let on. "All that talk around the weapon forges earlier made me realize there's so much I don't know about the history between your people and the fae of the seasons. I thought *some* of them were kind, and it's been hard to get totally invested in attacking them with that idea still in my head."

Madoc lets out a rough chuckle. "They're kind when they think it benefits them, not as a matter of character. It's understandable that you were confused, though. Given how badly the first fae you encountered treated you, even a little kindness must have felt like a lot in contrast."

"Yes. Well…" I look down at my feet and then back at him. "I feel like I need to see more for it to really sink in —how important this uprising is, how much I need to set aside all the things I believed before. I don't want to stand with you if I'm giving less than my full commitment. Everyone here in the Refuge seems to be doing all right. Are there other Murk colonies that the other fae have assaulted or something like that, that I could see to drive home just how bad things have gotten for you?"

To let me step beyond the walls of this place and hopefully reach out to Corwin, even if only for a moment? Hell, just getting a glimpse of the outside world might help me convey to Whitt where the Refuge is. And if I can get some of the rat shifters worked up about their hatred of the fae of the seasons, they might give away more about their plans for revenge.

If I could get just one useful thing out of this gambit, I'd be happy.

Madoc contemplates me with a serious expression that sends a pang of guilt through my stomach alongside the tension. Does he believe me? Is it kind of horrible for me to lie to him so blatantly?

It can't be more horrible than the fate they're arranging for the fae of the seasons. I can't imagine any way everyone back in the Mists could deserve the torment the Murk are planning.

"We keep our colonies scattered," Madoc says after a long moment. "Specifically so that if the other fae track down any one of them, it's unlikely to lead them to others. And there's no way we could keep your bond to your soul-twined mate shielded to make that journey. But there is something within the Refuge that I could show you. It won't be pretty. You have to be prepared for that."

A twinge of disappointment ripples through me, but I knew that getting out of this place immediately was a long shot. If there are more parts of the Refuge I haven't stumbled on before, it can't hurt to see them too.

I'll take whatever scraps of hope I can get.

"Of course," I say. "I know firsthand how savage the fae can be." My hand rises automatically to my scarred shoulder. The long-sleeved shirt I'm wearing covers all the marks, but from the tightening of Madoc's jaw, he knows what I'm thinking of.

Those scars are no secret, but abruptly I find myself wondering just how long he's been watching me. The Murk must have set up Aerik and his cadre to come across me and my family while in the grips of the curse—it was part of their plan that some vicious Seelie would discover the power of my blood.

"Were you there?" I blurt out. "The night I was attacked. Did you help with that part of the plan?" Have I just been feeling guilty about deceiving one of the people most directly responsible for the worst moments in my entire life?

But Madoc is shaking his head. I'm more relieved than I probably should be.

"I don't do much work for Orion above in the human world," he says, and touches his ears with their slight but obvious point. "He prefers to use the many Murk who could pass for human without a spell for those missions."

"That makes sense. The—" I cut myself off before I finish mentioning that the fae of the seasons used similar reasoning when sending people to the human world. I don't think Madoc would appreciate being compared to them, and I still want him to show me what I've been missing here.

Is his larger portion of fae blood in comparison to most of the Murk what earned him his spot in Orion's inner circle? But at least a couple of the other men I've seen the Murk king consulting with had ears as rounded as any human's.

"Come along then," Madoc says into my silence, looking as if he'd prefer we change the subject too. He motions for me to follow him farther down the tunnel, keeping a slow pace for my benefit, and I fall into step beside him.

My earlier thoughts are still spinning through my head, though. "It is true that the Murk have mingled more with humans than the fae of the seasons generally do, isn't it?" I venture. Most of the rat shifters around here lack pointed ears, for all their tails make it impossible not to know they're something other than human. And that dilution of their fae heritage is part of the reason they needed to make their own Heart to draw magic from.

"Yes. We don't choose our leaders based on the supposed purity of their blood here."

"But Orion looks almost true-blooded," I can't help pointing out. I'm surprised there were any Murk with enough fae heritage to produce a child that obviously fae.

I don't say that bit out loud either, but Madoc must pick up on my line of thinking.

"His parents and grandparents and perhaps more before that wanted to help us rise above the position we've been forced into, and purposefully sought out mates who were more... fae-inclined," he says. "You could almost say he was born for this, to be powerful enough to accomplish everything we needed."

And because of that lineage, he's also arrogant enough to think everyone should follow his whims, no matter how horrifying, I guess. I grit my teeth against that observation, remembering how well my criticism went over with Madoc last time.

"What exactly are you going to show me?" I ask instead.

Madoc just shakes his head. "It'll be easier to explain when I can show you. It isn't that far." He pauses and glances down. "Is your foot hurting you?"

I've been limping the entire time I've been living in the Refuge, so it isn't as if he could think it's a new injury. But he sounds honestly concerned—and maybe even a little chagrinned that he hasn't thought to check before. An unwelcome warmth flickers in my chest.

"No worse than usual," I say. "The longer I stay on it, the achier it gets, but I never have to walk too far around here."

"All right. If it becomes a problem, or if you need a replacement for the brace in your boot, let me know. I'm sure we can replicate it."

I don't know what to say to him after that. Does my minor discomfort really matter at all to him?

It's too confusing trying to untangle his motives, so I focus on setting my feet one after the other alongside him.

We walk all the way to the last station in this direction and clamber onto the platform there. Madoc walks up to a set of steel doors that I assumed went nowhere important, since I never saw anyone going in or out of them. He unlocks them with a few murmured words and a series of swift gestures I can't follow and pushes one wide for me to walk in past him.

On the other side, a linoleum floor leads down a short hall to a single door, this one unlocked.

Madoc rests his hand on the knob. "We're not sure what the humans who built this place meant to use this area for, but they never finished it. The air doesn't pass through easily, so it's not suitable for spending large periods of time in it. We've dedicated it to days past instead."

"What do you mean?" I ask.

He opens the door and ushers me in.

Right away, I can see what he meant about the unfinished part. The room is large, nearly half again the size of the station we just left, but the walls are rough concrete mixed with patches of bare bedrock, and the craggy ceiling adds to the cave-like impression. Only the floor has been sanded smooth.

A magical light drifts down from one glowing source in the middle of the ceiling. It catches on a line of metal chairs along the walls, stretching all the way around the room. More chairs form a series of concentric rings moving toward the center of the space, with gaps here and there where a person can step between them.

But the strangest thing is the clots of fog that hang over nearly every chair. They're like little dark clouds, churning in place a few inches above the seats. They remind me a little of the shifting light inside a Seelie's soul stone, but they aren't contained in any other object and they give off no light at all.

We aren't alone in the room. A Murk woman is sitting on one of the chairs at the far end of the room, the patch of fog there wrapped around her chest. Her jaw is set firmly, but a few tears have trickled down her cheeks.

"What is this place?" I say, my voice dropping to a whisper. The woman gives no sign that she's noticed our arrival.

"The vault of memories," Madoc says simply. "A way of keeping a record of the crimes done to us. Any Murk who's lost something to the fae of the seasons may offer up his memories here so that what was lost is never forgotten."

A shiver runs over my skin. The air in here is very still but cooler than the rest of the Refuge. "And what happens when you sit in one of the chairs?"

"You're absorbed into the memory left there until the part offered up ends or someone shakes you out of it." He gestures to the rings of chairs. "You can see whatever you'd like. Every memory in here shows how little the other fae think of us."

I can just... step into other people's memories? Traumatic memories, from the sounds of it. My legs balk. "I don't want to intrude on something private."

"We all have access to everything in the vault," Madoc says. "You'd be honoring the events by witnessing them and recognizing what was done to us."

"Can you tell me what I'd be seeing ahead of time?" I ask.

He shrugs, an oddly sheepish expression creeping over his face. "If I tell you which to view, encourage or discourage you from any of them, you won't trust that whatever you see is really representative of what we've faced. Pick a few at random, and you'll get a fair sampling."

He has a point there. I still find it hard to propel myself forward.

I walk along the line of chairs against the wall, peering at each of the churning dark patches in turn. They all look essentially the same, none bleaker or more violent than another. There's really no way of telling what each might hold—to my senses, at least. From what Madoc said, there must be some sort of magical trace the Murk can pick up on that gives an idea of the contents.

I said I wanted to see what the Murk have actually been put through by the other fae—and I can't see how I'm going to get anything else of use out of this place. There could still be information in one of these memories that'll get me closer to escape.

Madoc has hung back by the door as if to ensure there's no chance of me thinking he's influencing my decision. When I look back at him, his mouth has formed a crooked line, as if he's not totally happy I'm here.

It was his idea. But then, these are his people's deepest wounds.

Has he left a memory here?

I set aside that question and force myself to pick a chair at random, halfway along the room. Bracing myself, I sink into the chair.

As I settle into the seat, a chilly tingling sensation wraps around my torso and flows up to my head with my next exhaled breath. The world around me tilts, and I close my eyes instinctively.

And then I'm there.

A fire is blazing all across a small wooden cabin. The smell of smoke fills my nose. A man lies dead in front of the building, his torso slashed through from shoulder to waist so deeply the edges of his ribs glint against the bloody flesh.

As I watch from the perspective of whoever this memory belongs to, a woman runs toward me, shooing at me to run ahead of her. I shake my head, but the panic etched on her face convinces me. My view swings around as I turn. I glance back a moment later just in time to see a wolf lunge out of the shadows to tackle the woman to the ground. It plunges its claws into her chest with a savage grin.

I jolt awake to find myself clutching the sides of the chair, my breath coming short. For a second, the smoky smell lingers in my lungs. The still air cools the sweat that's broken out on my forehead.

Madoc watches me silently from near the door. The woman who was here before has left.

That memory doesn't tell me much, though. Who knows why the Seelie attacked those Murk? Maybe they'd already hurt the summer fae. It's easy to look like the victim when you're controlling what anyone sees of the story.

I push myself off of the chair, wavering as I catch my balance, and stride deeper into the room to one of the chairs closer to the center. Dragging in a breath, I sit down.

The chill wraps around me, I close my eyes—

And now I'm swinging high above an icy plain. There's a pain in my behind from an appendage I don't have in real life. The wind ruffles my fur, and I realize the memory is of a Murk in rat form.

A rat clutched by a raven. The black wings flap overhead, and the talons clutching my tail give me a shake so hard my bones rattle. Then the bird dives downward, plummeting toward the ground. It tosses me just as it lands, a few of those bones snapping as I hit the ice.

The raven shifts into an Unseelie woman. She jabs something I can't see into the base of my tail to stop me from running, though I'm too dizzy to be likely to anyway.

"Show yourself," she snaps. "I have questions."

Pain hazes my mind as I leave behind my animal form —other than my tail, which enlarges but remains pinned.

"What do you want?" I stammer. "I wasn't hurting anyone. I was only foraging—those woods belong to no domain, I'm sure of it—my mate is close to having our child; she needs—"

"Enough lies," the woman snaps, even though I can tell the Murk whose memory I'm in meant every word he said. Nothing but fear and anguish runs through his frame—and a pinch of hunger in his belly. "You don't belong in the winter realm at all. What tricks were you up to?"

"I swear, I only came through to the fringelands because I thought something grown in the land of the Heart might fill her more," the man says. "I don't want anything except to gather a few morsels of food and leave."

"We'll just have to pick you apart until we discover the truth, then."

The Unseelie woman turns as if expecting someone else, and a flare of panicked certainty shoots through my chest—I won't make it through this alive. My mate will never know what's happened to me. She'll be all alone.

In that moment of desperation, I spit out a string of syllables. Pain sears through my bottom—but I'm free. I leap away from the tail I've severed from my body, shifting into rat form at the same time, and dash into the shelter of the nearby woods even though every step is agony.

When I come out of that memory, I'm shaking. Madoc has come closer, standing over me as if he was considering snapping me out of it early. He peers into my eyes. "Have you seen enough?"

I swallow thickly. The man whose memory I just inhabited didn't deserve that treatment. But after all the Murk have done—so much the fae of the seasons haven't deserved either—I'm not going to say they deserve to be slaughtered over a few overly vicious sentries.

"I'll look at another," I say, annoyed that my voice wobbles.

Madoc frowns, but he doesn't stop me. He hangs back as I weave through the chairs again. But when I stop and swivel to sit down on the next one I've chosen, he clears his throat urgently. "Maybe not that one. That's... That's a particularly wrenching one."

I hold his gaze. "Shouldn't you want me to see it, then?"

He opens his mouth and then closes it again with a

sickly smile. "You're right. I should. Just—be prepared. If you react too strongly, I'll pull you out."

Is he putting on a show because he doesn't want me to see what this memory contains for some other reason? I sit in the chair, even more determined than before, and shut my eyes.

This time, I fall into a dimly lit tunnel that stinks of sewage. Because it's a sewer, I realize as I take in my surroundings. It's hard to focus on any details because my heart is pounding so hard. I'm standing braced in front of a doorway on a ledge that runs alongside the channel of sludge.

Several fae are approaching. I can't tell whether they're Seelie or Unseelie at first, but then a few bare their teeth to show wolfish fangs. "We'll take her for questioning," the one in the lead says. "Destroy the rest."

"No, please!" I cry, throwing my arms wide as if I can stop them with my body. "They're only—"

One of the fae punches me in the throat so hard my voice turns into a croak. Another yanks my arms behind me and snaps a magical binding around me as he carries me with his colleagues into the room I was trying to defend.

It's... It's full of children. Young fae ranging from toddlers to kids who don't look older than five or six in human years. They all freeze and stare at the sight of the intruders.

The few adult Murk who're standing among the children rush forward, letting loose their own rat claws, but the wolf shifters slice through their throats and bash their heads in a matter of seconds. Then they turn on the kids, some of whom are staring in stunned horror, others starting to wail or shriek.

The summer fae warriors barge through the room, catching every Murk child in their path with their fangs or claws. Blood splatters the little faces. Bodies slump like toppled, dismembered dolls across the blankets spread on the floor. And one of the Seelie—one of them *laughs*.

"This many fewer to grow up and become thorns in our side," another mutters, grabbing a toddler who was scrambling away from him with a whimper and slashing the poor little body right down the middle.

A scream of protest finally bursts from my damaged throat. The man holding me wallops me across the head— and I whip back into the vault of memories.

I double over in the chair, vomit burning up my throat before I have a chance to even try to rein in my nausea. Madoc springs forward, grasping my shoulder, pulling my hair back from the spray that spills from my mouth. I gag and sputter, those horrible images flashing through my mind on repeat. I can't shut them out, eyes open or closed.

"I'm sorry," Madoc says raggedly. "I shouldn't have let you anyway."

I stay hunched over for several seconds longer until I'm sure my stomach is done heaving. Then I bring my hands to my face. "That—who were all those kids? What were the Seelie doing there?"

Madoc eases back. "We have... what you'd call orphanages. For the Murk who aren't yet old enough to fend for themselves, who've been left parentless for a variety of reasons." His mouth twists. "I spent some time in one of those, though thankfully not that one, obviously. As far as what the Seelie meant to do, you saw it. One of them must have noticed the Murk living there when they were in the human world for some other reason, and they took the opportunity to exterminate as many of us as they could."

I don't want to believe it. Does Sylas know that kind of thing goes on? Do any of my mates? No matter how many spiteful pranks the Murk have played, no matter how many deaths they've caused, to rip apart tiny children who'd never done *anything*…

My stomach lurches again, and I wait until I've gotten it under control before I speak again. "I can see why you hate them so much."

Madoc sighs and helps me out of the chair. My legs tremble. He keeps his hand on my elbow to steady me and murmurs a few quick phrases. The dinner I threw up crumbles into dust that wisps away.

My cheeks flush with embarrassment that he not only saw me in that state but cleaned up after me too. He isn't acting disdainful of my reaction, though, the way I can so easily imagine fae like Celia or Laoni behaving.

He looks me over as if confirming I really am okay and then says, "It isn't so much about hate. I do hate the fae of the seasons for the things they've done—don't get me wrong. But I don't stand with Orion to punish them. I stand with him to make sure Murk like the ones you saw never have to be punished again."

He hesitates, and then adds, "The woman whose

memory you were just in came to the orphanage where I was living next. She managed to get away from the Seelie who captured her, but she lost one of her arms in the process. She never told us what happened to the children she'd looked after before us, though. I didn't know until I came here and sensed her presence in that memory."

I shiver. "I don't regret seeing it. I needed to know. But it was horrible."

"It was. And for her, and the other children like me, and every other Murk who's had to live in constant fear of the fae of the seasons stumbling on us at the wrong moment and deciding to rain their vicious judgment down on us all, I want us to have a real home. I want us to be able to walk around freely without that shadow hanging over us. Hell, I want us to be able to partake in the Heart of the Mist's magic again, if it'll have us, even if that's a pipe dream. We're fae… We shouldn't have to live as if we're only rats."

He averts his gaze as if he's ashamed of how much emotion he's shown. His frustration rang through his voice.

I want to tell him I understand, that I respect him more for the compassion and resolve he's just shown. But how can I when seeing that resolve through would mean destroy everything in the worlds that *I've* come to care about?

15

Madoc

The sun is bright overhead and the grass soft under my back, but for some reason no jolt of apprehension passes through me. Some part of me knows that right now, I'm perfectly safe.

I close my eyes, and a soft touch brushes across my cheek. When I look up, Talia is leaning over me. The waves of her vivid pink-and-purple hair frame her pretty face, her green eyes brighter than I've ever seen them up close—but then, the only times I've seen them up close before are in the dark of night or the artificial light of the Refuge.

She belongs out here in daylight. It gleams off her like some kind of magic.

But even more magical are the sparks that light up all through my body when she strokes her fingers over my cheek again and along my jaw. I don't even think about it;

I just reach for her. As I push myself up on one elbow, she lowers her head to meet me.

That first kiss is pure, glowing joy. Her mouth is sweet, and her breath hitches with a hint of a needy whimper. Just like that, I'm on fire with my own desire.

I pull her down over me, kissing her harder, delving my fingers into her silky hair. Exploring every inch of that hot, sweet mouth with my tongue. Reveling in the way her body fits against mine, smaller and softer with curves that nestle against me in all the right places.

I slide my hand down over her breast, swiveling my palm against the peak through the fabric covering it, and she gasps. She pushes upright, straddling me, and I realize for the first time that she's wearing that lacy, rosy dress she had on when I whisked her away from the summer realm. It's unmarked by the trip now, which some distant part of me recognizes is odd, but the rest of me doesn't give a shit.

Especially when Talia raises her hands to the neckline and tugs. The fabric slips down over her shoulders and chest, baring her to the waist. Her small breasts sway with the movement, peach-pink nipples hardening in the open air.

She tilts forward as if offering them to me, and how can I possibly resist?

I take one nipple and then the other into my mouth, working them over with my tongue until Talia is moaning and writhing against me. The shifting of her body against my groin is the most excruciating torture.

I can't wait any longer. I shove up the skirt of her dress and rip off her panties.

"Madoc," she pants, so full of wanting I nearly explode just like that. I fumble to free my cock, and then I'm plunging into her slick heat as if I'm meant to be nowhere else.

Talia clutches my shoulders, riding me with rolls of her hips. Pleasure like I've never known pulses through me with every thrust. My head tips back into the grass with a groan. I grip her hips to pull her into an even better angle—

And my eyes pop open for real.

I blink, unsatisfied hunger coursing all through my body. I'm staring up at the dark ceiling of my little room, sprawled on the inflatable mattress I set up there, my body flushed and my dick unbearably hard. Alone.

I rub my hand over my face, fighting to get my urges under control. Of course I'm alone. As far as Talia's concerned, I'm just the prick who stole her from her supposed mates and dragged her away from the sunlight. She has no interest in my actual prick. Even if *it* can't help noticing how appealing her lovely face and lithe body are.

But I don't think it's her good looks that provoked this dream. I haven't had one like it about her before. My thoughts travel back automatically to the past day, to our excursion to the vault of memories. To the way she looked at me after I told her about the woman from the orphanage, as if she wanted to take up a sword and fight to the death for me right there and then.

She felt our anguish. I'm not sure if she truly was turning against the fae of the seasons before then or if she was only digging for information the same way I have with her, but in that moment, she hated them too. She wanted to stand with me.

She let me hold her arm all the way to the door until I was sure she was steady, staying so close the warmth of her body grazed mine in the chilly air. And when she looked up at me after we left, so many unspoken words shone in her eyes that I wanted to drink them from her lips.

Maybe it's not surprising that not just the soul-twined mate Orion tied her to but three other high-ranking fae besides have fallen for her. There's a fierceness to her, an inner strength that burns inside her even now, even after everything she's discovered.

She *would* fight for whatever she feels is just, even against creatures with far more power than her, all the way to her death. I've seen that, clear as day.

I sit up, shaking my head to clear it. That fire also makes her dangerous, because it might be us she decides to fight. I've also seen enough of her, spoken enough with her, to be sure her interest in her mates was more than just fickle hero worship. She might be angry on our behalf for the crimes done to us, but I don't think her loyalty to those specific men has wavered. No matter how I've prodded, she's never said a word against them.

And there are times when I don't think she realizes that anyone's watching her when a sadness comes over her face that pricks at my heart more than it should.

Right now the only thing aching is my unattended erection, though. The lust the dream stirred up in me is refusing to leave me. With a hiss of frustration, I reach for myself through my clothes and shut my eyes, calling up the naked figures of other women I've actually bedded behind my eyelids.

As I stroke myself, the images keep shifting back into Talia's slim body, her pale face with its frame of vibrant hair. But she feels too ephemeral. I can't quite give myself over completely.

Muttering curses under my breath, I jerk my clothes into place and head down the stairs. My shoes make only the faintest rustling sound over the gravel.

Talia's new house is the closest to this end of the station where I built it. I don't even get up off the tracks, just walk until I'm level with it. The door flap is shut, but I don't need to see her. I take a long, slow breath, letting the tart scent of her, like freshly grown leaves, fill my lungs. I listen to her own breaths, the faint rhythmic wisp as she sleeps.

After several seconds, I know I've drunk in enough to get where I want to go. I scramble onto the opposite platform and duck into one of the bathroom stalls. Now, focusing on the false images of her from my dream and her very real scent, I come in less than a minute.

It's only a basic bodily urge now satisfied, but I feel absurdly uncomfortable afterward, as if I've somehow defiled Talia even though she wasn't really involved at all. As if it's such a horrible thing that a Murk like me might direct any lust her way. She's a human—a human who was shaped by my own king. She isn't *better* than me.

I've mostly pushed the uneasy feelings inside when I head back to the tunnel. I slip down onto the tracks—and the flap on Talia's house pushes open. I freeze.

"Madoc?" she whispers in her clear voice, which holds none of the passion it did in my dream but enough concern to bring back a pang of guilt. As she peers out at me, she swipes her hand across her eyes, obviously still sleepy. "Just getting another middle of the night snack?"

Did my thoughts manage to wake her up after all, or is she sleeping so badly in her new home that the simple act of my walking by pulled her out?

Either way, she doesn't appear to have any idea what I was actually doing, thank all that's holy.

"That's all," I say. "Nothing important. You look like you should get some more sleep."

She mumbles in agreement and lets the flap drop. I should set off, but I can't quite will my feet to move. I stand there as if guarding over her until I hear her breaths even out with sleep again.

She has no idea what went on in my head. And it doesn't matter anyway. Animals rut at each other. Whatever physical desire I've felt, it doesn't mean anything beyond my having a working dick.

I remind myself of all those things, but when I finally do make it back to my room, I don't get much more sleep myself. The images of Talia that haunt my mind now have nothing lustful about them.

She peers out at me from the shadows of her makeshift home. She thanks me for easing the pain of her headache. She answers Orion's questions in front of me, clearly nervous but refusing to be cowed.

She stares off toward the ceiling in a rare private moment, as if hoping she'll be able to peel back the layers of cement and asphalt with her hopes alone to see through to the world above.

She looks at me, pale and sickly but full of righteous horror, and says, *I needed to know.*

I finally get up when the rest of my people will be stirring, though my nerves are brittle from my fragmented sleep. Maybe the simple fact of the matter is that I know something isn't exactly right here. Talia might not be Murk, but in most ways that matter, she's one of my people too.

It's early enough that I can hope not too many people are hassling Orion yet. I catch up with the fae bringing his breakfast and help myself to a few tidbits on the way to his audience room. They know my standing with him well enough not to protest.

I fought hard for that standing. I've earned our king's ear. I don't think I'm really going to ask for all that much.

But when I come up on the platform that holds his throne and watch him get up from it with all his feral yet regal poise, my chest constricts.

I smile and take a seat across from him at his motion. He accepts a mug of coffee from another servant and sips it with great enthusiasm before digging into the food. "Well, then, my busy friend. Any progress?"

I've already told him about taking Talia to the vault of memories. "There hasn't been much time for new developments," I say dryly.

"Who knows what may happen while others are sleeping?" he says with a flippant wave of his hand, oblivious to the uneasy twinge his remark sends through me.

I choose my next words carefully. "I have been thinking more about my observations. It's obvious that Talia is coming around to fully support our efforts to claim the Mists. But it also makes sense that she's had a little trouble adapting to spending all her time down here after such a... different life before."

Orion hums and licks yolk from a soft-boiled egg off his fingers. "I hear what you're saying and ask you to get on with the point."

"I know we have to be careful of the soul-twined bond," I say. "But it would only take a small amount of energy to temporarily expand the shield a little, wouldn't it? If we could give her an hour or two above, outside or even in a building with windows—she couldn't see anything that could lead back to the Refuge's actual location anyway, and she'd have no way to communicate what she does see to anyone regardless..."

I trail off at the arch of Orion's eyebrows. He snickers to himself. "You want to coddle her? She's barely given us anything. She must know all kinds of inner workings of the arch-lords' courts, and she's keeping it all close to the chest."

I resist the impulse to bristle. "I don't see it as coddling. She's done a lot for us already, and we've *used* her a lot. Offering her a little kindness would be strategic, making her feel even more that we're on her side and that she should be on ours."

My king makes a dismissive sound and shakes his

head. "Of course we've used her. She's *mine*. I made her. That's what she's for. And she has more use in her yet if she wasn't so stubborn." He picks up a cherry danish. "I think we should take the opposite approach."

I study him warily. "What do you mean?"

"She obviously doesn't trust either of us enough to open up. There's an easy way to shift the dynamic. What is it humans call it—good cop, bad cop?" Orion smirks. "I'll get meaner to give you the chance to play her champion. Let's see what we get out of her once you've earned her full devotion."

Doubt winds around my gut, making the bits of breakfast I ate churn. This isn't how I wanted the conversation to go at all.

I've seen how close Talia already is to believing in us. But I can tell from Orion's tone that if I contradict him, he'll go from amused to scathing in an instant. I might make things even worse for her if he thinks he needs to teach me a lesson too.

Talia's voice rises up from my memory. *As far as I can tell, Orion is more interested in hurting fae—and not just the fae of the Mists.*

I shove that thought aside and focus on the present. "What exactly did you have in mind?" I force myself to ask.

"Oh, you'll see," Orion says with delight sparkling in his eyes. "Just make sure you swoop in and 'save' her thoroughly afterward."

16

Talia

The moment I step into the throne room, I can tell something has shifted in the atmosphere. Orion is poised on his throne, his tail slung over one arm and flicking idly but the rest of him absolutely still. His usual close companions, including Madoc, are standing as if at attention on the dais around him rather than lounging in their typical casual poses.

There are only a few other fae around, hanging back by the walls, tensed but with hints of anticipation in their faces. And the twitching orange glow of their Heart washes over them all.

I pause just inside the room, abruptly uncertain. When one of the Murk told me the king wanted to see me, I assumed Orion was going to offer to share another meal with me and chat a little like he has before. Or maybe suggest another job he thinks I could help with.

This... feels very different, in a way that makes my skin crawl.

Orion beckons me closer. "Come along, my pet," he says in a tone much more mocking than affectionate. "I don't want to be yelling across the room to talk to you."

I limp forward, even though every particle in my body is clanging with alarm. What good would running away do? It's not as if there's anywhere I could flee to that he wouldn't find me. My fingers itch to reach for my bronze bracelet, to rub the cool metal to remind myself I have that one secret tool, but I'm afraid of drawing attention to it.

"What did you want to talk about?" I ask, keeping my voice as steady as I can. He can probably pick up on my nervousness with his sharp senses, but I don't want to make it any more obvious than I have to. My gaze darts to Madoc of its own accord, and his mouth moves just slightly. I can't tell whether he wants to reassure me or warn me—or maybe it's neither.

"We're fine-tuning our plans for our invasion of the Mists," Orion says. He pauses until I've come to a stop right at the edge of the dais and motions for me to step up so I'm right in front of him. "We've been able to gather plenty of information, but our methods do still have a few limitations. I think it's time I saw through the rest of your purpose there."

A chill prickles through my nerves. I hold myself stiffly, just a couple of steps from his chair. "What do you mean?"

The Murk king gives me a narrow smirk. "You've spent

a lot of time among the highest ranking fae of the Mists. You've had access to an Unseelie arch-lord's entire mind. I'm sure you know all kinds of details about their habits and strategies that we couldn't glimpse otherwise."

My pulse stutters. Both he and Madoc have nudged me about my knowledge of the other fae from time to time over the past few days, but they've never demanded information. I assumed it was because they didn't think I'd necessarily learned all that much that would be useful to them. Apparently they were only biding their time, hoping I'd volunteer more than I have.

I can still attempt to play the ignorance card. I offer a sheepish smile. "There weren't any invasions or wars when I was with them. I don't think I know very much that would help you prepare, or I'd have mentioned it already. Mostly… Mostly we talked about more personal things."

I duck my head as if I'm embarrassed by the reference to the intimacy of my relationship with most of the fae who told me much of anything.

Orion's tail keeps flicking, his smirk still in place, his eyes glittering coldly. "*I* think you still have some loyalties to the fae who took you as their mate, and that's keeping you quiet. As if they aren't just as bad as the others when it suits them. Why do you think I chose a human to shape rather than one of my own kind? If you'd been a Murk, you'd never have made it out of that first cage."

Is that true? My gut twists with the question, but there's really no way of knowing.

And it doesn't change the fact that I believe the fae I trusted back home would be willing to consider that the

Murk might deserve more than the lot they've been given. That they'd be horrified by the violence I witnessed in the vault of memories yesterday.

"That might be true," I say, the lie heavy on my tongue, "but I still don't know what I could say that would help you."

"And that is why I've gotten tired of waiting for you to get your head on straight and fully embrace your true loyalties."

In one swift movement, so sudden I have no chance to react, Orion shoots forward to the edge of his seat and snatches my wrist. As he yanks me right up to him with a strength I wasn't prepared for, my warped foot stumbles. I nearly fall right into his lap.

But maybe he wouldn't have minded that, because the next second, he's swept out his own foot to knock my legs out from under me. My knees hit the surface of the dais, leaving me kneeling in front of him, my breath locked in my throat. When I open my mouth to protest, he grasps a clump of my hair and hauls my head back so I'm staring up to meet his gaze. His claws have come out, pricking my scalp like needles.

There's a rustling beside us. "Orion," Madoc starts, with a rough note in his voice.

But if he was going to speak on my behalf, his king doesn't want to hear it. Orion waves him off with his other hand. "It's time she understood who exactly is in control here, and just how much control I can wield." He grins at me, his face full of wicked amusement even as the pain of his grip radiates through my head.

I don't want to beg, and I don't expect it to do me any good, but the words spill out anyway. "Please. Ask me whatever you want, and I'll tell you what I can. I don't want—"

He jerks my head back and forth, sending another jab of pain through my wrenched neck. "I don't care what you want, little girl. You are mine. I made you. And now I'll take what *I* want."

He intones a few harsh words of magic, and the dissonant energy of the Heart hits me even harder. A burning sensation flares deep in my mind, spreading through my awareness as if my brain has caught fire.

I gasp, tears springing to my eyes. I try to blink them away, but something in Orion's spell holds my eyelids open as he peers into me as if seeing right inside my mind.

Which maybe he is. My thoughts jumble and whirl, and I nearly choke on the realization of how many things I *do* know that I'd hate for him to find out. But the burning is heightening into a full-out blaze, and I can't focus on anything except those gleaming yellow eyes pinning me in place.

However much he's dragging from my mind into his, he mustn't be able to control it perfectly. His pupils flicker back and forth like he's reading a book, and he snaps out a demanding question. "The illegal artifact collection the former arch-lord was keeping—your Arch-Lord Sylas didn't dispose of all of it?"

The answer tears up my throat as if dredged up by a barbed net. I can't hold it in. "I—I think he and the other arch-lords got rid of everything they thought was dangerous. But there might still be some things left." Has Celia held onto anything along with the collar she used on Corwin? I try to swallow down the words, but more crawl from my lungs. "I don't know where it would be, though."

Orion gives my head another brisk shake, but he seems satisfied that I've told him enough about that subject. "The magic used to create your new castle on the border. How did the opposing realms come together on it?"

I don't know much about that either, but what I do comes searing across my tongue. "They said they—they just had to appeal to the Heart of the Mists, and it accepted their intentions. And the border vow had to stay in place."

I can't feel my limbs anymore, not even my knees braced against the dais—only the scorching agony and the piercing of the Murk king's gaze. "What exactly did you say to convince Arch-Lord Laoni to back off on destroying that castle when she called you to attend to her alone?"

"I'm not sure," I gasp out. "She—she'd come down with the curse, and I reminded her that I didn't have to heal her. That it would probably be easier for me if I didn't. But I told her that she and her people mattered enough to me that I'd cure her even though she'd been attacking me. I think—I think she finally realized I didn't have any intention of hurting her."

But I am anyway. Nausea twines with the pain inside me. I'm betraying every one of the fae of the seasons right now, and I don't know how to stop myself.

The burning sensation is starting to ease back, though

it still hurts like hell. I don't know if Orion is exhausting his powers or if he's simply winding down on purpose. "What did your mates do to make the Heart of the Mists flare the way it did at your mating ceremony?"

My voice comes out in a croak. "I don't know. I had no idea that was going to happen. They didn't mention it before or after."

He lets go. My bones have turned to jelly. I collapse at his feet, my nerves jittering as if I've been stabbed by a thousand splinters all over my body. A dull ache fills my head.

"That's enough for now," Orion says, nudging me with the toe of his shoe. "Bring her back to her house and let her sleep it off."

I don't know who he's spoken to until firm but gentle hands slide over my shoulders and a familiar voice murmurs close to my ear, "I'm going to help you up now. Can you walk at all?"

Madoc eases my arm around him for support and lifts me to my feet. I wobble on my legs, my sense of the room around me still hazy. Orion has already turned to converse with his other men as if he doesn't care whether I even make it out of the room.

When I stumble with my first step, Madoc lets out a soft noise of consternation and hefts me right up into his arms. His thunderstorm scent fills my nose.

I don't want to be carried—I don't want to be handled like an invalid—but I can't convince any part of my body to move to my will.

Madoc strides out of the throne room with me. As we

head down the tunnel toward the station where he built my hovel, his voice drops even lower than before, his chin grazing my forehead. "I'm sorry. I didn't know he was going to do that."

What could Madoc have done about it if he had known? What would he even have wanted to do about it? It was all in the service of his cause, wasn't it?

How much did Orion see that will help the Murk ruin every part of the life I came to love in the Mists? How many fae are going to *die* because I didn't have the power to fight him off? Fresh tears well up behind my eyes.

"I'll talk to him, tell him you want to help, that he doesn't have to go about it that way," Madoc continues. "He'll see reason—he's just impatient now that we're so close to the goal. That doesn't excuse—" His voice goes raw. "You didn't deserve this."

Maybe not, but it happened anyway. And I have no doubt it'll happen again if I'm still here—maybe even tomorrow. I have the urge to crawl away inside myself as if that's even possible, as if Orion couldn't drag me out with his awful magic anyway.

Madoc sets me down in front of my "house." He speaks a few magical words, and the already fading pain pulls back even more. My head is starting to clear, but being able to think about what just happened only makes me more miserable.

"If I can do anything else for you," Madoc starts.

I shake my head before he can go on, not meeting his eyes. "Let me just be alone, please," I rasp.

My arms and legs have recovered enough that I can

crawl inside the hovel. I have the sense of Madoc lingering outside for a few minutes longer as if to make sure I don't change my mind and call out to him after all. Then he's gone.

I curl up on the blankets, staring vacantly at my hands. I have no idea how much Orion saw in my head that he could turn into a weapon against the men I love. I don't think he saw some of the worst things I could have given away, like my ability with true names or the fact that Whitt gave me his, maybe because it didn't occur to him to search for that. Surely he'd have remarked on it if he'd noticed.

But that doesn't mean he won't dig that out of me later. Soon. He could turn *me* into an outright weapon. In some ways he already has.

My gaze narrows in on the bronze bracelet. A wild, desperate impulse floods me.

I can make sure he never uses me again, that he can't steal one more thought from my head. The Murk haven't left any sharp weapons in my reach, but I could transform that bracelet into a knife right now and slash it across my own throat like I once threatened to in front of Ambrose.

Every awful thing Orion wants from me would drain away with my blood gushing over the floor. It'd all be done.

I sit up and touch the bracelet. "*Fee-doom-ace-own,*" I hiss, pouring all my fear and guilt into the words.

The band releases my wrist and straightens into a razor-sharp blade.

Staring down at it, I run my fingers over the warmed

bronze. I should just do it. It would be definite, final…
and easy. An immediate escape.

Something in me balks at that.

How much would I be leaving behind? I'd destroy any
chance of Orion getting more information out of me—if
there's all that much more he *can* get now—but also any
chance that I could escape the way I meant to before, to
warn the men I love of all the things *they* don't know. I'd
be abandoning them to a curse their enemy conjured and
a war they don't even know is on the horizon.

For several minutes, I grapple with myself. I bring the
bronze edge to my throat to see how the pressure feels. My
heart lurches, and I lower my hands again.

Something stronger than my panic rises up from deep
inside me.

I've gotten through so much. I've faced so much and
refused to give in. And part of me still believes that I can
do more by staying in this world than leaving it, as much
as I might want to flee the horror of what Orion's done
to me.

I close my eyes for a moment, and the resolve
solidifies. I'll get back to my home and my mates one way
or another. The Murk won't break me.

I'll just have to fight even harder in the few ways I
know how.

Heart help me, let it work.

17

August

As I walk across the polished stone bank to the still, glassy water of the Pool of the Clouded Past, my heart sinks. I'm not sure if I'm more worried that I'll spot something I should have noticed earlier, some mistake I made the night Talia vanished, or that it'll be clear the situation was hopeless from the start.

I kneel down at the edge of the bank. My reflection shines back at me, framed by the stark blue of the sky. I look… tired, my forehead creased, redness creeping into my eyes. I've barely slept more than a couple of hours at a time since the Murk stole Talia from us. When that letter arrived with her blood staining the paper, mocking us for losing something so precious to us…

The Murk could have no concept of just how precious she is to me, my brothers, and Corwin. What in the lands do they know about love?

And now we have other challenges too. The full moon is approaching, seemingly faster every day. We've started preparing the pack for undergoing the shift and discussing strategies to share with other domains, but the truth is, none of us are really sure what it might look like. How badly it might go.

On top of that, Sylas hasn't been able to confirm any wrongdoing on Tristan's part. His pack-kin gave a perfectly reasonable-sounding explanation for their activities near Hearth-by-the-Heart, claiming it was all precautions to help fend off a possible Murk attack on the Heart. We have extra guards keeping an eye on that area, but with it being free land, we can't force them to leave without a valid excuse.

Which naturally they know.

I catch myself gritting my teeth and force my jaw to relax. Right now I have to stay focused on what's in front of me—that is, my chance to take a glimpse into the past. I didn't have Sylas extend the request for the visit to our father only to sit around stewing over things I can't control.

"Show me the night of my mating ceremony," I say. "From the moment I left Talia at the platform to go get some refreshments."

The water shimmers. An image forms of a crowd of dancing fae. There's so much joy in their faces that my chest clenches up.

I watch myself moving through that crowd toward the refreshment table, my brothers on either side of me, Corwin just behind. Back then, I was only thinking of how happy I was to finally be able to say Talia was my mate in every possible way—and what sort of tart I wanted to eat first. Now, I scan the revelers around us, watching for any sign of ill intent.

Our pack-kin and the few Unseelie celebrating among them look totally innocent in their reveling. I don't catch a single hostile glance or conspiratorial murmur, not even a flicker of a frown. And I don't spot any suspicious figures among them who don't belong to either realm.

I guess we can hope that whatever magic the Murk have found, it hasn't let them mingle with us that closely undetected. The ones who took Talia did arrange to get her well away from the rest of the crowd before making off with her.

Of course, that means the pool won't be able to offer any clues at all. It can't show me what was far beyond my view.

I keep watching anyway.

We stop by the table and quickly pick out a few delicacies, none of us wanting to be away from Talia's side for very long. As Sylas turns back toward the platform, Whitt moves to the wine table, and I'm momentarily diverted by a couple of the guards I've been training with the longest, who clap me on the back and offer more congratulations. Their faces are ruddy with the alcohol they've already downed, but I don't see any malicious magic in them.

Then, as the me of the past moves to weave through the crowd, I spot a face that makes my gut tighten. Not because it's anything to do with the Murk, but because it's the cause of my other worries.

Tristan was standing maybe ten feet away from me at that moment, his cadre-chosen Jax beside him. He's saying something to her that the pool doesn't convey, but his lips curl with a sneer right before my view of him is blocked by the dancers.

His reaction isn't exactly a surprise, but it's a little disheartening to see that he couldn't summon any positive feelings about the occasion even on a night when so many other fae were full of happiness. But then, he's never seen Talia as anything other than a means to political power and a cure for the curse.

At least I can rest assured that he'd never have helped the rats take her *farther* from him and his interests than Sylas already had.

I peer at the pool as the rest of the scene plays out: the discovery of Talia's disappearance, the frantic initial search, the sight of Donovan's pack-kin unconscious in the woods. The Murk who carried out the crime must have been long gone by the time we made it there. I don't see anything I wasn't already aware of.

I sit back on my haunches, exhaling in a huff of frustration. There's been no further word from Talia. She hasn't reached out to Whitt again—the knowledge that he shared his true name with her without mentioning it to me until now sends a jab through my stomach, even if I understand the reasoning. Why didn't I think to do the same? And her connection with Corwin has stayed silent. He's sure she's still alive, but beyond that…

I wish the pool could show me *her* memories or what she's going through right now, as horrible as it might be.

My hands ball into fists. At the same moment, footsteps rasp across the rocky terrain behind me.

I stand and turn, my back stiffening when I take in my father approaching. I purposefully avoided flying my small carriage within view of the castle so that I wouldn't need to speak to Lord Eldris, since Sylas had already cleared my visit with him. Why he's insisted on seeking me out, I have no idea. I doubt it's for anything good.

"Did you find everything you were looking for?" he asks, offering one of his thin smiles. No hello, no acknowledgment of our relation to each other. He crosses his arms over his chest and lifts his chin imperiously.

"I'm managing just fine," I say. "If I'd needed assistance, I'd have reached out to your pack-kin. You needn't have troubled yourself."

The words themselves are as polite as I can manage, but a bit of bite might have crept into my tone. My father's eyes darken. "I don't need any guests telling me what I can do or where I should go in my own domain."

I'm not just a guest, I'm your blasted son! I want to snap at him, but I hold my annoyance in check. We have enough problems without my temper getting away from me.

"I would never think of doing so," I reply evenly. "I only meant that I had no intention of disturbing you."

He ignores that remark and comes up beside me, stopping a few paces away along the edge of the pool.

"You're looking for answers to do with that human girl of yours."

"Lady Talia," I say, with emphasis on her title. "Yes. As you must be able to imagine, we're very concerned with getting her back quickly and safely."

My father grunts, gazing across the pool rather than at me. "Such a shame a resource so important to our kind is tied up in a fragile mortal body."

I can't help bristling at that remark. "She's more than just her body and more than just a resource as well."

He glances sideways at me with a patronizing air that sets my nerves even more on edge. "You always were quick to emotion. It would have been better for you to have tied yourself to a proper mate, but I suppose there's no helping it now. You'll have plenty of time to choose more wisely when the dust takes her."

His tone is so matter-of-fact, as if he's discussing nothing more disturbing than the sunny weather, that it takes all my self-control not to lunge at him and slam his head into the water until he's drowned. My muscles flex all through my shoulders. "Would you say the same to your son the arch-lord?" I ask, a growl slipping into my voice.

Lord Eldris doesn't look remotely concerned by my anger. If anything, his expression only gets more disdainful. "Of course not. An arch-lord is allowed his whims. But I'm allowed my opinions, and there's no reason I shouldn't impart them to you. You obviously have too much of your mother in you."

In that second, I can only see red. He's lucky I don't tear his head right off his body. How *dare* he speak of my mother—the loving, kind woman he had brutally slaughtered in front of me on one of *his* whims—so callously.

I take a step toward him, and the breeze brushes over me. The wisp of it over my bare forearms brings the ghost of Talia's touch. I can almost feel her here, grasping my hand, reassuring me that she's here with me no matter what this bastard says to me. That he can't poison what we share.

And she would be right, wouldn't she? The pathetic, bitter man in front of me doesn't have to matter at all. I've left him behind; he has no more control over me. Once we get Talia back and she continues her campaign on behalf of the humans in the fae world, he won't even be able to control the people like my mother he still rules over either.

I don't have to worry one bit what he thinks of me. I don't have to give him a speck of emotional energy. He doesn't even deserve my rage, because that would mean I care.

My anger simmers down beneath a cool wave of soothing calm. I stare back at my father the way I've seen Talia face hostile arch-lords before. "I'm glad for every part of me that came from my mother, because I doubt what I inherited from you is worth anything. You're no longer my family. As far as I'm concerned, you stopped truly being my father when you ripped the one parent who actually parented me out of my life. So you can keep your advice to yourself. I have no interest in so much as speaking to you again."

I swivel on my heel and stride off without giving him a

chance to answer. Even after I've leapt into my carriage, I don't look back. His pride may be slightly stung, but I doubt he cares much what I think of *him* either.

As the carriage soars over the land, whisking me far away from him, it's as if a huge weight has washed off of me with the rushing of the wind. I've felt lost without Talia by my side, but she's still here in a way. All her sweetness and light have touched me and stayed with me.

I just need to keep being the man she fell in love with.

I don't have any new answers, but when I reach Hearth-by-the-Heart, I summon all the pack-kin who are currently present that I started training in combat back when we were less sure of our footing among the other lords. I've slacked off on that practice a little since we founded our alliance with the winter fae, but in this moment, taking it up again feels like the most productive thing I can do.

"We'll start with the warm-up exercises and move on to defensive forms," I say, walking around the group assembled by the pack village. "We know we have more enemies than we suspected we'd have to deal with, and that they're more powerful than we'd have anticipated. I want to be sure that you're all ready for them."

I may have let Talia down, but I won't let the rest of my pack down in my distress over her kidnapping. The best way I can protect them is to make sure they're prepared to protect themselves—against whatever threats might descend on us next.

18

Talia

Few of the Murk were around to witness Orion's assault on my mind, but I suspect word about it has gotten around. When I approach the ones stocking the food table the next morning, they accept my help but shoot me quick glances with what feels like a mix of wariness and pity. My skin tightens at the thought of what they might be wondering about me, but I'm not going to bring up the subject if they don't.

Instead, I pay close attention to the food they've brought. Most of it looks like it was nabbed from restaurant kitchens or even dumpsters, leftover catering trays maybe, nothing labeled. Some of the fruit has stickers on it, but knowing they originally came from Mexico or Ecuador doesn't tell me much when I know those countries export produce all over the world.

I'm not even sure I can draw any conclusions from the fact that there's quite a bit of breakfast food in the mix. My view from Madoc's telescope suggested that the world above the Refuge is on the opposite day-night schedule from how the Murk operate down here, but I don't know how close its source really is to our actual location.

Or this could be food that was prepared hours ago that the thieves have simply reheated after waiting until it's the appropriate mealtime. Hell, they could even be slipping through a couple of portals to some other part of the world completely, someplace where it is breakfast time even if it's not directly above us.

Even the boxes they're using are unlabeled, not giving anything away. Are they normally this cautious, or has Orion specifically ordered everyone to avoid bringing in anything that could give me a clue about where I am? The types of food don't give much away—there's always a mix of more familiar North American type items alongside dishes with Mediterranean or Asian or other influences I can't place with my limited human-world experience.

"It must be tiring, carrying so much stuff all the way here," I say in a casual tone as I rearrange a few apples on the table, just trying to look like I'm still pitching in.

The fae woman across from me shrugs. "Between all of us who work together, it's a pretty simple job. We all need to eat."

Which neither confirms nor denies that they're traveling a long way. I search for another tactic and then sigh. "I understand why I need to stay down here, but I do miss going outside. What's the weather like today? Maybe if I could picture it, it'd be easier not to be able to see it myself."

One of the other fae lets out a sound like a muffled snicker. The woman gives me a look that I suspect is all pity now. Not that her pity does me any good.

"I didn't pay that much attention," she says. "We have to be focused on steering clear of the humans and getting around locked doors and all the rest rather than what's going on in the sky."

And she's probably been warned not to tell me anything about the outside world anyway. "That's okay," I say with forced brightness, as if it doesn't matter that much to me anyway.

Just then, Bren saunters up to the table. He nudges aside a couple of other Murk who were picking out their breakfast and heaps several choice items on his plate, including the last four of the very popular sesame seed-dusted rice balls. The fae he displaced hang back until he's gone, glance mournfully at the now-empty plate, and take what they want from the rest of the offerings.

"Nearly disgraced and now he's rising in the ranks fast," one of the men mutters to the woman near me when Bren is gone.

"Because of the fight," I say.

He shoots me a cautious glance but nods. "He proved how far he'll go for the king. Orion rewards loyalty."

The woman shrugs. "I don't mind sticking to food duty if it means there's no risk of getting my guts clawed out."

"True. But once you've survived that, no one can touch you outside the king's circle."

"Do those kind of fights happen a lot?" I ask, not because it helps my escape but just out of queasy curiosity.

"Now and then," the woman says, not sounding at all disturbed by the fact. "Orion has plenty of ways of testing the ones who want to stand close to him. And some he trusts more than others to begin with. Or less. That Madoc." She shakes her head and then seems to decide not to say whatever she was going to follow up with.

My curiosity is immediately caught. "What happened with Madoc?"

"Better not to tell tales about anyone who stands with the king," the man mutters, and starts filling the now emptied plates with different food.

"It isn't 'tales' if it's true," the woman says, and turns back to me. "He was really just a boy when he made it here, and no one knew who his family had been. Orion and his close circle didn't make it easy for him. But Madoc was determined to show what he was made of, and he did. One of the fiercest battles I've ever seen, in the end. At one point I thought he was lost. He earned the spot he's got now more than some of them did, that's all I'll say about it."

She bustles off, leaving me wondering just what not making it "easy" for someone looks like around here, when fights to the death are a common event. What more has Madoc gone through to earn his spot?

I don't have to ask why he'd have put himself through anything. I heard how committed he is to helping the rest of the Murk have better lives. Every word he said to me in the vault of memories has stuck with me, adding to the uneasiness twined through my chest.

I linger by the food table for a while longer, nibbling on one thing or another even though I don't feel remotely hungry, listening to the pieces of conversation I catch as the Murk pass by and grab their own meals. Then I watch where they go. There's a doorway at the far end of this station that has a few fae coming and going fairly regularly. I see them each press their hands to a specific spot on the door before it opens though, so presumably it's tied to some kind of magic.

I don't think I'm going to convince the door that I'm Murk too. Talking any of the Murk into opening it for me seems even farther out of reach.

Orion hasn't called on me yet today. How much of a reprieve is he going to give me before he rakes through my mind again? I haven't gotten anywhere with the close-lipped Murk. I have to go back to the one sort-of solid plan I have.

I amble through the tunnels toward the maintenance room, pretending I'm just stretching my legs and looking around. Like in the past, no Murk are hanging around all the way down that final tunnel. I hesitate for several minutes, wondering if Orion will be able to pick this plan out of my head too. But I've already started it, so it isn't as if not continuing would stop him from finding out if that's the case.

I told myself I'd keep going, keep trying, so now I have to do that, or I might as well have slit my throat yesterday.

My muscles seem to be adjusting to the routine, at least. Clambering onto the machine below the vent isn't as much of a strain. I even manage to shape my bracelet into the right size of wrench on my first attempt.

I get to work on the bolt I started last time, heaving with all the strength in my arms. Imagining every twist is locking Orion and his hateful methods away as well as freeing me.

My shoulders start to throb, but I get a good enough rhythm going that I don't mind. Reposition and yank, reposition and yank, over and over until the bolt finally loosens enough to slip out.

A grin spreads across my face. I swipe at the sweat on my brow, poke the bolt back into its hole for appearances, and move on to the next one. Maybe I'll even get another fully out today.

I'm so caught up in that hope and the work that I don't register voices approaching until they're close enough that I make out actual words.

"—always so grimy out this way."

I jolt to a halt, my fingers freezing around the handle of the wrench. The chuckle that answers the remark sounds distant, but the rasp of footsteps is coming closer. Have they already heard my efforts?

My heart thudding, I mumble the true name for bronze as quickly as I can. With my focus scattered, the wrench doesn't bulge. I gulp a few breaths to steady myself and try again, keeping my voice as low as I can.

The tool wavers and curves around my wrist. I need to repeat the true name once more to fully smooth it out, my pulse hammering away the whole time. The voices sound like they're nearly at the entrance now.

I slide down the side of the machine, landing a little too hard on my warped foot. I have to clap my hand over my mouth to hold back a hiss of pain. With my limp more pronounced than usual and fighting a wince, I make my way through the machines toward the tunnel.

I'm about halfway through the maze of old equipment when the voices stop. Then one calls out, "Is someone there?"

"It's just me," I say quickly, hurrying into view as quickly as I can. "I was taking a look at all the machines here, wondering if there's something we can use for taking back the Mists. No such luck."

The two Murk who've wandered this way eye me, but neither questions my story. "It's all a bunch of junk," one says. "Orion's already had us scavenge what we can from here."

"I guess that makes sense," I say with a weak laugh. "I'll see how else I can help out. Did you need anything?"

"We're fine," the other fae replies, a little sharply.

I limp on toward the nearest station, but after several steps my foot hurts badly enough that I need to stop and give it a rest. I perk my ears, hoping I might catch a little more conversation from back down the tunnel.

The two fae who passed me have gone silent. That's odd. I stand there for a while, slipping my foot out of my braced boot to massage it, and I don't hear another peep from them, not so much as a rustle.

Then it occurs to me—that's because they aren't in the tunnel anymore. There must be another exit down there, one they've used to leave the Refuge.

Maybe it'll be just as locked to me as the others, but the next chance I get, I need to find out.

19

Talia

By lunchtime, my foot is still sore. When one of the Murk stops by my hovel to tell me that Orion wants to see me, I limp over on wobblier legs than usual, both because of the pain and my apprehension.

The Murk king is sitting off to the side of the dais with a spread of food and Madoc beside him. Orion doesn't seem to pay much attention to me as I make my way slowly over, but Madoc's gaze tracks my movements.

"Did you hurt yourself?" he asks in the low, hoarse voice that often has a strange gentleness to it.

It's hard to appreciate that gentleness when he's sitting next to the man who tormented me so gleefully yesterday.

I sink down at the edge of the platform a careful distance from both of them. "Just the same old hurt, acting up a little more than usual today. It happens sometimes." Definitely not because I was interrupted in the middle of arranging my escape.

Orion looks at me then, but only to nod in acknowledgment as if nothing at all horrible has passed between us. He motions to the food. "Help yourself. We don't want you wasting away."

Why, because then he wouldn't be able to pick any more thoughts out of my brain?

I bite back the snarky remark and pick up a stuffed pepper that fits easily in my hand. I'm not feeling particularly hungry, but I'll eat if it stops him thinking about other things he'd want me to do... and ways of forcing me into doing them.

I keep waiting for the other shoe to drop, for Orion to reveal his reason for calling me here, but he simply makes casual conversation about the day-to-day activities in the Refuge with Madoc and a couple of other fae who pass by. Maybe he simply wanted to confirm that I *would* come when called.

And to observe me up close. Is he checking for signs of hostility or rebellion after yesterday's spectacle? Waiting to see if I'll volunteer more information to try to avoid it happening again?

Is there anything I can volunteer that wouldn't hurt anyone but would put on a show of cooperating to buy me more time? I mull it over as I eat in wary bites, but I'm afraid even the details that seem innocuous to me might turn out to hurt the fae of the seasons in the long run. I've already inadvertently helped this vicious king far more than I'd ever have wanted to.

As I get to the point where I'm not sure I can force myself to swallow anything else, Orion turns to me abruptly with an audible sniff and a twitch of his tail where it's curved across the platform at his side. "You're getting pretty rank," he says in an offhand tone. "You haven't had a proper wash since you got here, have you?"

Shame prickles across my face even as my hackles rise. It's not my fault the only bathroom I have access to is a public-style restroom without any bathing equipment. I've been making do the best I can wiping myself down by the sinks.

"No," I say stiffly. "I didn't know there was anywhere where I could."

Orion snaps his fingers at Madoc. "You're not so fresh yourself. Why don't you take her down to the waterfall, and you can both get the grime off you. I've got to keep some kind of standards for the company I keep." He smirks, and I can't tell how much he's actually bothered by our state of cleanliness and how much he's just enjoying badgering us about it.

Madoc seems to study his king for a moment before offering a mild smile in return. "Of course. The waterfall shouldn't be busy at this time of day."

A waterfall… down here? That doesn't make much sense. Does this mean I'm actually getting to go outside? Is Orion giving me more leeway now that he's searched my mind?

I don't dare appear too eager about the prospect in case they pick up on my ulterior motives. When Madoc motions for me to follow him, I limp along, still slowed by the ache in my foot. He glances down at my boots as we reach the tunnel. "You're sure you're all right to walk?"

"What's the alternative?" I ask. "I don't need to be carted around like I'm helpless. As long as I *can* walk, I will."

"Fair enough."

We walk through the station and into the next tunnel. A few other fae pass us. When they've moved on far enough that I can no longer hear them, Madoc speaks again, in a lower voice even softer than usual.

"How are you doing otherwise? Are you having any lingering effects from the magic Orion used on you yesterday?"

A lump rises in my throat before I can catch it. I don't like how much relief I get from the concern in his voice, from the possibility that *someone* here might give a crap what happens to me beyond my usefulness to their war. That relief doesn't do me any good.

Maybe Madoc has gone out of his way to help me settle in and understand things more than the rest of his kind, but that doesn't mean I can trust him. He's still on Orion's side.

My head and really everything except my foot and my emotions feel just fine now. "No," I say. "But it wasn't exactly enjoyable while it was happening." I hesitate. "Is he going to do it again?"

I'm not sure whether Madoc would tell me the truth even if he knew. He glances away, swiping his hand across his mouth with an uncomfortable expression. "If he thinks he needs to. I've been talking to him about it, encouraging him to give you space to open up more… naturally. Like I've said, he sees his goals so close within his grasp, and he's gotten impatient. I'll do what I can."

Which might be not much at all. I swallow thickly and resist the urge to hug myself.

I have to get out of here. If this waterfall doesn't help with that, then maybe I can find another moment to work on the air vent today. I could go in the middle of the Murk's "night" while they're sleeping. Whatever it takes, as much as my arms can handle.

Partway down another tunnel, Madoc pushes open the door on a hovel built against the wall that I took for another house. Instead, it leads to a passage that was clearly fae-made rather than human.

The cement of the walls gives way to natural rock in a winding passage that rises a little upward and then dips down again, my hopes lifting and falling with it. The air is chillier here, the few specks of artificial light that glimmer on at our movements showing me only the outline of Madoc's form a couple of steps ahead of me.

Then the passage widens abruptly with a warble of sound. Water tumbles down into a sort of trough along a stretch of wall maybe twenty feet long. Shelves carved into the opposite wall hold folded towels and bars of soap. There's a bin in the corner heaped with used towels that I guess Murk from the Refuge must launder periodically like they have my clothes.

There are a few fae standing on the dry side of the room, just finishing getting dressed. At the sight of Madoc and maybe some gesture from him I don't pick up on, they toss their towels into the bin and scurry away at once.

I tread farther into the room cautiously. Warmth wafts off the falling water, its spray almost pleasant where it flecks my skin. A drain at ankle height sucks away the water in the trough before it can get close to overflowing.

"Where does this all come from?" I ask.

"There's an underground stream," Madoc explains. "It runs alongside one of the active subway lines, close enough for the heating systems to warm the water in this area. We simply diverted it a little." He shoots me a smile as if hoping to see I'm as pleased with that fact as he is.

I'd like it more if it wasn't just one more feature of what to me is a prison. "Definitely useful," I say, since he seems to expect a response.

"We won't be disturbed while we're here. You can take as long as you'd like. A warm soak might do your foot some good too."

Madoc says that and then kicks off his shoes. He goes through the motions so casually but quickly that I don't totally register that he's undressing until he's tugged off his socks as well and is reaching for the hem of his shirt.

I back up a step, my face flaring. "I, ah—I'd rather wash alone."

Madoc blinks at me as if it hadn't occurred to him that I'd object. "You can leave your undergarments on. I will too. It won't be any more exposed than if you were at a swimming pool."

The mention of swimming pools makes me think of the saunas in Sylas's castles—where I wore absolutely no clothes, and where I enjoyed August's company very much. Those memories make me feel more uncomfortable about this situation rather than less.

When I still don't move, Madoc's mouth forms an apologetic grimace. "I'm sorry. Orion wouldn't want you this far from the main areas of the Refuge unmonitored. I have no intention of gawking."

As if to emphasize that statement, he turns his back to me and continues stripping. I turn away from him too before I see any more skin exposed. I walk a little farther down the room, putting a good ten feet between us.

It won't be that bad, will it? I'll leave my bra and panties on like he said; I won't be anywhere near him. We'll just ignore each other and get clean, and then this will be over with. I can pretend he isn't even here.

I might not trust him, but since I've arrived here, he's never imposed on me physically, and he's had plenty of opportunities when he could have if he'd wanted to. I have to admit that even if I don't trust him in general, I can't picture the man who just apologized for the lack of privacy forcing himself on me in any way.

My nerves start to settle. I pull off my boots and take off the borrowed shirt and sweatpants. After my work on the bolts in the air vent cover, my arms look wirier than I'm used to, the thin muscles a little more defined.

Grabbing a bar of soap, I walk over to the falling water. The abrupt hiss of it to my right tells me Madoc has already stepped under it. Without glancing his way, I clamber into the trough and duck my head under the torrent.

Despite my situation and how many fears I'm holding in, there's something amazing about the rush of warm water over my mostly bare skin. It feels so comforting and almost normal. I lean into it, closing my eyes and just absorbing the heat and the soothing flow for a minute.

But I don't want to linger here very long. Wielding the soap, I scrub my face and body as quickly as I can. It gives off a light floral scent that reminds me of the summer realm with a jab of homesickness. As the bubbles are sucked away into the drain, I work more foam into my hair. I haven't been able to do much with it in the sinks, and the feeling of the strands turning squeaky clean is a relief all on its own.

Is it wrong to get any enjoyment out of this place? I have to think I need to take whatever strength I can from the few parts that aren't horrible. If having this moment makes it easier for me to focus on escape afterward, then it's working in my favor even if I'm here on Orion's orders.

As I stand in the water for several more seconds after the soap has all been washed away, Madoc's voice reaches me. "I'm glad you got to see that we do have a few luxuries here."

My eyes pop open. He's still standing several feet across the room from me, out of the water now with a towel he's rubbing over his pale hair, his back to me like before. But he must have picked up on my relaxed state one way or another.

I hadn't meant to look at him at all while he was partly undressed, but something about his comment—about the idea that even the highest Murk see something like this room as a *luxury* rather than a basic necessity, and what that says about the lives they've been forced to lead—sharpens my attention just for that moment.

The toned muscles flex all across his shoulders and back, but I don't find myself admiring them. No, the moment I focus on his body, my gaze is drawn to the flecks and lines—some white enough to stand out against his already pale skin, some a deeper pink—that mark nearly every inch of him. It takes a moment before understanding clicks in my head.

They're scars. He must have a few dozen of them just on his back and arms, which I've never seen before either thanks to the long-sleeved shirts he's always worn around me. More scars mottle his calves and knees beneath his damp boxer shorts. I'd noticed a few around his face in the past, but maybe he used to have more there too and simply put more work into healing the cuts and scratches that would be most visible when he was clothed.

The question spills out. "What *happened* to you?"

Madoc jerks around, dropping the towel to his shoulders. The folds of fabric partly cover his well-built chest, but what I can see of it has plenty of scars too, including a long, wide one that makes it look as if someone nearly carved through his ribs.

"What do you mean?" he asks, his stance tensing.

I step out of the water and feel abruptly naked. As I hurry to grab a towel of my own, I motion toward him, averting my eyes before I've stared for too long. "All those scars. How did you get them?"

It occurs to me a second later that the question is

pretty personal, but I can't bring myself to care. I've been forced to have my mind wrenched right open for his king to stare at—he can forgive a few prying questions in return.

Madoc wipes the towel across his torso and grabs his shirt. "I don't see how it matters."

That answer tells me immediately that the fae of the seasons weren't responsible. If he could blame it on their cruelty, he would have in an instant.

My mind trips back to the conversation I had with the Murk woman at the food table this morning.

"I heard that Orion put you through a lot when you were working your way up to being one of his main 'knights'," I say. "What exactly did he do to you? Is *that* where the scars came from?"

"I said it doesn't matter," Madoc replies, the hoarseness in his voice thickening.

I wrap the towel around myself like a dress, covering me from my chest to my knees, and turn to face him. "It matters to me. You want me to support him and his war. You want me to help all the fae here. How am I supposed to trust you if you're going to clam up the second I ask anything hard?"

Madoc glowers at me in his shirt and boxers. It's the first time I've seen him aim any negative emotion my way since our first conversation when I woke up in the Refuge. My back stiffens, but then he's glancing away. A ragged sigh slips out of him.

He drags his gaze back to me, crossing his arms. "It wasn't anything all that unusual. Orion tests the loyalty of anyone who wants to play a larger role at his side. You've already seen that."

"And testing your loyalty meant cutting you up all over your body?"

"I tried too young," Madoc says. "I didn't know what I was doing, and I had to be taken down a peg more than once. They needed to be sure of me. But I could have left any time I decided to. I didn't have to take on the dangerous jobs, or put up with being shoved around, or fight when I was called on to. I *wanted* to, so that he'd see I was stronger than all of that."

"And you really think that's okay?" I demand. "To beat up on—what—a teenager? To send you off to get hurt, just because he could? He probably laughed the whole time, watching you take it. He made you *kill* someone like he did with Bren the other day, didn't he? Rip apart another Murk, just because he likes seeing people being torn to pieces."

Madoc's eyes flash. "You want to talk about enjoying ripping people apart? Do you know why I was fending for myself like that at all? What you'd see if you found my chair in the vault of memories? The fae of the Mists you still want to protect, that you seem to think are somehow better than the man you're complaining about—a squad of the raven shifters tore my *parents* to pieces."

My frustration flames out. "What?"

He turns away, raking his hand through his hair, but the pain is clear in his voice. "All we were doing was living on the fringes of the Mists. It wasn't easy—there wasn't much food to scavenge and there were beasts to fend off—

but it was nice being a bit nearer to the Heart. My parents could use a little magic. I remember being able to feel it, distant but... *there*."

The hint of awe in his tone at the memory makes my own heart squeeze. He misses it, even with the monstrous Heart that Orion has created right here.

"And then one day my parents came running," Madoc goes on. "A sentry had spotted them—a squad of Unseelie was on the way. We ran for the portals, but there wasn't enough time. I watched one of the ravens chop my father's head right off his body and ram it into a tree branch like a trophy. My mother managed to push me through to the human world a second before they caught her too. The way she screamed..."

My stomach lurches. I can picture the scene far too clearly. My voice comes out thin. "I'm sorry."

Madoc just shrugs. "I'm lucky they didn't kill me too. I had no idea where I was, and I was a child and all tangled up in fear and guilt over leaving my parents—I stumbled into a carnival that was going on in with all kinds of humans around. If the ravens came looking for me there, I was lucky that a Murk who was passing by happened to notice me first. She brought me to the orphanage. I stayed there until I was old enough that I could convince them to let me leave, and then I traveled straight here. I'd heard about Orion and what he was trying to do. I wanted to be part of it."

Silence falls between us. I don't know what to say. I'm aching from throat to gut, and Madoc doesn't look as if he's feeling much better.

How much of that did he even want to tell me? He's avoided mentioning it before.

"I've never denied that the Seelie and the Unseelie can be awful," I say finally. "That doesn't mean I can't hate seeing Orion treat you or the other Murk awfully too."

"It isn't all awful," Madoc says. "You know that. And it'll be amazing when we've seen his plans through. There always has to be some sacrifice along the way."

"But… this much?"

"What exactly would you have me do differently?" he demands. "Walk away? I spent decades proving myself— what the hell was the point in enduring all that if I'm only going to toss the reward aside?"

I pause and then venture, "It just doesn't always seem to me like getting to stand beside him is such a reward."

We stare at each other for a long moment. Madoc is the one who breaks away first.

"Get dressed," he says brusquely, reaching for his pants. "We should get you back to the Refuge, where you'll find there are hundreds of fae who're a lot better off having Orion ruling over them than we ever were before."

20

Corwin

The Hall of the Heart isn't exactly where I want to be right now, while each passing hour without any sense or news of my mate weighs heavier on me. But the rest of life in the winter realm goes on even if I wish I could pause it.

And some of that life is ending.

"We've lost four to the curse since your mate vanished, with two more fading away as we speak," Laoni says, her hands braced on the top of the gleaming marble table. I wonder if the others can guess at the full reason for the glimmer of panic in the back of her eyes. "It's only coming on faster."

"It should taper off some once—once those who are undergoing it for the second or third time are no longer included in that number," Terisse points out, but she sounds pained. None of us want to think about those who got their second chance succumbing to the curse after all… least of all Laoni.

Uzziah frowns. "If we settle the matter within the next few weeks, it shouldn't come to that. Have you had no contact with your mate through your bond still, Corwin?"

"None," I say, with the jab of anguish that comes with the admission. I'd never tell them that Whitt has, but we haven't learned anything useful that way regardless. "You can be sure we've tried every other strategy we can think of to track down the Murk responsible. I actually have a proposal to make that might speed up that process."

Laoni raps her knuckles on the table. "Well, then, let's have it."

She wouldn't be so eager if she knew what I was going to suggest.

I prepare myself for the arguments I expect to come. "Talia was stolen on Seelie land. It seems most likely that her captors would have gone for the nearest portals to escape into the human world. One of Arch-Lord Sylas's cadre-chosen and I have made discoveries about the sort of magic the Murk have been using to cover their presence, but it's very subtle. Still, it may be able to lead us to the area where they left the Mists—and where their new spies are traveling from."

"Excellent," Uzziah says. "What are we waiting for then?"

I draw myself up a little straighter. "I think our best chance is to combine forces with the Seelie. A large squadron of our strongest sentries and soldiers alongside theirs, searching the fringelands and collaborating with our magic to draw out the traces of the Murk's passage. Sylas and I could oversee it together. We'd only need whatever manpower you can provide."

Laoni's lips twist as I suspected they would. "We send our people over to their realm to make up for their failings?"

I fix her with a hard stare. I'm past the point of being intimidated by her disapproval. "Laying blame is less important than recovering Talia, wouldn't you say?"

"It's not so much the laying of blame." Her hand clenches and then flexes as she forces her fingers to uncurl. "You know I want to see our people healed. But we can't sacrifice their future safety either. I'm only concerned about the precedent it might set—that the Seelie will feel we'll be at their beck and call in other situations as well."

"There must be ways to mitigate that risk," Uzziah says.

Terisse's head droops, her expression clouded. I can't tell what she thinks of any of this.

"I don't think it's risk at all," I say. "The Seelie understand as well as we do that these are extreme and unexpected circumstances. Is this an urgent matter or not? Coming up with vows or whatever else to try to offset any possible future entitlement will only delay our chances of success—and give the Murk more time to switch up their strategies."

Neve stirs at the far end of the table. It's never clear how much she's listening to these discussions, but her voice rings out perfectly clear if dry. "We must protect our people now. We've managed to find peace with the Seelie.

I don't see why we shouldn't work with them on this. I agree."

I offer her a quick smile, but Laoni is shifting her weight on her feet. "I'm not saying we *shouldn't* do it. I only want to be sure we don't commit to more than we're comfortable with."

I will the edge out of my tone. "We won't be committing to anything. It'll be a one-time operation, albeit on a large scale. This is the time when we need to decide what really matters. You've balked at and challenged the alliance with the summer realm plenty of times." I glance around the table at all three of my colleagues who've contributed to those challenges. "You've gone as far as deceiving our people to try to prove your point. None of that has exposed any true problems. Hasn't this resistance gone on long enough? Now our entire realm is threatened by your reluctance."

Laoni's eyes flash, but Terisse's shoulder's stiffen. Maybe she's thinking, like I was, of the moment during my confirmation ceremony with Talia when she pretended to be cursed. She speaks before Laoni can.

"Corwin is right. We've stretched out the conflict so long, and maybe that's why we lost the cure in the first place. Perhaps if we'd been more coordinated before, Lady Talia would have been better protected that night. If the Seelie will work alongside us, then I say we take all the help we can get."

She glances at me then with a look I think I can read an apology in, and my heart lifts just a little despite all that's weighing on it.

Uzziah lets out a huff, but he can't seem to find any argument to offer the three of us. And we could carry the majority if we wanted anyway. "All right," he says after another pause. "If we're going to do it, we should get on with it and make this happen now."

Laoni's lips have flattened, but then her shoulders come down. She looks more defeated than accepting as she nods to me. "So be it. I have people adept at seeking spells whom I can ask to join the effort. Are there any other sorts of magical affinity that would be helpful?"

At least she's asking practical questions now that she's done balking at the idea. "Yes," I say. "The Murk's primary method of disguise seems to involve a reflective element. Skill with detecting illusions or rebounded light would be particularly welcome."

Terisse snaps her fingers, the clouds that appeared to be hanging over before having departed with her newfound conviction. "I have just the man who'd be an excellent addition. Shall we all confer with our flocks and then send along those who'll be participating?"

Everything's proceeding faster than I'd dared to hope, but I can't complain about that. "I want to put word out to the nearest flocks as well so we can gather as large a group as possible, and I'll need to inform Arch-Lord Sylas so he can do the same, but we do want to act quickly. Have your people head to Heart's Cadence within the next two hours. We'll set off then."

We disperse from the Hall, my steps toward my palace much lighter than they were entering. Zelpha and Verik join me before I've made it halfway there.

"We're going ahead," I say before they need to ask. "I'll see to our own flock folk. You and the others reach out to any nearby domains you think will contribute."

Zelpha's lips curl with a tense smile. "I'd imagine they all will, if it's toward bringing Lady Talia back. And we *will* bring her back." She gives my arm a companionable bump with her elbow that's the most reassurance she can offer while maintaining her professional demeanor in public view. Then the two of them leap from the ground in raven form.

By the time the two hours I asked for is up, I've gathered two dozen of the most adept magic-users from my own flock, and a couple hundred fae from other flocks have assembled around the palace. They've already been at work conjuring carriages.

I leap into my own carriage, Verik and half of my flock folk accompanying me in that one, and motion to the others. "Follow my route. We'll meet up with the Seelie forces on the other side of the border and head to the fringelands as swiftly as we're able to."

On the summer side, the warm air washes over me with a rush of leafy scents I'm coming to appreciate. Sylas is waiting with his own squadron of wooden carriages, containing nearly twice as many fae as I'm bringing. Whitt stands by his side. We exchange quick nods of encouragement and set off without another word. There's no argument between the three of us about how urgent this mission is, both for our people and for ourselves.

Taking in all the vehicles soaring across the summery landscape, a little more hope blooms in my chest. With all of us put to the task, combining our talents, surely we'll get closer to rescuing the woman we lost.

I just have to try not to focus on worrying about what state we'll find her in when we do. I will not be crippled by my grief. I'll take all the love I have for my mate and turn it into the strength to get her back.

During the journey to the fringelands, my coterie and I take to raven form to fly from carriage to carriage and make sure all of the fae with us are clear on our strategy. All the gazes that meet mine are bright with determination. I may feel the loss of my mate deeply, but I'm not alone in missing her.

The weather grows hotter and muggier as we near the hazy forests at the very edge of the Mists, the opposite of what we'd face on the winter side. The heat turns my stomach, and many of my fellow Unseelie look uncomfortable, but no one complains. I pass on the suggestion to adjust the warming charms on our clothes to cooling ones, which eases the discomfort a little.

Deep within the fringe forests, where the portals glimmer with their dark sheen here and there just up ahead, we halt the carriages and disembark. Normally even when we've assembled together, the summer and winter fae have kept to their own kind. Now, Sylas urges everyone to mingle.

"We want to make full use of our varied skills," he says. "We can't fully collaborate if we're still keeping ourselves separate."

I step up beside him to show I'll be working closely with my own Seelie counterpart. After a few hesitant murmurs, the two groups of fae merge, until it's hard to pick out who's wolf and who's raven at a glance. Then we set off.

Sylas and I chant the first spells, and the others raise their voices to match ours. The Heart's reach is thinner here, but between all of us, magic thrums through the air. It ripples over my skin and across the landscape. I walk slowly amid the crowd, every sense alert for the slightest hint of one of the lingering spells we're scanning for.

We're starting the search with a relatively small area to condense the power of our efforts. When one stretch of forest turns up nothing, we move on, continuing our chant. Sweat beads on my face and trickles down my back, but I ignore it.

The first shout comes after perhaps half an hour. There's a trace of a shadowy illusion at the base of one tree, with an odd quaver to the magical energy that sits uneasily with me. We mark that spot and tramp onward. My spirits are lifting, but one hint isn't enough to be sure it's more than random chance.

Then another call rises up, and another, and I taste a prickle on my tongue that leads me to the faintest glimmer where a few beams of sun seep through the fog. We mark all of those as well. Then, across a few more miles, we find nothing.

Sylas calls a halt to the search and tells everyone to refresh themselves with the drinks and food we're all carrying. He turns to me, his expression both pleased and serious.

"It's still a somewhat large span, especially considering how the portals shift around."

"It is." I inhale slowly, and a small smile crosses my lips. "But we've narrowed it down. More than one of the Murk have passed through that stretch, and none nearby elsewhere. Many of them must be coming through one of the portals in that general area. At least now we have a starting point instead of wandering the human world aimlessly."

"Indeed." Sylas looks toward the portals. "Now the real search can begin."

21

Talia

Silky sheets slide across my limbs. They feel like a warm breeze licking over my skin.

I roll over on the bed, and Corwin is there beside me. He slips his arm around my waist and tugs me to him, love shining in his dark eyes.

My heart swells with joy and longing. I hug him to me, abruptly choked up.

He's here. My soul-twined mate, with me again. It's been so long. I started to wonder if I'd *ever*—

The thought shivers up from some distant part of me that this doesn't make sense. How *can* I be with him? Where even are we? There was— I'd been—

The doubts wash away with another rush of warmth and a deeper longing. I can't focus on anything except the hunger to get closer to the man I'm lying next to.

The same desire echoes into me from Corwin. He grasps the sides of my face and pulls me into a kiss.

Our lips meld together, our tongues tangling, and heat flares low in my belly. I want to be with him in every possible way, to feel him around me and inside me, to have him flood my body with all the amazing sensations I know he can bring.

As if in answer, Corwin wrenches down the sheets. I'm nearly naked underneath, only my panties on. He dips his head to suck one of my nipples into his mouth, and the pleasure I was seeking rushes through me. I press my head into the pillow with a gasp.

He works me over with strokes of his tongue that draw the tip of my breast to a hardened peak and squeezes my other nipple between his fingers. Giddy sparks shoot through me straight to my sex. I squirm against him, whimpering, eager for more.

"Please," I mumble. "Please."

With an urgent noise, Corwin pushes up to kiss me hard on the mouth. At the same time, he yanks at my panties. They whip off me with a snap of torn fabric. Then the hard length of him is pressing against me. I lift toward him, bliss throbbing through my core where he's rubbing against my slickness, encouraging him on. An instant later, he's thrusting right into me, stretching me, filling me.

I'm so wet already that he slides in deep with a burn that's nothing but welcome. A moan escapes my lips. I buck to meet his thrusts, claiming every ounce of pleasure he can bring to my body. We're here in this together, passion searing between us, and nothing will ever break us apart again.

My release comes with such force that I shudder and cry out, my back bowing up against the sheets. As Corwin reaches his peak with a stuttered breath, three more figures gather around us.

All my mates have come to me. Sylas's mismatched gaze raises more heat as it travels over my naked curves. Whitt licks his lips, which have curved into a wicked grin. August's strong hands descend to pull my face to his.

In a matter of moments, I'm lost between them, kissing one and then another, arching into their caresses, more whimpers and gasps tumbling out of my mouth. Whitt enters me with one quick thrust while Sylas works me over from behind to prepare my other opening. August fondles my breasts. It's all so much I can barely catch my breath.

Bliss rolls over my body in waves. I writhe between them, tipping over the peak only to be tossed up toward it again, soaring higher and higher with every burst of heady delight—

And then a raucous laugh rips through the haze of pleasure. I flinch, and my eyes snap open. The cocoon of passion and love I was wrapped in an instant ago vanishes, though my body is still throbbing with desire.

The sight around me snuffs out any lingering hunger like a bucket of icy water dumped over my head. I'm lying on my side at the edge of Orion's dais, the erratic orange light of the Murk's Heart wavering over me. A small crowd of fae has gathered in the throne room around the platform, all their eyes fixed on me. Many are leering, several are chuckling. It's one of them whose laugh woke me up.

From a dream. My hands drop to my sides, with a surge of relief to confirm that unlike in that dream, I'm fully dressed. But I— Did I fall asleep here?

My head feels muddled—I don't remember the last moments before I drifted off. It's hard to imagine being relaxed enough to doze off here. Did Orion carry me from my house… to put me on display…

As I push myself into a sitting position, my heart beating wildly, the king steps up beside me. He grins down at me with a twinkle of vicious amusement in his yellow eyes. "Thank you for that lovely performance, my pet. My people have found it very entertaining—and provoking."

Performance? Provoking?

A few of the watching fae make gestures that mimic sex, and my stomach plummets even as scorching heat shoots to my cheeks. There's nothing lustful in that heat now, only shame.

I might not be naked, but I must have been making some of the sounds from my dream in reality, maybe even moving my body without realizing it. And they all watched…

"I—I—" I stammer, but I don't know what to say. My face burns even hotter. I pull my legs up in front of me as if to shield me from all those stares.

"All right," Orion calls out. "The show's over. Get back to work—or if you haven't got work to do, maybe you'll be inspired to enjoy each other as much as my pet enjoyed her dream."

The fae around the room start to turn, drifting toward the entrance, but their leaving doesn't give me much relief. A shiver wracks my body.

Orion crouches next to me, still with a sharp smile on his face, and speaks low enough that no one else will be able to hear. "Nothing in your mind is safe from me. This is only one of many demonstrations I could offer."

I cringe away from him and bump into the legs of someone who's come up at my other side.

"I think she's gotten the message," Madoc says, his voice casual but with a thread of tension running through it. "Maybe we should let her get some proper rest now?"

Orion straightens up and waves his hand dismissively. "Do what you like with her. I've had my fun. For now."

He saunters away with his tail swinging as if I'm a toy he's done playing with. I can't contain another tremor that races through me.

Madoc peers down at me, a frown tugging at his mouth. *He* saw all that too. He saw me moaning and squirming with desire in my sleep…

Another rush of embarrassment nearly suffocates me. I rub my hands over my face. I just want to curl up into a ball tiny enough to drop through a crack in the floor and never be seen again.

But that's not an option. Madoc waits without speaking as I gather myself. Part of me wants to ask just how bad it was, how much of the dream I acted out in front of the audience of Murk, but I can't bring myself to even mention the topic with him.

He probably thinks it's awful that I'd still want my mates at all, even in a dream, after everything I've seen and heard about the fae of the seasons.

Slowly, I pick myself to my feet and limp alongside him toward the door. I'm not sleepy—and from the glow of the magical lights, it seems to be daytime by Murk standards—but my sense of time has been upended. Still, I'm exhausted in a way that has nothing to do with wanting sleep. The uncertainty and fear I've been living with, amplified over the past few days, has been wearing away at my inner strength. I hate how weak I feel.

"No one will remember it in a day or two," Madoc says in an obvious attempt at being reassuring. "They don't really care. It was just Orion wanting to remind everyone of his power."

"Especially me," I mutter.

Madoc pauses as we come out into the tunnel. The fae who watched my humiliation have totally dispersed—there's no one nearby. He ducks his head. "It was a horrible way to do it. Do you need anything? Food, or something to distract you?"

The fact that he's trying to help in his hesitant way only makes me feel worse. He *can't* do anything for me. Would he even want to try anything that would actually get me out of this nightmare when it'd bring Orion's rage down on him—destroy everything he went through so much already to gain? I doubt it.

It's probably a risk even admitting he doesn't agree

with his king's tactics.

I glance up at him, a strange mix of affection and anger twisting in my chest. I'm glad he's at least trying and frustrated that he won't do more all at the same time. He offers me a pained smile, which brightens the planes of his not-at-all-unpleasant face just a little, and an even more horrifying thought strikes me.

If Orion can peer inside my head and manipulate my dreams, what else could he compel me to think? To feel? To *do*? He'd probably delight in the idea of forcing me to betray my mates with one of his inner circle—or maybe even with himself?

My skin crawls at the idea. I step a little farther away from Madoc. I don't know if there's any real chance of what I've just imagined happening, but even considering it is making me jumpy. I don't want to be near any of them right now.

"I think—I think I just need to walk a bit and clear my head," I say. "On my own."

Madoc opens his mouth as if to say something and then closes it again. After a moment, he nods. "Of course. If there is anything I can do, just seek me out."

At the nearest station, he moves away from me to speak to a few of the fae carrying boxes through a doorway. My gaze lingers on the entrance for a moment, my memories stirring.

I have to get out of here before I find out just how far Orion is willing to go. Is there a way I haven't tried yet that would be even easier than the air vent?

As innocently as I can manage, I wander around in the

other direction and head toward the far end of the Refuge where the maintenance room is.

As I step into the final tunnel, voices ahead of me catch my ears. I creep closer, staying close to the wall. A glimmer of light illuminates a fae face for just a moment before the three shadowy figures at the far end of the tunnel vanish.

I wait a few minutes to be sure they're really gone and that no one else is coming, and then slink over to check the end of the tunnel. There *is* a doorway there, one I thought was just part of the tiled wall that closes off this section of the Refuge. When I run my fingers over the grout, I can now feel a thin seam around one chunk of them that must open up.

But it won't open for me, no matter how I press and pry at it. I can't get any grip with my fingers at all. Even if I could, it's most likely sealed with magic as well.

Hugging myself, I step back before anyone can come through or otherwise stumble on me tugging at it. Orion might enjoy terrorizing me, but that doesn't mean he'd want to know I've gotten so desperate I'm trying to leave. How would he punish me for that infraction?

I can't just stand around doing nothing, though. My restlessness drives me over to the air vent. But as I scramble up onto the machine beneath it, I catch a rustling sound somewhere nearby.

I freeze, my pulse hitching. The rustling comes again —not so close I'm worried anyone's seen me, but it could be right near the entrance to the room. A Murk in rat form patrolling the borders of the Refuge?

Hell, it might even be a normal, not-at-all-fae rat, not that I'd be able to tell the difference.

I crouch by the machine for several minutes, but the rustling continues. It starts to get a little louder, coming this way. If it is a sentry, what will they think of me hanging around here? How closely might they examine this place if they suspect I have a special interest in it?

Gritting my teeth in frustration, I push away from the machine and meander back to the tunnel.

Isn't there *anything* I can do to get closer to escape? With every passing minute, the darkness feels more constricting, the air thinner. My heart is still beating fast, and sweat is forming beneath my shirt even though I'm far from hot.

I limp onward, desperation nipping at my heels. If I could even just get a few seconds when I was sure I was completely alone, that no one would hear me…

Halfway down the next tunnel over, I pass a workshop room that's currently unused. The furnace is still running, its crackling thrum filling the room. A smoky, metallic scent trickles into my lungs, but a flicker of hope rises up at the same time.

I dart into the room and squeeze behind the furnace where I can't be seen from the tunnel and where I can hope its noise will cover any hint of my voice even to fae ears. There's no one nearby right now, but someone might come along at any moment. I have to be fast.

I cup my hands over my mouth, picture Whitt's bright eyes, and whisper, "*Wye-con-ell,*" with all the hope and anguish in me.

An ache opens up down the center of my skull, but a glimmer of my mate's presence catches in my awareness at the same time. *Whitt,* I think at him, ignoring the quickly building pain. *Whitt, hear me. Speak to me.*

His voice carries to me from so very far away. *Talia! We're trying— —think we've narrowed— Are you—*

The connection I've been able to forge is so tenuous his words are already fragmenting. I have no idea how clearly he'll be able to hear me. *I'm trying to find a way to escape. Still no clues about where I am. Be careful. The Murk have a Heart. They have so much more magic than we thought. I—*

Anything else I'd have conveyed to him is lost in a sharper sear of agony that feels as if my scalp is literally peeling away from my skull. A choked gasp breaks from my throat. I drop my head, pressing the heels of my hands to my forehead.

Whitt's voice and any sense of him I had vanish. There's nothing in my head but a thrashing pain. It's all I can do to hold back a sob.

Tears trickle from my eyes anyway. Even this physical distress isn't enough to drown out the anguish swelling through me.

Did I manage to tell him anything useful at all? Why couldn't my magical abilities be just a *little* stronger?

I wrap my arms around my knees and bury my face against them, my tears soaking into my pants. I don't know what to do. I don't know how to get out of here.

What if I never can?

22

Whitt

Talia's voice quavers through my mind, splintering and fading in and out despite my best efforts to hold it in focus. *—trying to find— —no clues about where— Be careful. —a heart. They have so much—*

And then she's gone, with a jolt of agony that radiates from her into me, lingering even after I've lost any hint of her.

My fingers clench against the map I'd spread on my desk as if I can catch her and pull her back to me. An even deeper anguish digs into my gut.

So much urgency and turmoil reached me even in that brief, frail connection. She was upset, maybe even desperate. And I don't even know what it is she was trying to tell me.

I slam both my fists down on the desk, my frustration

cracking the outward nonchalance I've gotten so adept at putting on. In the privacy of my study, it hardly matters, although I'd have teased August about such a show of temper. My fangs have leapt from my gums, as if there's anything in front of me I can tear apart to save my mate.

All I have are the same books and scrolls and other bits of aged paper I had before.

I glare down at the specific piece of aged paper spread out in front of me, the map I was studying when Talia called on my true name. It isn't giving me answers anywhere near quickly enough.

With a combination of magic and ink, the map holds as accurate a record as we can maintain of the main portals to the human world from the Mists. Of course, those portals do move around some and so need frequent updating, and minor ones regularly emerge into being or vanish. It's a partial picture at best.

Still, I've been making note of the most longstanding portals in the area where Corwin and Sylas found consistent traces of Murk presence along the fringes and comparing them to our sentries' observations from the human lands on the other side to see if any place jumps out as a hotbed of rat activity. The pests are likely to be less careful in the human world, where most of those around them can be easily deceived.

So far I haven't found any evidence from past reports that would make one spot or another seem like a particularly good target to focus on, though.

We have other sentries investigating every portal currently there in the meantime, not to mention stalking through those distant woods hoping to catch one of the vermin on their way through. We've worked out traps that should be sprung by the magic they're typically using. But there's no way of knowing if it'll be enough.

And Talia may be running out of time. What are the blasted vermin putting her through?

I scan several more pages of old notes and then shove back my chair with a sigh and the start of a headache prickling at my temples.

Is there something better I could be doing with my time? The part of me most aware of my role as Sylas's cadre-chosen nags that I should be making more plans for how we'll deal with the curse when the full moon arrives in less than a week's time, but to the rest of me, that feels like defeat. Like acknowledging that there's no way we'll have brought Talia home before then.

How can the mangy rats have gotten the better of us so thoroughly?

I'm about to go out so I can meet the most recent sentries as soon as they return from the fringelands when one of the castle attendants knocks on my study door. When I open it, he cringes a bit, and I school my expression into something less fierce. It won't do any good going around looking as if everyone I encounter is a rat I'm planning to eviscerate.

"My apologies for interrupting," the attendant says quickly. "One of Lord Tristan's cadre-chosen wishes to speak with you. She's waiting outside."

She is, is she? My senses automatically go on high alert. Tristan only has one female cadre-chosen, that woman named Jax, and I haven't been happy about their odd but not explicitly imposing activities near our domain either. What does she want with me specifically, and why now?

"Thank you," I say with a brisk nod, and go down to find out.

Jax is indeed standing several paces from the castle's front door, her toned frame clothed in a casual but form-fitting dress that seems more appropriate for a revel than a business call. She flicks her black hair over her shoulder and fixes her heavy-lidded eyes on me with a small, sly smile that raises my hackles.

Why is she looking at me as if we're in on some kind of secret together when I've barely spoken to her before today?

"Whitt," she says smoothly. "I'm glad you were able to meet with me on such short notice."

"If there's trouble or a new development involving the Murk, I'd want to hear about it at once," I say, keeping my tone coolly polite. "What is this about?"

"Walk with me, and I'll explain."

I'd rather she spit it out right here, but I do have to maintain more decorum than saying as much. She's probably enjoying the thought that she'll irritate me by drawing out her report. So I'll just have to irritate her right back by showing as little annoyance as possible.

She walks toward the woods that lead to the edge of the hill—toward the small outpost she and a few of her pack-kin have set up on the unclaimed land beyond Hearth-by-the-Heart. She doesn't expect me to go all the way down there with her just to find out what she wants, does she?

I keep pace with her, taking no pleasure from the bright mid-morning sun. "Feel free to begin explaining at any time."

"To be honest," she says, "I'm mostly concerned about you. You've been running yourself ragged over these past several days, haven't you?"

As we step into the shadows of the forest, I shoot her a puzzled look. "Of course I've been working hard. My mate has been stolen by the blasted Murk, who pose who knows how many other threats to the rest of us as well. It'd hardly make sense for me to be taking it easy."

One corner of her lips curls upward as if she finds my statement amusing. Abruptly, I find I *would* like to eviscerate her, rat or not.

She speaks smoothly but lightly. "And is your lord working himself quite as hard as you, or is he leaning on you to do the heavy lifting, as lords so often do? Not that I'm speaking from experience or anything."

Her wry tone implies the opposite. Is she suggesting she's unhappy with Tristan's leadership? Perhaps this unexpected overture will be useful to us after all, if she's going to reveal something that he wouldn't want us knowing.

I'm not going to besmirch Sylas to draw her out, though. "I'm quite satisfied with my pack's leadership," I say evenly. "But I'm sure such situations do arise in other packs more often than is ideal."

"I'm glad to hear you haven't encountered that

problem yourself. I've often thought it must be difficult for you, being so close to true-blooded and yet reduced to little more than a servant simply because of a younger brother's birth." She tsks her tongue.

It takes a concentrated effort to hold in my wince at her words. The rancor I've felt in the past toward Sylas has faded a great deal since we've gotten any misunderstandings and missteps between us out in the open, but she isn't wrong to have guessed at it. I suppose it isn't *difficult* to guess, though. Most fae in the same position would probably have resented it more than I did, considering I have very little interest in taking on Sylas's responsibilities anyway.

I shrug. "It leaves me more time for revelling and requires less stern adherence to duty, which suits me just fine. I'd hate to see what chaos any pack I ran would end up falling into."

Jax lets out a soft laugh and pats my arm, her hand lingering by my elbow just long enough for a renewed sense of uneasiness to wash over me. She isn't trying to lead up to any confession about her own feelings with this line of conversation—her family isn't high enough that she could ever have had a lordship in her sights. I can see how far she is from true-blooded in the shell of her ears, only slightly more pointed than August's human-like ones.

"I suspect you sell yourself short," she says. "I've seen how well your pack responds to you. They're at least as much yours as Sylas's."

I don't like the direction she's heading in at all now. "Is

that all you brought me out here for?" I ask. "To compliment my rapport with my pack-kin?"

Jax stops in a small clearing, turning toward me as I stop with her. She touches my arm again, letting her fingers rest on my wrist as she peers up at me through her eyelashes. "I came to speak to you out of a fellow cadre-chosen's concern and the respect I've formed for you across our dealings with your pack. I didn't think you'd want to admit to any difficulties with your pack-kin around, but we all need our chances to shed the pressures on us and enjoy a little escape."

She reaches into the folds of her skirt and draws out a small bottle. "I gather you're a particular fan of absinthe. We got quite a fine vintage brought in not long ago—consider it a gift and a recognition of your worth."

As I stare at the bottle in her hand, I can't stop my spine from going rigid. Bile has risen in my throat. Images of another woman in a different forest crash through my thoughts, scattering every impulse but the urge to destroy the threat in front of me as quickly and thoroughly as I can.

It isn't my worth or respect she's focused on. The scheming woman is trying to *seduce* me. Like Isleen, with the flirty touches and the wine—is it only absinthe in that bottle or did Jax think she could blot out my self-control just like that snake of a—

My claws and fangs have already sprung free before I get a hold of myself enough to realize how I'm reacting. I catch myself just shy of lunging for Jax's throat—and not with a love bite. The only lust her overtures have stirred up is a desire to see her dead and strewn across the forest floor.

That can't be the reaction she was hoping to provoke, I realize. I cough and step back, trying to cover the rage that's still searing through my veins. She can't have any idea what happened between Isleen and me, let alone how the encounter ate at me and nearly destroyed my relationship with both my brothers and the woman I love. She's simply using common tactics toward a goal she doesn't know has already been accomplished in a much more dire way.

That may very well be only regular absinthe in that bottle. She may simply have hoped to shatter my faithfulness to my mate.

But the shame and fury over that encounter with Isleen haven't totally healed, I can see now. I'm still itching to gut the woman in front of me for even suggesting I betray Talia like that. I drag in a breath, forcing more of the vitriol in me down.

Lashing out at Jax might not have been the response she was expecting, but it could have harmed me and my pack even more than if I'd succumbed to her advances. The cadre-chosen of an arch-lord's pack savaging that of another lord over offering him a beverage? Imagine all the concerns about my stability and unfairly hostile intentions toward Tristan's pack he could raise.

She has no idea how close she came to unraveling me in entirely the wrong way.

"I appreciate your offer," I say, managing to clear all but a little gruffness from my voice. "I'm afraid I can't indulge right now, as I'm keeping my head as clear as possible given the current threat."

Jax peers at me, no doubt picking up on some trace of my intense reaction and puzzling over it. She twirls the bottle between her fingers. "Well, it's a gift for whenever you'd want to enjoy it. Take it with you, and I hope you'll find yourself a moment to relax before too long."

She hands the bottle to me, so I take it. Then she taps my chest. "If you should feel you'd like to talk to someone with no ties to your own pack, I'll be just down the hill tonight."

I doubt she imagines I'm likely to take her up on *that* offer after the way I just recoiled, but perhaps she feels she has to make the attempt just in case. I give her a brief nod, and she saunters away with a sway of her hips designed to draw the eye.

As I head back toward the castle, the last shreds of my horrified rage subsiding, a deeper discomfort wraps around my gut.

Why did she come to me and make this proposition *now*? Is it random, or is there something in particular she'd be aiming to achieve with the timing?

Sylas and August are home at the moment, getting fae from our pack and others organized for another search effort, but both of them planned to make excursions later in the day that would take them away from the domain until well into tomorrow. Astrid has already gone to supervise our sentries traveling around and out of the fringelands. Tonight, for the first time since Talia's disappearance, I'd be the only member of the cadre present at Hearth-by-the-Heart.

How interesting that Tristan's cadre-chosen seemed intent on distracting me at this precise moment.

Even as my stomach twists uneasily, my thoughts sharpen at the sense of a scheme. I spring forward into wolf form and lope off to inform my lord of this ominous development while we still have time to respond.

23

Talia

W hen the ache in my head eases back enough that I can move without falling over, I make my slow, wobbly way back to the station that holds my hovel. As I pull myself onto the platform near it, a couple of Murk amble by. They shoot me a quick glance and chuckle to themselves, their tails twitching with amusement.

My stomach sinks. I can guess pretty easily what they find funny. Even if those two didn't witness my humiliation earlier today, the fae who did have probably passed on the story all through the Refuge by now.

I glance around the station and catch several more piercing glances, some of which jerk away when I notice them, others that linger for a few seconds in what's close to a leer. My gut knots even more. I crawl into my "house" and huddle there, waiting for more of the ache in my skull to subside.

I haven't eaten anything yet today. After a while, my head starts to spin more than throb, and my stomach pinches with enough hunger to cut through my other discomforts. I grit my teeth and head over to the meal table.

The two fae who've just brought a fresh load of food aren't ones I've spoken to before. The woman sees me coming and arches her eyebrows with a hint of a sneer to her lips. She mutters something to the man, who glances over and grins in a way that makes me want to run right back to my hovel.

I grab a few items that are the easiest to carry and hustle away without a word. One of the Murk on the tracks brushes close to me, murmuring, "Maybe you could dream about me sometime."

I don't answer, dashing the rest of the way to my house. Inside, I pull the door flap tightly shut and crouch against one hard plastic wall. I have to force down the dumplings and pear I grabbed, and my stomach doesn't feel much better afterward.

Simply lying there doesn't help me relax. My whole body may as well be a live wire. Nervous energy thrums through it, sparking occasional fresh bursts of pain in my head.

The small space starts to feel suffocating. I don't know what's going on outside, what new horror could be descending on me.

I ease back the flap just a bit and watch the fae passing

by outside. Seeing them doesn't exactly reassure me, but it takes the edge off my panic.

What am I going to do if I can't get into the air vent in time? Are there any other escape routes I might not have noticed? I'm not sure how to find that out, though. It'll look suspicious if I start poking around at the walls and structures here more than I already have.

As I'm mulling that problem over, Madoc's familiar form comes into view. He's picked up a tortilla wrap from the table, and he's walking along the tracks past me as he swallows his first bite.

I'm momentarily torn in two directions, but trying *something* seems better than staying shut away in here doing nothing. I push myself out of the hovel and hobble over to catch up with him.

"Madoc!" I call, careful not to pitch my voice too loud. I don't really want to draw anyone else's attention if I can help it.

He glances over and stops so I can catch up. My frayed state must show more than I realize, because he frowns, his brow knitting with concern. "Are you all right, Talia?" His gaze darts through the station, mainly in the direction of the throne room. "He hasn't—"

"Nothing else has happened," I say quickly. Nothing worth mentioning, anyway. I fall into step with him, and he continues on toward the tunnel, keeping a slower pace to account for my limp. "I just—I was wondering, are there many other little side passages and rooms in the Refuge like that one you have?" Maybe one of those would have some kind of vent or crevice a slim human woman could fit into that's escaped Orion's consideration.

Madoc nods, his expression still worried. "A few, here and there. Why do you ask?"

"I—" I need a good excuse. A couple of Murk pass us as we enter the shadows of the tunnel, and their smirks provide enough inspiration. "I was just feeling like I need to get away from everyone here for a little while. Farther away than just in my house. Maybe it sounds silly, but—"

"No," Madoc says, in the gentle tone that always surprises me a little even though his hoarse voice falls into it so easily. "I can understand. But those hideaways have all been claimed by one fae or another. You wouldn't be guaranteed privacy." He pauses. "If you wanted, you could make use of mine. I was going to pick up something there, but then you'd have it to yourself for at least a few hours."

That isn't what I was hoping for, but it's at least more of an opportunity than I had before. If Madoc has kept anything related to his work for Orion in his private space, I'll have a chance to find it.

And maybe if I play up how unsettled I am by Orion's treatment, I'll earn even more of his sympathy. Not that I need to do much playing up. I just have to resist the urge to hide my discomfort.

"That would be great," I say. "If you really don't mind."

"Not at all." He gives me a smile that looks a little sad. "I'm glad I can do something to make things easier for you."

"Thank you."

Just as we're coming up on the entrance to his room, another Murk saunters toward us. The fae man's eyes travel over me, and just as he passes me, he reaches out to grope my breast.

I yelp, jerking away with a flinch, and Madoc leaps in so quickly his tail lashes through the air.

He slams the fae man against the wall of the tunnel. There's nothing gentle about his voice now. "She isn't a toy for you to play with. Don't you dare treat her like that again."

The other man stammers, his eyes growing wide. "I— I'm sorry, I thought— Of course, she's Orion's. I would never— I'm sorry."

Madoc steps back with a look of disgust, his stance still tensed, and motions to me. "Apologize to *her*."

The groper meets my eyes much more warily this time. "I'm sorry for touching you." He scurries off down the tunnel without a backward glance.

Madoc scowls after him. When he looks at me, his expression somehow softens even as something fierce lights in his eyes. "Has that been happening a lot?"

I hug myself. "Not—not like that. Not actually grabbing me. But people are definitely looking at me differently."

He mutters a curse under his breath and stands there a moment, as if he feels he needs to do something else but doesn't know what. Finally, he ushers me on into the passage with the stairs, keeping a respectful distance behind me.

Is he upset because he thinks the other fae are going to

mess with what Orion obviously considers his property, or because of how it affects *me*? His insistence on the apology to me seems to suggest the latter.

But how much does it really matter if he can't—or won't—do anything to protect me from his king?

At least his obvious horror at anyone else manhandling me eases any anxiety I might have had about being alone with him in his private space. I sink onto one of the pillows scattered along the wall, and Madoc sits on an overturned crate on the other side of the room. He studies his mostly uneaten wrap and sets it aside as if he isn't hungry after all.

"You can spend as much time in here as you need to," he says. "I can bring you food and escort you anywhere you need to go in the rest of the Refuge. I know that's probably not how you'd want to live, but—it'll get better, it's just that the… events from this morning are still fresh in everyone's minds."

I rub my forehead. "Until he does something else to me."

Madoc knows who I mean without me needing to name him. He sighs. "I don't agree with all of Orion's tactics, but he's handling things the way that's worked for him for centuries before now. It isn't about you personally, I promise you."

Does he really believe that? I gaze back at him steadily. "But it is. I'm not fae. I'm hardly even human to him. He calls me his 'pet.' As far as he's concerned, he made me and I belong to him. There's no way of knowing how far he'll go, how much worse he might treat me than anyone else here, is there?"

Madoc's mouth twists. "I *have* been talking to him. I'll bring up the current situation too—that it's affecting the respect the others should have for you after the way you've helped us. And—if you'd open up to him, he'd see you more as an equal collaborator. Tell him everything you saw in the Mists, anything that might help us. He just needs to be sure he can trust you to be on our side."

I recoil from the idea inwardly, my back going rigid. "You expect me to betray my mates to a man who's enjoyed torturing me more than once in the past few days."

Madoc looks away, his jaw working. When he brings his gaze back to me, his eyes have hardened. "You've seen how the fae of the seasons have treated us. We're only defending ourselves from a continuing existence of being hunted down and slaughtered at every turn. Would you still rather side with *them*?"

"It's not about picking sides," I snap, my nerves finally fraying completely. "There are plenty of horrible Seelie and Unseelie, and I've never denied that. Back when I was in the Mists, I was doing everything I could to change things to help everyone they're being horrible to. But it isn't all of them. I know my mates, I fell in love with them for a reason, and I haven't seen one thing that's made me question my faith in *them*."

"They're all part of the same system," Madoc says, sounding frustrated, but I don't want to hear any more.

"And so are you. Trying to tell me that I should just give in to whatever Orion wants so he won't hurt me, that I can't expect any better because your war is so much more important. You know what? I can admit that I was wrong to assume that the Murk were all as awful as the other fae said. I know now that you've got reasons for being angry, and lots of you aren't just looking to make other people miserable."

"Of course we aren't."

"Right," I say without slowing down. "It isn't fair to judge an entire people based on what some of them do. And if you think I should recognize that when it comes to the Murk, then maybe you should realize it applies to the rest of the fae too."

Madoc stares at me, apparently lost for words. "I—" he starts, and cuts himself off. He seems to gather himself, but there's something awkward in his posture, as if he's no longer comfortable in the room. "I'm sorry," he says, not quite meeting my eyes. "I meant to give you some space and instead I've upset you. I'll go."

He picks up a couple of papers that were on the floor by his telescope and slips down the stairs without waiting for my response. Not that I have any idea what I'd say next. My throat is aching now, with all the anguish that leaked into my voice with my last words.

Maybe it's too much to hope that anyone here would ever see my point of view. It was hard enough getting the summer and winter fae to relax their guards enough to recognize that they didn't have to be enemies, and they'd only been in real conflict with each other for a few decades. It seems like they've been at odds with the Murk for pretty much forever.

A sense of hopelessness rolls over me, making me want to curl up and wallow in it, but I gather my resolve. Ignoring the heaviness in my heart, I get up and examine every inch of Madoc's room, rifling through his snack stash, checking under the blankets of his makeshift bed, peering at the star diagrams stuck to the walls.

I don't find anything else that feels like a clue I can use. Another wave of hopelessness hits me, thickened by my growing exhaustion. I sink down on the pillows again, thinking I'll just rest and recover for a little bit.

But I must fall asleep, because sometime later I find myself blinking awake with a jolt of adrenaline, my mind taking a moment to remember why I'm waking up in a different place from usual.

The artificial light overhead has dimmed to the faintest of glows. I can barely make out Madoc's form across from me, mostly covered by blankets. His breath rasps in and out in the slow rhythm of sleep.

I must have been here for hours. He came back, found me sleeping, and didn't want to disturb me even though he needed to get his own rest.

I sit up carefully, not wanting to ruin his sleep either. Then I notice the plate of food he's left for me next to the pillows: some kind of flaky pastry that gives off a meaty scent when I inspect it, an orange, and a powdered donut. Even though he was probably annoyed with me after the way I talked back to him earlier, he didn't want me going hungry or to have to navigate the tunnels outside on my own to get a meal.

A strange sensation squeezes around my heart. I look at the vague shape of the fae man across from me and wish I knew the right way to thank him. The right thing to say to make him understand.

Because I meant it when I said that I don't think the Murk are all evil. *He* isn't evil, even if he's gotten caught up in Orion's awfulness. After what I've seen, I'm not sure I can blame him for assuming that's the only way to get a better life for him and all the other Murk. What other options have presented themselves?

I don't want to let Orion get away with his plans for the Mists, but I don't like the thought of Madoc suffering because of his king's choices either.

I can't do anything about that in my current situation, though. The sleep has given my emotions a chance to reset, and the thought of venturing out into the rest of the Refuge is no longer quite so intimidating. Especially considering that it seems to be the Murk's "night" now, so almost everyone will be asleep.

That makes it the perfect time to get back to work on my escape plan, doesn't it?

Taking the meat-filled pastry with me and filled with a rising sense of purpose, I creep down the stairs and through the tunnels toward the maintenance room. As I expected, the Refuge is dark and silent. I have to step carefully to avoid stubbing my toes when I can barely see a few inches ahead of me.

I gulp down the pastry, which turns out to be stuffed with spiced chicken and some kind of dried fruit, and am just wiping the crumbs from my fingers when I reach the collection of abandoned machines. I make my way to the one by the vent, clamber up, and whisper the well-practiced true name. The bracelet reshapes in my hands. Balancing myself on the machine's sloping top, I get to work on the next bolt.

This one seems to come easier, or maybe that's just because of my renewed surge of energy and determination. I twist the wrench with all my strength, picturing myself managing to loosen not just one but two or maybe even three tonight. Then I'd be more than halfway to my goal.

I've just heaved on the wrench one last time, feeling the bolt give completely, when a skittering sound reaches my ears. It's so unexpected that I startle. My hands jerk on the wrench—and the tool tugs the bolt right out of its hole. The metal cylinder clinks off the top of the machine and falls to the concrete floor with a louder clatter.

My pulse lurches. I freeze instinctively, and footsteps thump toward me. Down—I have to get down so they don't see what I was doing. With no time to transform it, I toss my wrench behind the machine and start to slide off.

Before my feet have even reached the ground, a Murk woman who must be one of Orion's sentries darts into view. She takes in me and my guilty pose. Her eyes, better suited to the dark than mine, lower to inspect the ground. She leaps forward and plucks the bolt off the floor.

When she straightens up, she's just a foot away from me. I'm afraid to move.

She holds the bolt up between us. "I think Orion needs to hear about this right away."

My voice tumbles out of me. "Please, I was only— I wasn't hurting anyone—"

The fae woman mutters a few magical words, and the words die in my throat. I feel as if my mouth is stuffed with some invisible substance. My limbs have gone rigid too. I couldn't move now if I wanted to.

She prods me and nods with a look of vicious satisfaction with her spell. "You stay right here, and we'll see what my king makes of this disobedience."

24

Talia

From when I first woke up in the Refuge of the Murk, I've done my best to keep my composure, to hide how terrified I am, to put on a show of resilience. The moment I see the cage, that self-control flies out the window.

My legs stiffen, my heels attempting to dig into the ground to stop the two fae men escorting me from dragging me any closer. My pulse lurches and starts to rattle through my veins. My body shakes with the frantic rhythm.

It isn't exactly like the cage Aerik held me in. The bars look like steel rather than bronze, and there's no door, just an entire side that's folded down to make room to shove me in. But it's even smaller than that one, only a little bigger than I am. There'll be no room to pull away from any of the walls, no way to do more than sit in a crouched position.

The cage is set off to one side of the dais. Orion stands over it, grinning eagerly as his men haul me the rest of the way over. Even though it's still very early in the morning by Murk standards, a couple of his close associates have arrived to stand around him. A few dozen regular Murk have drifted into the throne room after hearing of the commotion.

Not one set of eyes I meet holds a trace of friendliness. Madoc hasn't appeared—I don't know if he's even aware of what happened.

I don't know if there's anything he could do if he is.

"In you go," Orion says briskly with a clap of his hands. "If you can't be trusted to roam free, we have to make some adjustments to your living situation."

"I wasn't going to run away," I lie, unable to stop my voice from quavering. I've tried these arguments before when the king first confronted me in the maintenance room, and he didn't believe me then, but I can't give up on the tiny chance that they might sway someone else who'll speak up for me. "I just missed the fresh air. I only wanted to get a taste of it and then I'd have come right back."

Orion snorts. No one else makes a sound except the huff of the guards as they toss me into the cage. I sprawl on my hands and knees, and someone shoves the side of the cage up to close it. A lock snaps into place. Orion seals it with a tap of his hand and a few words of magic.

There are bars all around me, everywhere I look. The smell of the newly forged metal clogs my nose. The orange glow of the Murk Heart flickers over me, the quaking pulse of its energy feeling somehow mocking.

I wrap my hands around my knees, my chest constricting. My heart is thumping so fast I'm half afraid it'll fly right up my throat.

I squeeze my eyes shut, but images of the past flash through my mind regardless. Aerik's disdainful stare. Icy Cole jabbing me with his sharp fingers and elbows. The stink of my own filth all around me, the endless days without a glimmer of hope. The snap of my warped foot.

I've conquered those fears. I've held the panic at bay before, getting better at it every time. But since then, I've never been thrown into a cage by fae who are my enemies. This isn't just a reminder of past horrors—it's the same horror repeated.

It could become even more horrifying. Orion has no reason to care about keeping me alive and reasonably healthy like Aerik did.

My lungs clench tighter. My breath squeezes in and out with a painful wheeze.

"Look at her shudder," the Murk king says in a mocking tone. "Pitiful little human girl thought she could get the better of us. Of me." He cackles and smacks the top of the cage, making the bars and my nerves jangle. "What were you using to loosen those bolts, pet? I know those spindly fingers wouldn't be strong enough on their own."

Pain pierces my skull like it did when he questioned me before. He's trying to wear me down—but I've already told him the truth. The words tear out of me like they did the last time he raked through my mind. "I made a wrench. I used that."

The spell he's put on me doesn't seem to force me to give more details as long as the statement itself is truthful. And whatever powers Orion possesses to reach inside my thoughts, he hasn't been able to determine that I *am* being truthful—or that I used a true name's magic—so far. Maybe the possibility is so far-fetched to him that he'd never recognize it.

"*Made* a wrench?" he sneers. "Someone here made it for you or maybe with you, you mean. Who helped you with your little plan?"

"No one," I say truthfully. "I did it on my own."

"Then someone's going to have to pay for not keeping a close enough eye on the workshops, I suppose." Orion peers over the growing crowd as if he thinks he's going to spot someone to blame right now. Even in my muddled state, I notice a few of the nearer fae cringe.

I close my eyes again, tuning out the Murk king, our audience, and my panic as well as I can.

Focus on something else, I tell myself. *Focus on something better.*

The tickling of the sweet-smelling grass in the fields of Hearth-by-the-Heart. The sweep of Corwin's wings when he carries me through the chilly winter air. August shooting me a smile across the kitchen as we cook together. Whitt, spinning me slowly in a dance during one of the revels. Sylas's powerful hands caressing my body as he kisses me.

I am more than a pitiful human. I'm more than a pet.

I have to hold on to all those other parts of me and not let this setback shatter my spirit completely.

Even if I can't think of any way I could possibly get out of this.

My pulse evens out enough that I'm no longer dizzy. I draw a breath into my chest and then another. My ribs still feel as if they're closing around my lungs, but not quite as painfully as before.

When I open my eyes again, my gaze catches on Madoc's pale hair where he's moving toward the dais through the gathered fae. When he spots me, the tendons around his jaw tighten. I think he nearly stumbles. His gaze darts from me to Orion, and he walks the rest of the way to the platform even faster.

I doubt he'll be able to convince Orion to let me out, at least not any time soon, but knowing he's here, knowing he's bothered by what's happening to me, gives me a shred of comfort.

Orion stalks away from the cage across the platform, pacing from one end to the other and back again. He rubs his hands together. A manic gleam has sparked in his eyes that makes my skin crawl in uneasy anticipation.

"I shaped this girl as a tool of our own," he says, "and it seems she doesn't appreciate the special role I gave her. But there are other ways we can still use her against our enemies, hmmm."

"What did you have in mind?" one of his other associates asks with a broad grin.

"Let me see." Orion comes to a stop by my cage again and taps his lips. "So many of the fae of the seasons have staked all their hopes on this fragile human. They see her as the answer to all their problems, as some kind of blessed being sent by their Heart to protect them. How much do you think it would crush their spirits to watch us crush her?"

Twittering laughter spreads through the crowd. A chill of starker fear seeps through me to pool in my gut. What's he talking about?

Orion smirks down at me. I get the impression he can tell just how much he's unnerving me and enjoying every hint of my discomfort.

"Yes, that would be perfect," he says. "We'll make a show of it. String her up for them all to see, let them watch as we snap every bone and slice through her skull. It won't do to kill her, of course, because then they'll be able to mourn her loss. We'll leave her paralyzed and lobotomized, a broken shell they'll still be scrambling to reclaim. And in the middle of their distress, we'll sweep in and slaughter them as if we're the wolves and they're nothing but lambs and lame ducks."

A cheer rises up, but I barely hear it, I've gone so numb with horror.

No. To be locked inside my body even more fully than I'm trapped in this cage, to have my mind cleaved apart so I can barely form a coherent thought—to be made utterly helpless, nothing more than a doll he's dangling as bait—and for my mates and all the other fae who've come to support me to have to watch—to know I'm being used to bring about their doom—

Tears are streaming down my cheeks before I even

realize I'm crying. I press my hands to my eyes, but nothing will hold them in. I'm starting to wheeze again with the contracting of my lungs.

Oh, God, maybe I should have slit my own throat while I had the chance. My bracelet is gone now; I've got nothing at all here in this cage.

How can I stop this from happening? How will I not go insane waiting for him to carry out his awful plan?

I swipe at my tears and grasp the bars of my cage. "Please," I say in a ragged voice. "I could help in other ways—there's so much else I could do—" If I could just buy myself a little more time...

But Orion only scoffs, his yellow eyes offering nothing but vicious amusement. Instinctively, I look to Madoc, who's come up beside the throne. His pale face has turned almost sickly, but he hasn't said a word yet. *Please*, I think at him.

His king follows my gaze. Orion snorts and pats his hand on the top of the cage again, sending another vibration through it. "Looking to my faithful servant for help, are you, pet? Do you really think he gives a damn what happens to you as long as you serve our cause? He did well then, if you fell for his act. Excellent work, Madoc."

Madoc... dips his head in acknowledgment of the praise. When he lifts it again, he's focused completely on his king, as if I'm not there at all. The bottom of my stomach falls out.

Orion strokes the top of the cage as if petting a cat. "I choose who stands beside me carefully, little girl. You obviously didn't realize that. Has he seemed to dote on you, to be there for you when you needed it? Anything he offered you, it's because I ordered him to win you over. You're a tool to him as much as you are to me. He doesn't care about you any more than he does a bar of lead. But illusions are his speciality, and from the expression on your face, he wove quite a good one."

I try to swallow, but my throat won't work. There's a sob lodged in it. Madoc gives no sign that contradicts anything his king said.

And why would I expect him to contradict it? That all makes sense, doesn't it? Throughout all the kindnesses he's shown me, he's never stopped trying to convince me to join their war, to turn against the fae of the seasons and tell Orion everything I can. Even last night, he was encouraging me to betray my mates.

I'm as alone here as I was when I first arrived. I never should have allowed myself to imagine I'd gained even a partial ally.

Despair descends over me again, wrapping around me like a suffocatingly thick blanket. I lean my face against my knees and focus on only the pressure of my arms hugging my legs, the hard floor of the cage beneath me, and the coolness of the air.

In their eyes, I'm nothing, and I've never felt more like that's true than in this moment.

"Well, then," Orion says, apparently satisfied that he's traumatized me as much as he possibly can, "let's leave my pet to reflect on her many mistakes and get to work on finalizing our invasion."

He steps away from the cage. Footsteps scrape across the dais, and lowered voices fall into discussion at the other side of the room. There's a rustling and an excited murmuring as the gathered fae go back to their work.

And I'm left with nothing to do but hold onto myself as hard as I can.

25

Madoc

I didn't know it was possible for me to feel the same anguish now as I did on the day the Unseelie warriors slaughtered my parents. I was a child then, and I've had decades upon decades to harden myself since. I've seen and heard of so many horrific acts. They fuel my determination, but they don't shake me anymore.

Until this moment, watching an act dealt by the hands of my own king.

I already had the sense that something was wrong from the energy in the air as I hurried to the throne room. When I emerged from my rooms after waking and finding Talia gone, there were murmurs of "traitor" all through the tunnels.

I hadn't realized they meant her, though. I walked into the throne room not at all prepared to find the woman who's come to haunt both my dreams and my waking hours hunched in a cage, shivering in terror.

As I make my way to the dais, the voices around me blur into a wordless din. I keep my head high and my strides steady, because if Orion catches any hint that I disagree with his approach, that she's won any loyalty over what I feel for him, it might be even worse for her as well as for me. But inside I'm aware of little other than her slim form contorted by the size of the cage, the panic in her wide green eyes, the effort I can tell she's making to try to hide her distress—and the agony the sight provokes in me, twisting through me from throat to gut.

What has she done? What could she *possibly* have done that would require a punishment like this? She hardly had the means to commit any major betrayal.

But what she said to me yesterday is true. Orion doesn't see her as one of his people but as one of his belongings, a pet. Caging her after she's stepped out of line probably makes perfect sense to him.

My king is pacing the dais now with an air more like a lion than a rat. I can't ask him what she's done or say anything on her behalf while he's putting on this display for the audience that's gathered. Hopefully I can draw him aside soon after he's done with his spectacle and convince him that outright traumatizing her is only going to make it harder for any of us to earn her support.

Not that I think there's much chance of getting her to completely abandon her devotion to her former home after the way she spoke to me yesterday. But it's an argument Orion will understand. We can at least allow her to be comfortable while we keep her cooped up in the Refuge, until we can finally move in on the Mists.

"I shaped this human as a tool of our own," Orion says now, "and it seems she doesn't appreciate the special role I gave her. But there are other ways we can still use her against our enemies, hmmm."

My body tenses. Does he mean to take this punishment even further?

What *did* she do—try to kill him? That's the only crime I can think of that would warrant this kind of viciousness.

Ridiculously, I both can't believe Talia would resort to that kind of violence, and also wouldn't entirely blame her if she had. I wouldn't want her to succeed, of course, but it'd be understandable for her to want to after the way he's mistreated her already.

My king has stopped by her cage, putting on a show of contemplating his options when I'm sure he knew exactly what he planned before he even ordered that cage constructed.

His voice comes out with a lilt that's both playful and cutting. "So many of the fae of the Mists have staked all their hopes on this fragile creature. They see her as the answer to all their problems, as some kind of blessed being sent by their Heart to protect them. How much do you think it would crush their spirits to watch us crush her?"

My hands start to clench before I catch them. He can't really—after all the ways she's advanced our goals, even if she didn't know what she was doing—she's been more instrumental in paving the way for our victory than anyone in this room other than Orion, and I have to admit that includes me.

But there's no respect or even pity in his gaze as he peers down at her, only sadistic glee.

"Yes, that would be perfect," he says. "We'll make a show of it. String her up for them all to see, let them watch as we snap every bone and slice through that skull. It won't do to kill her, of course, because then they'll be able to mourn her loss. We'll leave her paralyzed and lobotomized, a broken shell they'll still be scrambling to reclaim. And in the middle of their distress, we'll sweep in and slaughter them as if we're the wolves and they're nothing but lambs and lame ducks."

What? My stomach flips, sending bile up my throat. Nausea clamps around my gut.

The memory flickers through my head of the ravens cackling as they rammed my father's severed head on that branch, echoing into the cheer that's lifted up around me. For just a second, the world tilts.

The orange light of the Heart catches on the tears that've dampened Talia's cheeks. As she presses her hands to her face, her shoulders shake. When she reaches out again, grasping the bars of the cage, there's nothing but blank panic in her eyes.

"Please," she says to Orion. Her voice spills out in a babble, offering other help, other contributions, anything to save herself from the fate worse than death he just described.

How can he just smirk at her as if this is all a game?

And then she looks at me. She doesn't speak—for

fuck's sake, she cares enough about me and the position I'm maintaining here not to call out to me overtly, even now—but the desperate plea in her gaze is unmistakeable.

Which means Orion doesn't miss it either. He laughs and taps the top of her cage, and just when I thought the moment couldn't get any more horrifying, he aims his smirk at me. "Looking to my faithful servant for help, are you, pet? Do you really think he gives a damn what happens to you as long as you serve our cause? He did well then, if you fell for his act. Excellent work, Madoc."

Oh, no. At the crumpling of Talia's face, misery written all through her expression, I feel as if he's stabbed a knife right into my chest.

It isn't true, I want to tell her. *It wasn't an act—not all of it.* If I'm being honest, in the past few days I've had to do more acting to *avoid* showing how much I'm coming to care rather than how much I don't.

But Orion is grinning at me in the wake of his compliment. How can I throw it back in his face? I nod just slightly, fixing my gaze on him, keeping my posture as still as I can. If I look at her now, I'm not sure I can hold onto my self-control.

Some part of *me* wants to kill him now.

Orion glances down at Talia again and speaks in a croon. "I choose who stands beside me carefully, Talia. You obviously didn't realize that. Has he seemed to dote on you, to be there for you when you needed it? Anything he offered you, it's because I ordered him to win you over. You're a tool to him as much as you are to me. He doesn't care about you any more than he does a bar of lead. But illusions are his speciality, and from the expression on your face, he wove quite a good one."

With every word, he drives the knife deeper—into both my chest and Talia's, from her reaction, which I can't help marking. Her whole body folds in on itself even tighter than before. The panic in her eyes dulls, but only because it's shifted into a sort of dazed hopelessness that brings my claws prickling to the tips of my fingers.

She looks like that fierce spirit of hers has already died.

I drag my gaze back to my king as he says a few dismissive remarks. He waves off the crowd and motions for me and a few of his other knights to join him at the other end of the dais. My feet move of their own accord, carrying me away from the wounded figure in the cage.

It takes a minute before I'm sure enough of my voice to speak. The conversation has started around me, but I've barely heard it. As soon as there's a lull, I tip my head to Orion and then toward Talia. "What's the reason for all this? Did she hurt someone?"

Orion guffaws, as if the notion of Talia managing to harm one of us is absurd—which it actually kind of is, knowing her to the extent I do now. I don't think he's assuming that based on his knowledge of her personal values, though.

"She thought she'd flee," he says in a derisive tone. "Got her hands on some kind of tool and was working at the bolts on an air vent in the maintenance room that someone missed as a possible exit. Now she's seen what her lies and her commitment to the fae of the seasons earn her."

He goes back to discussing the best timing for his gory demonstration and our attack to follow. Should we launch it while the Seelie are wild with the curse, when they'll have little control but won't understand what's happening, or afterward, to amplify their helplessness? Are the other colonies prepared to march within the week? Have we stockpiled enough equipment?

Practical considerations in the lead-up to destroying the woman crouched just twenty feet from us, bit by painful bit. All because she wanted to get away from this place, to return to the mates she loves. *That* is the treachery Orion objects to so violently.

I'm standing right next to him, but I watch him as if from a great distance, adding little to the conversation other than occasional nods and noncommittal murmurs. I note the way he cuffs one of the young fae who comes with a report across the ears, for no reason except the girl stutters a little. I observe as Bren enters the room, and Orion jokes to the others about the scars that the fight he incited will leave behind. And all the while, Talia's clear, soft voice filters through my thoughts.

There's no way of knowing how far he'll go, how much worse he might treat me than anyone else here, is there?

He made you kill someone like Bren the other day, didn't he? Just another Murk, just because he likes seeing people being torn apart.

You want to save your people. As far as I can tell, Orion is more interested in hurting fae—and not just the fae of the Mists.

I told her she was wrong. I told her he only wanted to

make us as strong as we could be, that his methods were necessary to have brought us the power to win against the other fae. But she's chipped at my certainty, and now...

Now I'm not so sure she wasn't seeing things more clearly than I ever have, when I was so focused on both the vengeance and the brighter future Orion promised.

Our king has done amazing things. No one could deny that. The Heart blazing away beside us is the clearest possible testament. But is this what I want a new era for my people to look like? Celebrating torture, reveling in violence and pain...

Are we really better than what the fae of the seasons think if we'll stand back and even cheer Orion on while he breaks every part of the woman in that cage, who's done nothing worse than try to live her own life? Who's managed to care about at least some of us regardless of what we've put her through and what she's heard about us before?

Although it's hard to imagine she cares after this latest assault. We've just proven everything the fae of the seasons would say about us true, haven't we?

And I helped, by standing there saying nothing to challenge it. By acting as if I appreciated Orion's praise and his plan.

Nausea grips me all over again. I said to Talia once that all the tests I went through were worth nothing if I threw away what I won with them. But what are they worth if I don't use the position I won to fight for a future where we really aren't living in fear—of the wolves and the ravens, and of each other? Of this man who calls himself our king?

I go through the rest of the conversation and then my other duties of the day as if sleepwalking, most of my focus inward. There is a line I'm not willing to cross, and my king has just drawn it for me. So what am I going to do about it?

The pieces of a plan of my own start to come together in my mind alongside a growing resolve.

Every time I enter the throne room, Orion is there, but that's not unexpected. I have to wait just a little longer, even though that means more time for Talia to dwell on the threats and the claims he made.

When the lights dim, I head off to my room as if I mean to turn in for the night. I know Orion will do the same soon, down the tunnel to the large chamber carved into the rock beyond the throne room walls. He casts enough magic around its entrance that he doesn't bother posting guards there. He trusts his skills more than any of us.

After I'm sure he'll be asleep, I intone the words of one of the illusion spells I helped perfect around me. Orion didn't lie when he said that kind of magic is a particular affinity of mine, and it'll hide me from my fellow Murk as well as any other fae. Then I shift into rat form and slip down the stairs and through the tunnels.

Talia has lain down on the floor of the cage, curled into a ball. There isn't room for her to extend her limbs much more than that anyway. Her eyes are closed, her face blotchy with past tears and present stress. Seeing her like that wrenches at my heart all over again.

She's stayed so strong through so much… He hasn't finally broken her, has he?

I glance around the throne room once more to confirm that there's no one here before shedding my rat form. Then I weave a more detailed illusion, one that'll reflect the image of Talia I'm seeing now to anyone who glances this way. It doesn't do any good to keep myself hidden if a random passerby could notice she's talking to someone.

I ease within that illusion and pull back the one that was hiding only me. Reaching through the bars, I brush my fingers over Talia's hand.

She jerks awake in an instant, faster than I expected. All at once she's scrambling as upright as she can get, shoving herself against the far side of the cage.

"What do you want?" she asks, but the fierceness I'd have expected in her voice has faded. It wobbles with a trace of fear.

She thinks I might have come to inflict some new torture on her.

Staring into her strained but still pretty face, taking in the distrust in the eyes I never meant to admire, I have trouble remembering what I wanted to say. My hesitation dredges up a wash of shame. *She's* adjusted her opinions about the Murk after the things I've shown and told her, admitted to being wrong. How can I still balk at doing the same for her, after all the suffering she's faced since I brought her here?

"I want to help you," I say. "I don't agree with what Orion's done to you or anything he talked about doing to you."

Talia makes a noise of disbelief. "Are you still trying to trick me into trusting you, after he's already told me that was all his idea? How stupid do you think I am?"

I swallow thickly. "Not stupid at all. Smarter than me in many ways, I've come to realize." I glance away and then back at her, not knowing how to convince her. "It's true that he ordered me to be friendly with you to try to get you to open up about your knowledge of the Mists. But the rest of the things he said aren't."

Her gaze is still full of doubt. I force myself to go on.

"I might not agree with all your allegiances, but there's so much I respect about you. Your bravery, your resilience, your compassion, your willingness to listen..." We won't get into the emotions I've felt that went beyond respect, but the thought of those compels me to add, "Even your loyalty to your mates. You're not just a pet, and you don't belong to Orion. You're your own person. I *have* come to care about you, and you don't deserve this."

"But somehow Orion isn't aware of any of that," she says.

"Orion is... Orion. He wouldn't have appreciated me feeling conflicted over the job he'd given me, so I've let him continue thinking I was only spending time with you on his orders. But I can't stand with him if this is how he's going to rule. I'm drawing that line."

Talia studies me through the bars. Her expression doesn't give away any clue of how much she believes me.

When she speaks, her tone is skeptical. "And how are you drawing that line? By coming to talk to me? Because you talked to me plenty before, and it didn't stop this from happening."

"No, it didn't." I rub my hand over my face. "I didn't think it'd come to this—maybe I should have realized. Maybe I was too caught up in my own hopes for the future to see clearly. But I see now."

"What does that even mean?" she asks.

"I—" There are things I still need to be sure of. It's not just Orion but all of the Murk I have to consider. "If you went back to your mates, what would you say to them about the Murk? Would you tell them to slaughter us all?"

Talia frowns. "Is this some trick to get me to reveal something about how they work or what their strategies are? I'm not falling for it. Why don't you just go away, if all you're looking to do is ask me more questions?"

She turns her head, leaning her cheek against the bars and closing her eyes, shutting me out the only way she can.

I sit there, torn. But the answer isn't really all that difficult to arrive at, is it?

She's taken more than one leap of faith for me. I can't expect her to make another if I won't offer one of my own. And deep down, I do know what her answer would be, don't I? It's only selfishness that makes me want to hear her say it in so many words before I trust it.

I trust her. I trust the love and determination I've seen burning in her soul.

"That's not all I'm looking to do," I say, summoning all

the firmness I can into my voice. "I'm here to help you leave the Refuge."

Then I reach up to the top of the cage and mutter the words to bring the side of it swinging down, opening up the way to her freedom.

26

Talia

The wall of the cage hits the ground with a faint clink. My eyes have already popped open at the shift in the air with the movement of the bars. I stare at the lowered wall and then at Madoc poised next to me on the edge of the dais, now visible without any barrier between us.

He's letting me out. He really—

My first surge of relief snaps away with another flare of suspicion. This could still be some kind of trap. He's trying to lure me into betraying Orion all over again to give Orion an excuse to torture me even more.

I never should have believed a single word that came out of his mouth.

He's watching me expectantly. I turn away, leaning my head against the bars on the opposite side. "Go away. Whatever you're trying to do, I'm not falling for it."

"Talia." There's an edge of frustration in Madoc's voice. Did he really think I'd fall for his conflicted supporter act that easily a second time?

He inhales roughly and releases the breath in a rush. "Fine. I understand that you don't trust me. I can't really blame you. But if you don't come with me now, I don't know if we'll get another chance. Orion's talking about making his move after the next full moon, which is in just a few days. I don't—I don't know what else he might do to you in the meantime. What could I possibly be leading you to that'd be *worse* than what he's already planning?"

His words and the rawness in his voice sink in slowly through the numbness of my despair. It's true that Orion couldn't really hurt me worse than he's already declared he's going to. He's said he's going to break every part of my body and deaden my mind in front of all the fae of the seasons—what could be more awful than that?

If there's even the slightest chance that Madoc really does mean to let me escape, that he isn't as loyal as Orion thinks, wouldn't it be better to take that chance than to throw it away when I don't have any others? I know for sure no one else in this place is going to help me, and I've got no tools that'll open this cage on my own.

The only advantage I have left is whatever difference the things I've said to Madoc might have made in the way he sees me and his king.

I look at him warily, taking in the urgency in his gray eyes, turned thundercloud-dark in the dimness of the room. The pallor of his face, still a little sickly. His hand, gripping the side of the cage so tightly the knuckles have whitened.

He's giving every appearance of being desperate to get me out of here. But I just don't know whether I should believe it.

Maybe it doesn't matter whether I believe it or not, only whether I'm willing to let my uncertainty keep me here where I know my situation is hopeless or to take whatever tiny chance I might have with him.

But I can't stop myself from asking, in a steadier voice than before, "Why would you help me escape? Aren't you worried that I'll bring the fae of the seasons down on the Refuge, destroy all those dreams you have about making a better life for the Murk?"

It might not be the wisest idea to remind him of just how badly this situation could go for him, but I need to hear his answer. I need to understand how he could see this betrayal of his king—and possibly his entire people—as a reasonable option.

Madoc's throat bobs, but he holds my gaze. "No, I'm not," he says. "The way into the Refuge isn't that easy; we'll be safe here regardless of what you tell your mates. Am I worried about how it'll affect our chances of getting a better life in general? Of course. But—I think I know you well enough now to say that you aren't going to go back to the Mists and tell them we should all be butchered. You'll do whatever you can to avoid bloodshed on both sides. And maybe by getting you back to them, I'll have shown enough proof for *them* to trust that there are at least a few of us who deserve better than the brutality they've aimed at us."

A touch of emotion passes through my chest, like a feather brushing between my ribs. It takes me a moment to recognize it as a flicker of the hope I thought I'd lost.

I still don't know what Madoc's full intentions are, but he has been listening to me, and not just for strategic information he can pass on to his king. He understands what matters to me.

He maybe even believes I could pull off a miracle beyond any magic I've possessed so far.

"You'd want that?" I say. "You'd rather settle things with negotiations and treaties, if that's even possible, than with a war where you'd get to rule over all of the Mists if you won?"

"If there's a way to end the attacks on us and to give us a proper home in the Mists without even more of us dying, without us resorting to savaging people who don't deserve it, then I'll take it," Madoc says. "I didn't think it *was* possible. But from what I've seen while I watched you in the Mists and now here… I trust that if anyone *can* make it possible, it's you."

A strange note comes into his voice with those last words, one I can't decipher but that sends a wobble through my pulse. I don't trust him, but then, I never did, not completely. But he's said enough that the chance I'm taking doesn't feel quite as precarious. That's enough.

I didn't slit my throat the other day because I refused to give up. I'm not going to roll over and die on Orion's whim now either.

I ease forward out of the cage, and Madoc pulls back to make room. His gaze darts around the throne room. He doesn't look all that reassured by the fact that he's convinced me, which reassures *me* that this isn't some gambit just to trick me.

"The one other thing Orion said that's true is that I'm good with illusions," he murmurs. When I've crept free of the cage, he closes the side again. "I can make it look as if you're still in there to anyone who doesn't come too close. But as soon as Orion is up for the day, he'll check on you. I'll have to dispel the illusion before then, which means you'll need to be well on your way at that point."

I'll need to be well on my way—which means Madoc isn't coming all the way to the Mists with me. In spite of everything, my pulse stutters with concern. "Isn't he going to know you helped me? What's he going to do to *you*?"

Madoc smiles tightly. "I'll be laying down more than one kind of illusion. I think I can cover my tracks well enough. He already knows you've been able to surpass his assumptions of what you're capable of—and one benefit to his single-mindedness is that I don't think it'd even occur to him that someone who's worked as hard to earn his favor as I have would ever throw it away. Come on. We need to go to the maintenance room first."

I follow him out of the throne room and through the tunnels, sticking close behind him, walking as quickly as my warped foot will allow. My legs and back ache with stiffness from being cramped in the cage all day, but stretching them in motion brings some relief along with the soreness.

Once, my toe hits a bit of gravel that rattles against the tracks, and I freeze. But no one comes running our way, and Madoc urges me onward. A little while later, a small furry body scurries past us on the opposite side of the tunnel, briefly lit by one of the few dimmed bits of illumination still on for the night. The rat-shifted Murk doesn't pause or even glance toward us.

Madoc must have one of his illusions wrapped around us even now. At least I've got proof that he's as good as he said.

When we reach the maintenance room, he peers around the walls and points to the vent. "That's the one you were working on?"

I nod. He walks over and climbs onto the machine below much more easily than I ever did. With a few muttered words, he's loosened all of the bolts and let them fall to the floor. He sets the vent cover on top of the machine. Then he beckons me closer.

Is he sending me out by that route after all? Now that I've spent nearly a full day in a cage, the thought of squeezing myself into the small opening makes my chest clench up.

But when I step over, Madoc just reaches to take a strand of my hair between his fingers. "I need to use this to make sure they believe you went this way. It'll keep them off your trail for longer—hopefully long enough for your soul-twined mate to get to you once he can hear you again. All right?"

All he wants is to pull out a hair, for my own protection—and he's asking my permission rather than simply taking it. Some part of me that was still a little afraid that he was leading me into a trap relaxes, and my heart thumps faster.

This is really happening. He's getting me out of here. I *will* speak to Corwin again, soon.

"Go ahead," I whisper.

There's only a brief pinch in my scalp when he tugs out the hair. Madoc turns to the vent and holds the root of the hair in front of his mouth. He speaks a few magic-laced syllables and then blows into the tunnel.

I'm not sure exactly what effect he's conjuring, but a moment later he snags the hair in the corner of the opening and hops back down. "That's done. Now for our actual route."

He leads me away from the maintenance room to the nearest station, and then to a doorway locked with magic in one corner. I'm not sure what illusion he draws with his murmured words, but the sentry stationed just a few feet away doesn't so much as blink when Madoc opens the door and motions me through.

I find myself in an even darker, mildew-smelling space. I can barely make out the walls around me, which I find by stretching out my hands—the space is just wide enough that I can touch both with my arms completely extended. Madoc is little more than a blur in front of me.

"I can't see," I say.

The air shifts. I think he's going to offer his hand and balk at the idea of taking it, but instead he simply steps a little closer. "Hold onto the back of my shirt. Try to adjust. This is the easiest part of this route."

Wonderful. I grope through the darkness and curl my fingers into the fabric of his shirt. Something brushes my ankle and then jerks away—his tail, I realize.

He moves forward slowly enough for me to follow behind him, gradually picking up the pace when I show I can keep up. My boots tap against uneven bits on the floor, some of which slide at the contact, but I can't tell what we're walking over. I don't even have a sense of how far this hallway stretches. Madoc stays silent, so I do too.

How many fae travel this way regularly? What are the chances we'll run into some?

How far do we have to go before I can reach out to my mates?

Those questions whirl in my head as I tramp on, essentially blind. The darkness starts to close in on me, shortening my breaths. I drag air deep into my lungs to steady myself.

Madoc slows before he comes to a complete halt, so I don't walk right into him. As I let go of his shirt, there's a grating sound like something mechanical turning. He speaks a few more words of magic under his breath. Then, with a soft creak, a door swings open. A waft of cool, damp air washes over us.

There's a little more light on the other side, a faint glow that seeps down from somewhere above. The passage ahead of us appears to slant upward and then veer to the side through solid rock, roughly carved into a narrow tunnel.

This isn't part of the original station, clearly, but a route of the Murk's own making.

The rocky floor gleams with a hint of moisture. A faint trickling sound reaches my ears. I hesitate, staring into the passage. "How much farther?"

"It's a long route, and a little twisted," Madoc says. "The shape of it is a spell in itself—to prevent discovery. I'll lead you all the way to the surface."

There really isn't any way to go but forward, is there?

I square my shoulders. "Then let's get going."

27

Talia

Madoc was right when he said the first hallway was the easiest part. The rocky passage may be slightly better lit, but my feet wobble on the uneven ground. Any place that's smooth is also slick with dribbles of water. When I brace my hands against the walls to catch my balance, the rough stone there scrapes my palms.

He doesn't hurry me, even though he has so much more on the line than I do. I was going to be worse than killed anyway. His entire standing among the Murk hangs in the balance right now, probably his life as well.

But he stops every few steps to check that I'm coming along all right. A few times he opens his mouth as if he's going to offer to carry me over the tricky terrain, but then he shuts it, maybe guessing—correctly—that I'd rather stumble along than have his hands on me. He keeps his tail tucked close to his legs so it doesn't risk tripping me.

"We can talk in here," he says. "I still have a spell on us to deflect any notice of our presence, and it's unlikely anyone will be coming through this passage at this time anyway."

That makes sense, or why would he have chosen it? I nod, clambering over a particularly steep bump in the floor. "I guess this isn't a route you'd generally be bringing cargo through." I can't imagine trying to carry boxes of lead or whatever while constantly stubbing your toes and risking tumbling on your face.

The corners of Madoc's lips twitch upward. "No, we have other passages for that. This one is typically used by travelers who'll be bringing back information and observations rather than supplies."

Spies, he means. Like he was in the Mists. Like other Murk must be right now, watching over my mates and our people.

I wet my lips, abruptly noticing the pang of thirst in my throat. I haven't eaten or drank anything except a few scraps Orion tossed to me several hours ago, and my nervousness isn't helping.

Madoc must catch the motion or something in my expression, because he digs a small bottle of water out of his pocket. "I thought you might need this. I have a few bags of snacks as well. Nothing especially filling, but the dinner spread didn't offer any items I could easily store for later."

"That's okay." I accept the water with a gratitude I'm

not totally comfortable with. My gaze slides over the contents, which look perfectly clear. The seal on the lid is still in place—but of course that doesn't mean much when you're dealing with magic.

Being suspicious of the drink is kind of ridiculous at this point, though, isn't it? What could Madoc have gained by bringing me all the way out here only to drug me that he couldn't have achieved much easier? I twist open the lid and take a few gulps.

When I glance at Madoc again, a shadow has crossed his face. He's noted my hesitation too. "I am sorry," he says, looking awkward. I'm guessing he's not very accustomed to apologizing. "For—for not being able to step in sooner. For not doing more before it got to this point. I didn't think it *would* get to this point. He's never— It isn't—" He doesn't seem to know how to go on.

There's something heart-wrenching about the fact that he sees the scars that Orion and his followers left all over his body as *normal*, so much more acceptable than the way his king treated me. But I suppose it is different in plenty of ways, even if I don't think what I've been through is that much more awful.

"He's never had a human whose genetic code he altered around to toy with," I say. "He's still the same person he was before. You just gave him a pass because of what he could do for you."

Madoc's mouth twists. "It seemed necessary—the way he ran the Refuge, the way he pushed us to prove ourselves. War isn't a kind thing, and that's what we've been preparing for. But you paved our way toward victory so much, and all you wanted was to go home..."

He pauses. "I can understand why you'd want to go back, and it worries me that Orion apparently can't. I thought that's what the war was about—reclaiming our home. But if he could torment you like this for wanting the same thing, then maybe you're right. Maybe causing pain is more important to him than anything else."

He starts walking again, and I shuffle after him, watching his careful, steady paces over the undulations in the stone floor. I feel like I have to offer something in return for his admission.

"After what happened to your parents, it might be understandable if you'd want to cause the other fae a lot of pain too," I say, not really sure what I'm getting at. I just want to understand, to get a sense of what I'm leaving behind, what I can tell the other fae when I reach them.

Madoc shrugs without looking back at me. "Many times, I've imagined inflicting a *lot* of pain on the savages that tore my family apart. I'd bet you're not completely immune from those kinds of thoughts either."

I think of Aerik and his cadre, of the blood that splattered the forest on the edge of my childhood town and the scars marking Jamie's face, and have to admit, "I'm not. I wouldn't toy with them if they were helpless in front of me, but I've been glad to see them get put in their places as well as we've managed so far." Every time I see Aerik's cruel face, I'd like to punch it or stab him in the gut. I can own that.

"There've been a lot of crimes committed against my

people," Madoc goes on. "There are a lot of Seelie and Unseelie I'd like to make pay. But... I can't say it doesn't ring true to me, what you said about not judging everyone by the actions of some. I can accept that it wasn't fair of me to assume your mates didn't care about you for who you are, just as you do them. You're obviously very good at inspiring emotions one wouldn't necessarily expect."

There's a sort of self-deprecating wryness to his tone, but it's the weariness underneath that niggles at me. "What are you going to do after I'm gone?" I ask.

"I'll pretend to help with the search that'll no doubt go out for you, and maybe lay a few more misleading clues to confuse matters. Then we'll get back to planning the war. Without the spectacle Orion was planning and knowing that you'll be able to prevent the full-moon curse from taking the Seelie, I'd imagine he'll delay the attack he was hoping to carry out a little longer. Hopefully for long enough for you to make some progress encouraging the wolves and the ravens to consider negotiations."

"I'll do what I can." It's hard to think beyond reaching my mates again, setting my feet back on familiar ground. I have no idea what *they've* been through while I've been missing. And... "I can't see telling them that Orion is worth bargaining with. I wouldn't trust him to mean a single word he says. We can't even count on him sticking to the letter of an oath he gives when he's not governed by the Heart of the Mists, can we?"

"No." Madoc rubs his mouth. "We'll take it as it comes. I can feel out others subtly and see who might be inclined to support a peaceful change rather than full-out war. And maybe there'll still need to be some fighting, just… not quite as much as otherwise."

"If we can resolve this without all of any kind of fae ending up dead, that'll be better than what he's planned," I mutter.

"And if it comes to that, then it comes to that. I can't say I'm all that optimistic about the fae of the seasons caring one bit about how we feel about anything." A trace of bitterness comes into Madoc's voice. He shakes himself. "That isn't the point of this. The point of this is *you* don't deserve the fate he had in mind for you. That one thing I can change."

A lump rises in my throat. "And if I can't make any arrangements quickly enough, or there aren't enough Murk who'll compromise? Will you be with them fighting to slaughter all of the other fae, trying to rule over the entire Mists?"

Madoc is silent for a long moment. When he stops and turns toward me, the expression on his face echoes the hopelessness I felt locked up in that cage. "I won't strike out at anyone who isn't striking at us," he says firmly. "I can promise you that much. The rest is up to them."

Staring back at him, I feel as if I can suddenly see the bars that have snapped into place around *him*—maybe back when his parents were killed in front of him, maybe from the moment he was born. He's been caged in his own way by the hostility toward the Murk, by the way the leaders he had stoked the urge for violent vengeance.

Is it any wonder he has trouble seeing another way?

Neither of us has been dealt a good hand among the

fae. But he's trying to do something better with it now anyway. That does count for something.

"I hope it goes much better than that," I say, but I can't say I have all that *much* hope myself.

Just about anything would be better than the picture his king painted of our near future, though.

Another thought hits me with a sudden chill. "Do you know—when Orion reached into my head and was searching through my mind—did he find anything he was planning to use against the other fae that he didn't mention in his questions?" Just how much did I end up betraying my mates yet again?

Madoc blinks as if confused before understanding flickers through his expression. "You don't have to worry about that. He didn't search your mind at all. He only wanted you to think he had—that he *could*—to intimidate you. The questions he asked were based on observations we've made in the Mists, and he used a spell to force you to answer truthfully, but he can't actually see right inside anyone's head."

"Oh." An unsettling mix of relief and embarrassment trickles through me. There's yet another trick I fell for. But at least that means I can be sure Orion doesn't know any of my few remaining secrets.

We walk on in silence for a time. The passage veers one way and then another, seeming to double back on itself at least twice, sometimes sloping downward again before it heads back up. My warped foot is starting to ache. I feel as if I've walked at least a couple of miles.

Then we take another turn, and the passage widens—

well, the space between the walls does, anyway. The floor, not so much. A deep chasm appears to have pushed the wall on the right a few feet farther away, leaving a strip of stone just wide enough for us to comfortably walk along next to the perilous drop.

My legs balk. I peer down into the chasm, unable to see the bottom, only total blackness.

"We're almost there," Madoc says. "Stick close to the wall, and you'll be fine." He has his own hand resting against the wall at our left, the end of his tail braced against the ground by his feet.

I gather my resolve and limp after him, setting my own feet as far from the chasm as I can. At least this section of the path is pretty straight.

"You said the passage is a spell," I say. "That's why it's so long and twisted. What kind of a spell?"

I'm actually only asking out of curiosity, no thought of scheming left in my head other than the desire to get out of this place, but Madoc tenses a bit before he answers in a careful tone. "Only to ensure that those entering this way don't reach the Refuge unless they actually know where they're going."

That's why he isn't concerned about me bringing an army down on the Refuge. The fae of the seasons won't know "where they're going" even if I lead them to the place where I exit. There must be some kind of incantation or similar you need to make sure the path leads you right. It makes sense as a security precaution.

It also explains why it'd be *very* difficult for the other

fae to have found me, even if I'd managed to give Whitt any real clues.

"How long have I—" I start to ask, just to break up the gnawing silence before it descends too heavily again.

Madoc cuts me off with a jerk of his hand. He freezes in front of me, staring at the passage ahead of us. Apprehension washes over me.

Then I hear it too. A metallic squeak like unoiled hinges, carrying down through the dim space.

Someone's coming.

They're coming quickly. Just a couple of heartbeats after I caught the squeak, distant but audible voices reach my ears. I can't see the figures who're talking yet, but I have the sense it's only a matter of seconds before they turn the bend to come into view.

Madoc's head swivels sharply, taking in the passage around us. He scrambles several paces farther up and leaps across the chasm to a small ledge that barely juts out far enough to support his feet. He motions to me. "My illusions can stop them from seeing and hearing us, but it won't let them walk right through us. We have to get off the path."

I hurry after him, my heart hammering. As I come up across from him, the two figures step into sight at the top of this section of the path. They're hustling toward me, one behind the other, talking in excited voices.

But not so excited that they'd miss running straight into a solid body, whether they can see me or not.

My gaze whips back to Madoc and the ledge he's braced on. There's room for another person to stand there next to him, but only just—and I'd still have to *make* it to that spot. Jumping over a fathomless crevice with a crooked foot that's now outright throbbing.

The image flashes through my mind of me careening down into the vast darkness below. My pulse hiccups and thumps even harder.

"I don't think I can do it," I whisper. "My foot—I'll fall."

Madoc stretches out his arm. "You just need to get close enough for me to catch you. *Quickly*."

My focus narrows in on his open hand. He wants me to trust him with my safety, to put all my faith in him...

Haven't I already done that by coming this far with him anyway?

The Murk sentries are coming up on us fast. I don't let myself second-guess my last thought. With a gulp of air, I step backward to give me a bit of a running start, and then throw myself toward the ledge.

For a second, with nothing solid beneath my feet, my stomach starts to plummet as if I'm going to fall with it. My eyes have squeezed shut of their own accord.

Then Madoc's hand clamps around my elbow, yanking me the rest of the way to him so his other arm can slide around my back and swivel me toward the wall. He holds me there, just inches from his body, his thunderstorm scent wrapping around me too.

My feet wobble and settle on the ledge, but I don't dare nudge him away. He's become my entire sense of balance. I can feel the faint, nervous thump of his own pulse echoing through his embrace into me.

The two fae dash on past us. Their voices are drowned out by the pounding of my heartbeat in my ears. Madoc and I stay there, locked in place and perfectly still, until I can't hear them at all.

Tentatively, I dare to look over my shoulder. I can't even see them now—they've gone around the turn at the bottom.

Madoc adjusts his grip on me, and a jolt of panic shoots through my veins. But he keeps the same firm but gentle hold he's offered from the start.

"I should leap back across first, and then you jump to me like before," he says in a low voice, his breath tickling over my forehead. "Can you find a position where you feel steady?"

I swallow hard and manage a nod. Gradually, he eases his arms back and I lean against the wall, keeping most of my weight on my good foot. Madoc watches me closely, making sure I'm okay.

He pushes off the wall and lands solidly on the path with a swish of his tail to help steady himself. When he turns and holds out his hands to me, my pulse still skips a beat at the thought of the drop between us, but I don't hesitate as long as before.

Going back to safety is easier. And I already know he can catch me.

I fling myself toward Madoc, and he grasps my waist for just long enough to set me fully on the stone floor. I exhale shakily. "Let's skip that part next time."

Madoc lets out a startled laugh. He gazes down at me for a moment with an expression I can't read and then points me toward the top of the path. "Let's hope there isn't a next time."

Despite the pain in my foot creeping up into my calf, I pick up my pace, knowing escape is close but that we can't be sure no other Murk will show up unexpectedly. Thank God, we make it to the top of that steeper strip and leave the chasm behind without incident. Madoc directs me along a couple more brief passages to reach a short ladder that leads up to a circular panel in the ceiling.

He climbs up the ladder, murmurs a little magic, and shoves the panel to the side. Air fresher than anything I've breathed in over a week washes down over me, and a gasp escapes my lips. Madoc peers down at me, an emotion I don't recognize flitting through his eyes again.

He isn't reconsidering letting me go, is he?

But he leaves the panel open, coming back down the ladder to where I'm standing. He touches my shoulder so lightly I barely feel the press of his fingers through my shirt.

"Talia," he says, his gaze so intense I get worried about what he's going to say all over again.

Before he can go any further, he stiffens, his attention flicking away. He spits out a curse and turns back to me with so much more urgency than before.

"They've already noticed you're gone," he says. "They'll be searching all the passages. I have to get back to divert them. Move fast as soon as you get outside. Get away from the entrance, stay hidden, and call your raven. I'll do what I can to keep them off your trail. And—thank you."

I'd ask what he's thanking me for, but he dips his head

to graze his mouth against mine in the most fleeting of kisses. It's there and then gone before I can react to that either. The instant he pulls back, he nudges me toward the ladder. "*Go!*"

There's no time to say anything at all. I spin toward the ladder, grasp the rungs, and haul myself toward the world outside as fast as my muscles will move me.

28

Sylas

"Nothing yet," August mutters under his breath, as if I can't see that nothingness just as well as he can. He shifts on his feet next to me, his boots rustling against the dry needles scattered on the forest floor.

Even at this late hour, long after sundown, the summer air is warm against our skin, laced with a sweet cedar scent. I don't find that smell as soothing as I normally would, not when we're braced for a treacherous attack.

All around us, dozens of our warriors and other pack-kin August has trained up to competency are waiting with us. With Whitt's help, we've devised a variation on the deflection spells the Murk have been using to avoid notice, ensuring that no one can tell we never ventured much beyond the bottom of the hill when we gave the appearance of setting off this afternoon. We've been lurking hidden in one of Hearth-by-the-Heart's forests with a view of the castle for hours.

"Maybe they've thought better of it," Astrid murmurs at my other side. "Or we've misread their intentions."

I incline my head in acknowledgment. I'm not sure whether I'd rather either of those possibilities were true than see us launch ourselves into battle tonight.

We held back from the larger search effort I'd planned for yesterday after Whitt gave his warning, concerned about an attack from Tristan's pack. When nothing came of that, we decided to lay this trap.

By all appearances, my castle is currently vulnerable, most of my pack's warriors absent, only my strategist who's a fine but not extraordinary fighter as a figure of authority. Whitt even made a show of walking around the fields outside pretending to take swigs from his gifted bottle of absinthe after we left.

If Tristan's pack means to attack, now would be the ideal time. And if they do, then I need to be here to prevent the violent uprising from succeeding. No doubt Tristan thinks he can slaughter all those of my pack who remain and then catch me and the rest of my cadre by surprise on our return, making it easy for him to claim the domain that was once his cousin's for his own.

But if they don't, then we've wasted nearly two days that might have brought us closer to finding my mate over nothing.

My gaze slips away from the castle toward the edges of the pack houses that I can make out through the trees. We instructed those who can't fight to shore up their entrances with magic and stay inside if they hear sounds of a battle tonight. I hope that's enough to protect them. If Tristan's forces arrive, they should tangle with our sentries first, but I wouldn't put it past him to send warriors to quickly deal with our weakest kin who might raise the alarm.

We had the sentries draw back from their typical patrols to remain within our hearing. I have no doubt that any attackers would aim to dispatch them as swiftly and brutally as possible for the same reason they might target the village.

The minutes slip by. An owl lets out a low hoot from a nearby tree. Our warriors stand still and on guard around us, not letting the impatience and uneasiness I'm sure they feel show. Despite my own apprehension, a flare of pride fills me at what an admirable force we've nurtured within our pack.

I only have a moment to enjoy that sensation when a scuffling sound reaches my perked ears. There's a faint noise like a yelp cut off, barely audible unless you were listening for it.

My fangs spring from my gums in an instant. I jerk my hand toward the castle, and we charge forward as one being, leaping into wolf form to make the sprint at a faster pace.

At least a dozen attackers have surrounded the nearest sentry—he might already be cut down. More sounds of a struggle carry from the far side of the castle. There's already the crunch of splintering wood as the doors are forced down. Rage sears through my veins, pulling my lips back from my teeth in a snarl.

That wretched mangy traitor of a lord. But he misjudged me if he thought I'd make this easy a target. He'll regret ever threatening my pack, taking advantage of the harrowing situation we're in. I'm already itching to tear him to pieces myself.

Half of our fighting force, led by August, splits off to fall on the intruders on this side of the castle. Some slash at the warriors in wolf form while others rise up as men and women to fend them off with swords.

I race with Astrid and the rest around the side of the castle, pushing my limbs as fast as I can go. There will be blood spilled here tonight, but I'll do whatever I can to ensure most of it is on Tristan's side.

Instead of surprising us, we've turned the surprise around on them. The attackers who marched on the front of the castle whirl around and flash fangs and claws, but they're surrounded in an instant. We plow into them without giving them more of a chance to react.

For the first several minutes in the fray, I remain in wolf form, lunging this way and that, ripping through a throat here and carving open a belly there. When one of Tristan's cadre-chosen advances on me with sword swinging, I shift with a violent stretch of my limbs, snatching up my own blade from my belt and plunging it into his chest before he can do more than nick my cheek.

One more small scar to add to my existing assortment.

I spin around, panting and gripping the hilt of my sword tight in my hand. Bodies are littered across the field in front of the castle I so painstakingly built. The sight sends a pang through my heart, but there's no time for regrets now. More of my brethren are still struggling between those bodies.

Tristan brought more warriors than I expected—but I haven't left anything to chance. As I spring at a woman about to skewer one of my guards, a fierce cry rises up from the lands to the south. A moment later, a brigade of Donovan's pack-kin rushes in to help us defend our home as I did once for him. The messenger I instructed to race to his castle and raise the alarm made the journey even faster than I'd hoped.

But where is Tristan in all this? I know the assault is his doing because I recognize many of the attackers from his pack, but I haven't seen the lord himself. Surely he didn't send forward this offensive without even being here to oversee it?

That would make him not just a traitor but a coward as well.

The scent of blood is thick in my nose, and growls and the clang of blades fill my ears, but as I topple one more warrior, an even more alarming noise pierces through the din. It's a bark of pain that sounds distinctly like my older brother, coming from inside the castle.

I knew a few of Tristan's pack had breached the walls, but I'd assumed we'd caught most of them before they'd made it inside and that the guards stationed within could deal with those who slipped past us. As I burst past the front doors, I realize I've been at least partly mistaken.

Bodies of both my warriors and Tristan's lie slumped

in the entrance hall, and more sounds of a commotion filter from deeper within the castle. There's another grunt that I'm sure now is Whitt, followed by a dark chuckle that makes my blood run cold.

"With me!" I holler, summoning any warrior who can break from the battle outside to follow me, and race down the hall toward the fighting.

There are a few more bodies in the rooms beyond. One of my guards is struggling with a fae man who's slashing out with a dagger in one hand and clawed fingertips on the other. I barrel into him before he has time to register my presence, and my guard stabs him in the heart the second he's knocked to the ground.

"Thank you," she gasps, clapping her hand to a wound on her side that's bleeding.

"More help is coming," I tell her. "Find a healer as soon as you can." I have to get to my brother before even a healer won't be enough.

Blood dapples the wooden floor, mixed with larger smears here and there. I dash along that trail, worry clenching my chest. Then there's a loud metallic clatter up ahead, and I know exactly where I'll find them.

I hurtle into the kitchen in time to watch Whitt hurl one of the pots he knocked off their hooks at Tristan's head. The lord dodges with a sneering laugh, but he stops in mid-step at my entrance, his sword still held at the ready.

August will not be pleased with the mess our intruders have made of his favorite room. Shards of broken glass and china litter the floor. A few of the cupboard doors are bashed in. And there's blood streaked all over the place.

Perhaps a little is from Tristan, a few small wounds leaking through his clothes on his forearm and thigh, but I have to think most of it is Whitt's. He's favoring one leg, his trousers stained crimson from a gouge by his hip, and his opposite arm—his dominant one—hangs limp, the shoulder carved open to the bone. More blood colors his vest from somewhere on his abdomen.

He's holding himself upright, his teeth bared and his eyes sharply determined, but his forehead gleams with a sheen of sweat. He's barely holding himself together.

I step forward, brandishing my own sword. "It's over, Tristan. We saw through your plot. Most of your pack-kin have already fallen. Back away, and you might leave here with your life if not much else."

Tristan meets my gaze with a wild, vicious light in his eyes, as if the curse has come over him three nights early. But he's fully coherent when he speaks. "You killed my cousin; you stole his domain. You sent my entire family into disarray—for what? Some dust-destined dung-body with a few pretty tricks?"

I don't think there's any reasoning with him, but he's closer to Whitt than I am to either of them, and I don't like those odds. I move carefully forward, pressing my advantage without any sudden moves to provoke him.

"Your cousin was scheming to murder one of his fellow arch-lords, as you no doubt well know, since most likely *you* were the one he meant to put in Donovan's place," I have to point out. "Talia had nothing to do with it. Don't blame me or her for the fact that he faced the rightful consequence for his crime."

Tristan laughs again, this time more of a sputter. "See it however you want. If I can't have the throne Ambrose meant to give me, I think I'll take at least one of *your* family down on my way out."

Without any more warning than that, he springs at Whitt.

I fling myself around the island that's standing between us. Whitt has grasped a heavy pan, which he swings at Tristan's temple. But this time the lord doesn't even bother to dodge. He takes the blow with a sharp exhalation and stabs his sword toward Whitt's chest.

My brother could try to wrench himself backward. But he sees me coming, and he has all the faith in me I could possibly ask for. Instead, he blocks the strike with his good arm, hissing as it chops into his flesh, and shoves Tristan toward me in the same instant.

I slam into the lord and tackle him to the floor. With one harsh smack, Tristan's sword goes spinning away. Whitt slumps against the cupboards. I bring my own blade to the traitor's throat.

"You have me at your mercy," Tristan says with a sickly grin, pinned beneath me. "But what if I say I—"

I plunge my sword straight through his neck before he can say the word *yield*.

His head rolls back to thump against the tiles. The blood that spurts up and flows out to puddle beneath him looks like justice—for all the ways he's betrayed our people, for all the harm he's tried to do to those I care about. Not a speck of guilt settles in my gut.

Whitt makes a choked sound that I think might have been an attempt at a chuckle. If that's the best he can do, then he's even worse off than I realized.

I push away from Tristan to kneel by my brother's side. He's nearly as bloody as the man I just killed—Heart help me, maybe even more so.

"Technically you should have given him his lawful opportunity to surrender," my strategist says, somehow taking on his usual wry tone even with the strain in his voice.

"*Technically* the bastard met a better end than he deserved as it was," I retort, and get to work muttering what spells I can to stem the bleeding.

"I have no complaints myself, to be clear," Whitt mutters, and then lapses into silence. He's starting to fade.

I grit my teeth, speaking the spell words faster, drawing as much of the Heart's energy through me as I can. Then the sound of pounding feet reaches my ears.

Several of my pack-kin and a few of Donovan's burst into the room. With a rush of relief, I spot my best healer among them. He's probably come worried he'd need to tend to me, but I can't say I feel any better about it being Whitt who needs him instead.

"Quick!" I wave him over. "And anyone else with any strength in bodily magic as well. He's bleeding out fast."

"I'll be fine," Whitt says, but it's more of a mumble now.

When I've done what I can and have drawn back to let

those more skilled do their work, I pace the kitchen, worried it won't be enough. I have the urge to stab Tristan a few more times for nearly taking my brother from me, not that the treacherous lord would feel it.

But it turns out Whitt was right, as he so often is. By the time the rest of my pack and those of Donovan's who came to our aid are gathering in the castle, the rest of the attackers now dealt with, all of Whitt's wounds are sealed, and the healer has rejuvenated him enough for him to look clear-eyed around the kitchen and remark, "You'd better get me to my room to finish recovering, or August is going to finish the job Tristan started."

"It's better you don't move at all for at least an hour or two," the healer informs him. "Take your rest here."

And so Whitt sprawls out with a pillow and blanket I have a guard fetch, dozing for a while, as the rest of us deal with the bodies and the damage done.

Tristan and his men we heap at the edge of the forest for the rest of his pack or his extended family to claim. Our own, the fourteen who took fatal wounds in the defense of our domain, we clean as well as we can and lay out by the pack village for their families to say their final farewells through the day. In the next evening, we'll hold the funeral ceremonies.

Dawn light is just peeking over the horizon when I step back, looking down at the row of the fallen. So many good men and women we've lost over that family's greedy quest for power. The sight weighs on me, all the heavier with the knowledge of how much else we still have to face.

"Come on," August says to me softly, and leads me

back to the kitchen, which looks remarkably like it did before other than Whitt still snoozing in the corner. I suppose the pack-kin August trained know how much this space means to him and took particular care setting it right.

He gets out the fixings for a hot drink, and Whitt stirs from his sleep. Our older brother glances around the room with a smile. "Excellent, I got to skip all the clean-up."

August snorts, and I shake my head, and for a second the moment feels normal, all the loss we've experienced far in the distance.

Then there's a flutter of feathers by the window. A raven swoops inside, transforming into a man the second he's entered. Corwin's eyes are bright with a mix of hope and worry.

"I can sense her again," he says in a rush. "Talia. It's not totally clear yet, but—I'm going to her now."

29

Talia

The second I scramble out into the thin light of what's either early morning or evening, Madoc jerks the lid shut over the passage behind me. I sway on my feet, overwhelmed by the rush of sensations.

The fresh air gushes into my lungs like a drug. The open space around me feels eerily vast compared to the narrow tunnels I've spent most of the past several days in. And then comes a jolt of awareness inside me, the abrupt recognition of Corwin's presence somewhere distant but filled with hurried joy.

My soul! Can you hear me?

I can, I think back at him, nearly choking on my relief. *I can. I'm here.*

I'm coming as quickly as I can, Talia. I was by the Heart —it'll take a little time to reach the fringes. Where are you?

That... is a very good question. I stare around me,

taking a few hesitant steps and struggling through the mental upheaval of my sudden change in surroundings to take in the details of the space around me.

I've come out into a courtyard of stone tiles in what appears to be a park. A few stone benches border the wide circle, and grassy fields and small hills dotted with occasional trees spread out around it. I spot a playground with a slide and climbing equipment in the distance.

None of that tells me where *here* is, though.

Another jolt races through my chest, this one less pleasant. Madoc told me to get away from here, to hide. How quickly will the Murk reach this spot to search for me? Will his attempt at diverting them work at all?

I set off as fast as I can limp, hugging myself. There's a path winding between the trees, and I make out the rooftops of buildings in the near distance. If I can check street signs or a map or a local newspaper, I should be able to figure out where I am.

I should have asked Madoc before he sent me out here so I'd know right away—but it's too late for that now.

Corwin can read my impressions and the emotions they stir up as well as he always could. *Even at my fastest, it'll take a few hours. Get yourself to safety and you can confirm exactly where you are afterward.*

I'm not totally sure where is safe. Where might the rat shifters be lurking in the human world? Are there others around—would they recognize me?

I wish I had some way to at least cover my hair, my most distinctive feature.

I hustle faster, ignoring the reawakened pain in my

foot. A rustling sound makes me jump, but it's only a shift in the wind rippling through the branches of the nearby trees.

No one else is around. The light is gradually brightening, a pinkish tint hazing the sky. It must be very early in the morning here—no one's really up and about yet.

As I get closer to the edge of the park, I make out a wrought-iron gate up ahead and a road beyond it. Occasional cars are already cruising by. Even though I'm no longer used to the rumble of engines that was so familiar when I was a kid, seeing them gives me a flash of reassurance.

I'm not totally alone here, even if I can't ask any of the people in those cars where exactly I am.

As long as I can reach you, you're never alone at all, Corwin says through our bond, with an impression of his arms wrapping around me.

My heart tugs with a desperate longing to be in those arms for real. It's been too long since I was with my soul-twined mate—with any of them, really, but the bond between Corwin and me makes the pain particularly acute. My skin is quivering with the need to fully reconnect with him. The same urgency ripples from him into me.

If I could be there in an instant—oh, my soul, I've missed you so much.

I've missed you too. Thoughts of all the things I've been through without him start to rise up, but I shove them down. He's worried enough without knowing how the Murk treated me or the reason they stole me away. I'll be able to explain everything better and more coherently when we can talk face to face—and all the other arch-lords need to know too.

But there's one warning I have to give him now. *When you get here, you'll need to be careful. The Murk have a lot more magic than we thought. It's hard to explain, but they may be able to overpower even a true-blooded fae like you when you're so far from the Heart of the Mists.*

I can feel the truth of what you're saying, even if I can't understand how it's possible, he responds. *But we can deal with the Murk themselves later—once you're safely home. I'll avoid tangling with them. I only want to reach you and bring you back.*

Yes. The start of a sob clogs my throat. *Yes, I want that too.*

As I come up on the gate, the thought of one specific other arch-lord and his cadre grips me. *Are my other mates okay? Has the next full moon already passed? I lost track of the days…*

Corwin's voice washes over me, managing to be soothing even in its urgency. *Don't worry about any of that. Nothing matters until you're back with us. But the full moon hasn't arrived yet, and the others are—*

There's a moment's hesitation, and I can tell he's muffling impressions he doesn't want to pass on to me. Enough slips through for me to get the sense of an injury. *Were they hurt?* I ask with a flare of panic. *What—*

Focus on making sure you're *not hurt for now*, Corwin says firmly. *Sylas, August, and Whitt are all well—they're following behind me as quickly as they were able to get themselves together. There was only a… brief conflict that's now dealt with, which did no lasting harm to any of them.*

I know he's not lying, but that there's a lot more he isn't saying as well. Unfortunately, he's also right that this isn't the best time to discuss what's been going on in the Mists any more than it is for chatting about everything I've experienced.

I step through the park's gate and glance around. The street signs on the corner don't reveal anything about my larger location other than the names appear to be in a language I don't know. I wait for a break in the sparse traffic, dart across the road, and start glancing through the windows of the shops and restaurants lining the other side of the street.

Their names are all in that other language and so are the smaller signs hanging in some of the windows. But a café on the far corner has a laminated newspaper clipping pasted next to the door that includes an English quote: "The best croissants in Munich!"

Germany, Corwin says, catching my observation before I need to purposefully pass it on. *I know which portal to look for. It won't take long at all once I've reached the fringelands. Can you find somewhere you'll be out of danger to wait?*

I don't know. I dart a glance around and hurry onward, my heart thumping. Where can I go that I'll be sure the Murk won't track me down in the hours it's going to take Corwin to make it here? I don't know how to speak the local language—even if I did, the humans around me can't fend off fae magic.

I've got a head start, at least. That's something. As long as I can stay ahead of them...

But now that the initial burst of adrenaline is wearing off, I can't help noticing how tired I am. I'd barely gotten any sleep when Madoc woke me up to help me escape. My warped foot is aching, and my other limbs are starting to stiffen from all the walking and climbing and the stress that's gripped me for much longer than that.

Besides, as long as I'm out wandering the streets, there's *more* chance of a search party spotting me. I need somewhere I can take shelter and stay out of view. Somewhere I won't get kicked out of by the local citizens either.

I hobble onward, looking over a bus shelter, an alley, a coffee shop that's just opening for the day. None of them seem like ideal options. I can't shake the sense that I'm running out of time.

I turn one corner and then another, taking a weaving path so at least I'm not directly down the street from the park. How well will the Murk be able to sniff me out and know which route I took? Is there a bus I can hop on to give myself more distance?

How can I when I don't have any money to pay for the ride?

That thought has just passed through my mind when footsteps tap against the sidewalk somewhere nearby. Instinctively, I throw myself down behind the low wall around the patio of a restaurant that's currently closed.

I reacted not a moment too soon. As I peek through a small gap between panels in the wall, two figures come around a bend at the other end of the block—perfectly human-looking, but with a feral glint in their gazes that makes my muscles tense. One of them sniffs the air and heads my way. That and the intensity of their stares as they scan the street convinces me that they're Murk.

How did they get here so quickly? Or does Orion just have so many followers that they're everywhere? They clearly are sniffing me out, though. In a matter of seconds, they'll be on top of me.

I scramble for a solution and abruptly remember Madoc taking my hair and blowing his magic into the vent.

Can I push my scent away from me? I know the true name for air. I've used it to carry sound to me, so why not smells away from me?

It's the only real chance I have.

"*Briss-gow-aft,*" I murmur in as quiet a voice as I can manage, summoning the memories of leaping to August as he taught me the syllables.

The breeze stirs around me. I whisper the word again, compelling the current away from me, to wash over the ground where I walked and waft across the street in the opposite direction. Pick up every trace of my presence and disperse it elsewhere. Carry it away. Please.

The Murk keep walking toward me. I risk one more hissed repetition, putting all the mental energy I can into the magic—and they hesitate.

The one who sniffed before raises his nose. "That way,"

he says, pointing away from me in the direction I sent the breeze. They trot across the road and hustle around the next corner.

You did so well, my soul, Corwin says, with a tremor of distraught emotion that he isn't here to protect me.

But he's coming. I just have to hold out a little longer.

I don't know how long my trick with the air will divert my pursuers. I wait only a minute, until I'm sure they're well on their way, and then I backtrack the way I came, hoping any fresh scent I leave behind will mingle with the old and confuse my trail. I also mumble *"Briss-gow-aft"* under my breath at regular intervals, washing away whatever traces I can.

What else do I know about the Murk that might help? They're used to enclosed spaces, like I was starting to become… They're used to slinking through dimness and darkness, avoiding the full light of day, which is creeping up on us even now. That might help me.

And maybe they'd be less likely to look *up* rather than along the streets at the level where they're in the habit of finding things.

I spot a building with a metal staircase running up the brick wall to a side door on the third floor and scramble over to it. Wincing at every soft clink of my boots against the metal steps, I make my way up to the highest point and tuck myself behind a solid wall in one section of the landing that hides me from view.

I murmur the true name for air over and over, dispelling any trace of my scent from the area, until my throat starts to get hoarse and an ache spreads through my skull. Surely I've blown away enough traces of my path by now?

My head droops against the metal wall.

I'm almost there, Talia, Corwin says. *Hold on just a little longer.*

I can do that. I can. I fight back my weariness, scanning the terrain below for any sign of pursuers.

A yawn stretches my jaw. The sun beams down over me, draping me in more warmth than I've felt in days. My head lists to the side again, my eyelids drooping—

And a raven dives out of the sky.

Corwin lands next to me, shifting into the form of a man with his wings still spread, and pulls me into his arms. My hands shoot up to cling to him. The sob I've been holding in for what feels like days now tumbles out of me.

"I've got you, my soul," he says out loud, the same sentiment echoing through our inner connection. "We're going home."

30

Talia

Corwin must have cast one of the fae spells to hide us from human eyes, because he carries me away from the stairway where he found me with a flap of his wings and no concern at all about who might see us below. I cling to his shirt, tucking my body as closely against him as I can, but it doesn't feel like enough.

Even though he's right here, both physically and within me through our inner connection, the bond demands more. I'm burning to meld right into him, as if I can get close enough to make up for the days and days when we were much too far apart, when even our bond was muted.

And it isn't just me. The same need sears through him, making his arms tighten around me.

Soon, he says, even his inner voice ragged with urgency. His wings flap harder, the speed of his flight making the wind whip through my hair and tousle his dark curls. *We're almost there, almost away from them.*

I sense it when he spots the portal he arrived through. He dives with a warble of the wind and careens through it so quickly the passage is little more than a brief blurring of my vision and flip of my stomach. Then we're whooshing through into the fog of the Mists' fringelands.

Corwin spins, still holding me tightly, and snaps several magically charged syllables at the portal we've just come through. It wavers and contracts to a much smaller shimmering surface, and I can tell from the impressions that trickle through him to me that he's sealed it off to ensure no Murk follow us. It'll only hold a day or two, but they have no hope of reaching me right now.

Relief washes over me, with a sharper surge of desire right on its heels. I lift my head, and Corwin is already dipping his to meet me.

The impact of our first kiss after so long apart sizzles both of us like an electric shock. I find myself twisting in his arms, wrapping my own around his neck and my legs around his waist, kissing him harder.

I need, I *need* to reinforce the bond that was nearly severed by confirming just how entwined we are in every possible way. I've never felt this kind of carnal longing before, ringing through every nerve and amplified by the answering desire radiating through my mate, as powerful as the lightning bolt that first bound us together.

No coherent thoughts pass between us now, only that flaring of emotions and errant words. *You... My soul... So long...*

As our lips crash together, tongues tangling, I'm only vaguely aware of Corwin moving us until he's laying me down on the floor of the carriage he must have ridden here in. His wings are still spread above us like a dark canopy.

He devours my mouth and then kisses my jaw and my neck. Everywhere his hands and his hot breath touches me, my skin lights up with giddy quivers.

The twist of need between my thighs burns deeper. I wrench at his pants, and he tugs down mine as he kicks his the rest of the way off. His shaft slides against my core, setting off a pulse of pleasure so intense I moan.

Corwin buries his face in the crook of my neck as he lines himself up. My hips arch to meet him, but he hesitates just for a second, with a wild spark of recognition. *It's your time. You're fertile.*

I've avoided full sex with all of my mates during those days of the month before, but not a single particle of my being can bear to wait now. *I don't care. I* need *you.*

And I need you, he replies with a strangled sound, and plunges into me.

Another moan escapes me with the heady rush of being filled so swiftly and completely. My knees lift to grip Corwin's thighs. I sway into his thrusts, urging him as deep as he can go. As the pleasure and pure joy of being completely connected again swells through me and flows between us through our bond, our mouths collide with more frantic kisses. Our hands roam all over each other's bodies. The muscled planes of my mate's body flex beneath my fingers.

My mate, Corwin thinks with a shudder of breath. *My soul. Mine.*

Mine, I echo back to him, clutching him with all my strength. The wave of ecstasy builds and builds, carrying me higher with every gasp and rocking of our bodies. My fingernails dig into his shoulders, and he groans at the delight that sparks with the pinch of pain.

I'll never let them take you from me again. Never.

Corwin bucks into me, his rigid length finding that perfect spot inside me again, and again, and—

My release blazes through me, tossing me over the peak and leaving every nerve tingling, spurred higher by the burst of bliss as my soul-twined mate follows me.

In the shaky aftermath, Corwin hugs me to him, as if we really could melt into one being. I inhale his cool, foresty scent, letting it wash any remaining hint of the Refuge's dank tunnels from my lungs. Then my mate raises his head.

We're no longer alone. Sometime in the middle of the mad collision of our bodies, my other mates reached the fringes. Sylas, Whitt, and August have come up by the side of the carriage. August looks awkward, but his expression is bright with love and relief. Whitt's lips are curled in an amused smile, and the intensity of his gaze heats my skin all over again. And Sylas…

I've never seen my Seelie arch-lord so overcome with emotion. He holds himself as tall and noble as always, but I don't need a soul-twined bond to recognize the mix of anguish and elation in his mismatched eyes.

We're bound together too, me and the three of them,

in every way *we* possibly can be. We swore ourselves to each other what now feels like years ago—but we never had the chance to even start to consummate that official commitment.

A fresh surge of longing rushes through me. I need all of my mates—I need them with me; I need them *in* me.

Corwin recognizes my hunger, and perhaps my Seelie mates do too, even with only sight and scent to go by. Without a word, he draws back, giving them a soft smile and a nod. As I sit up on the lightly padded floor, I reach for them. They leap in to join me.

"You're all right?" August says, nuzzling my shoulder, trailing his fingers down my back.

Sylas strokes his firm hand over my hair with a growl. "If those mangy rats hurt you—"

They did, but not in any way that seems to matter right now. "I'm okay," I say, my voice quavering. "I just— being so far away from you—not knowing if I'd ever—" My throat chokes up. I catch Whitt's gaze where he's knelt in front of me. "I'm sorry I couldn't reach out to you better."

Before I can say any more, he touches my cheek. I can see all the same love glowing in his eyes as when he gave me his true name. "You did everything you could. It killed me not being able to reach out to *you*. But you're back with us now, and that's what matters."

He tugs me in for a kiss, nearly as urgent as the ones I just shared with Corwin. A hum of approval resonates from Sylas's chest, and he dips his head to nibble my earlobe. August switches from nuzzling to marking my shoulder with his mouth. The same need buzzing through me thrums in the air between us.

My body seems to move of its own accord. I can't resist the yearning in me any more than I could with Corwin. I yank Whitt closer, run my fingers into the thick waves of Sylas's hair where they fall to his shoulders, and lean into August's embrace.

In the haze of passion, I'm not totally sure who's stroking their hands over my breasts, who's lifting my shirt to kiss a path down my spine, who's delving deft fingers between my thighs where I'm still slick from my first homecoming. All that matters is the growing inferno we're caught up in. Even Corwin, watching from the bow of the carriage, gives off nothing but approval and a sense of rightness.

I unfasten Whitt's slacks first. As his hardness springs free, he groans and pulls me onto his lap to straddle him. His mouth reclaims mine, one hand braced against the floor of the carriage for balance, but I can't help noticing that his other arm moves stiffly as he reaches to tug my shirt right off.

I pull back just an inch, remembering the vague answer I got from Corwin about what my other mates have dealt with while I've been gone. "Are you hurt? What happen—"

Whitt cuts me off with another desperate kiss. His answer spills across my lips. "Nothing that isn't already healing, mighty one. And being with you makes me feel as if it's all already behind me."

I can't help kissing him again, making a note in the

back of my mind that I need more answers later. That thought is swept away a second later by the thrust of Whitt's shaft into me.

I whimper and sink into him, wanting all of him. He kisses me hard, cupping my breast as he rocks me up and down on him, my other lovers caressing me everywhere else.

"I love you," he murmurs between kisses. "My mate."

When I choke up this time, it's with nothing but happiness. "I love you too. All of you. So much."

He slides his hand down to fondle the sensitive nub just above where we're joined, and my second release surges over me. I tip back my head, and my cry is swallowed by Sylas's lips. The giddy wave crashes over me.

Whitt sits me down on one of the side benches, panting in the aftermath of his own finish, and August is there in front of me in an instant. My gentlest lover dapples kisses across my lips, cheek, and neck until I'm whimpering for more. When I grip him through his pants, he lets out a strangled sound.

"Oh, my sweetness," he says roughly. "Nothing was right without you."

"I'm here now," I say. "I never want to be apart from you again."

His next words come out fierce. "We won't give them a chance." Then he's kissing me with ardor to match, stealing my breath.

The moment his pants are loosened, he enters me, filling me to the brim, his tongue delving between my lips at the same time. I'm so sensitized now, so adrift on the pleasure of this moment and the moments before, that I'm spiraling toward my peak with just his first few thrusts.

I try to hold on, reveling in the exquisite stretch of August's hardness inside me, in the tender words that tumble from his mouth, but it's a losing battle. I clench around him, and he joins me with a ragged grunt.

August caresses my cheek as he gives me one last, lingering kiss, so sweet my heart aches with it. Then he eases back to make room for Sylas, who's been stroking his fingers over my naked skin.

The Seelie arch-lord gathers me against him. He steals a quick kiss before pulling back to meet my eyes. "Will you welcome one more of your mates, my love?" he asks hoarsely.

As if he needs to protect me from himself. As if I don't want him, need him, just as much as the others.

"I couldn't want anything more," I say, tugging him back to me. I didn't realize how just empty I felt trapped among the Murk until now, with all my mates around me.

Sylas lies me back down on the floor of the carriage, his powerful frame braced over me. He kisses my mouth and down my neck to my chest, where he sucks one nipple and then the other into his mouth. I squirm with the sparks of pleasure, my sex throbbing again for this final act of completion. My chest hitches. "I need you."

Sylas growls, and if he meant to take this slower, that intention must vanish with my plea. I raise my knees, and he presses forward to meet me, filling me slowly but steadily until I'm gasping with the blaze of sensation. At this point, it's all I can do to cling onto him and ride the maelstrom, spinning into bliss with every pump of his hips into mine, losing myself with a shudder that spreads even more delight all through my body.

The Seelie arch-lord comes in me with a fresh flood of heat. Then he rolls off me and eases my body up into a sitting position again, so all of my mates can gather around me.

In their ring of heat and adoration, I let my muscles go slack. Now that the wrenching compulsion for connection has been satisfied, my previous exhaustion is rolling back in.

But it doesn't pull me completely under. As my mates murmur more words of affection and fond caresses, memories of everything beyond this moment start creeping back in.

The impending war. The curse. Orion and his horrible Heart.

I jerk back into alertness. "We have to get back. There must—in the winter realm, the curse, it's taken more people. And the full moon is in two days?"

Corwin kisses my temple. "You needed this closeness to be yourself again," he says. "We'll speed back—if you're up for the journey now? It won't help anyone to push yourself after the ordeal you've already experienced."

I squeeze his hand. "I think I'm up to a carriage ride." I can nap during the trip back. And then—

Another thought strikes me, so hard and piercing I flinch. My mates ease back. "What's wrong?" August asks, his body already tensing to leap to my defense.

"I—" I don't know how to tell them this. I've just

realized that they don't know the facts I've come to accept over the past several days—they don't know how entangled both I and my powers are with the leader of the Murk and the magic he wields.

Would they even have wanted to share this interlude with me if they did?

My expression brings a shadow across Sylas's face. "Whatever you're facing, we'll see it through with you. You can tell us."

How can I admit to them that I'm the tool of their greatest enemy, an instrument meant to bring about their downfall?

But I have to. I can't hide this from them. The fear of what could happen to *them* is already gnawing at me with every moment I stay silent.

"There's a lot I have to tell all of you," I say, the words stinging my throat on the way up. "But we should go back to the Heart as quickly as we can. I'll tell you on the way there."

Whitt glances across the hazy forest toward a wooden carriage that he and his half-brothers must have arrived in. "Why don't we take our craft, then? It's larger."

"Of course." Corwin glances at me with curiosity and concern, but he doesn't press for me to speak right away.

We pull our clothes back into order and clamber out of the gleaming winter carriage. The Unseelie arch-lord dismisses it with a few words and gestures, leaving a sheen of frost on the ground that melts within seconds. We settle into the summer carriage without delay.

I sit in the widest middle seat with August and Whitt

on either side of me, Corwin across from me, and Sylas setting the vehicle into motion from the helm. As it weaves between the trees, he moves to lean against the starboard side between the two benches, watching me.

Whitt gives my knee a gentle squeeze. "Go ahead, mite."

My throat constricts. All at once, my eyes are burning with tears.

I force the words out before my mates get too caught up in worrying about me to really listen. "I—I found out where my powers come from, and why I can heal the curse. It's all because of the Murk."

My mates stay still and silent as I lay out everything important that happened and everything I learned, from the moment Donovan's pack-kin led me into the woods through to my escape from the Refuge. When I stumble over some parts, August grasps my hand, and Whitt slips his arm behind my back.

I can sense the tension in all of their stances, but they don't withdraw from me. Not yet, anyway.

When I finish, there's another long moment of silence. Corwin extends a tendril of affection and horror at my mistreatment my way, but I can tell he's disturbed by more than just that.

He glances at Sylas. "Can we trust the cure she offers, then? The Murk may have worked something worse into it, something that'll harm us more in the long run."

"Orion didn't mention anything about it working that way," I say. "He said the point of the curse was so that all the fae of the Mists would start counting on me, so it'd hurt you when he took me away. But... there could be more to it that he didn't talk about."

"It could all have been lies," August says abruptly. "There's nothing *stopping* them from lying. Even if they've made some kind of false Heart, for it to give them enough power that they could cast a spell that huge... It's impossible, isn't it?" He sounds more hopeful than certain.

Sylas shakes his head. "I don't know. I'd have thought an awful lot of things we've seen the Murk do in the past few months were impossible, but yet they happened. And it explains a lot of things that I didn't fully understand before." He pauses. "Aerik even told me that the reason he and his cadre came out of the Mists the night they stumbled on Talia, they were hunting down a rat. One of the Murk led them right to her."

A shiver passes through me, even though it's only confirmation of what I already knew. "I thought I was connected to the Heart of the Mists—everyone was saying I was blessed. But it's not that at all. It was the Murk's magic all along." The power in me comes from that horrible orange mass with its jittering light. Just the memory of it makes my skin crawl.

"That might not be true," Whitt says thoughtfully, still running his hand up and down my back in a soothing motion. "You said this Orion and the other Murk didn't show any sign of suspecting you could use true names. They left the bracelet on you and had no idea you might have used it to form a wrench. *That* power didn't come from them. Perhaps the Heart of the Mists recognized what you could do for us and welcomed you regardless of the Murk's intentions."

"Its powers do work in inexplicable ways," Corwin says.

"So what do we do now?" I have to ask.

Sylas rubs his jaw. "I think we'll return to the Heart of the Mists as quickly as we can and consult with our fellow arch-lords. Talia is ours far more than the Murk's now. We'll let nothing challenge that. But how to proceed with the curse—we should come to a consensus that the entire rulership is satisfied with."

I don't know what's worse: the thought that people might die while I stand back because the arch-lords are too suspicious of the source of my cure, or the thought that I might hurt the sickening fae worse if I do cure them. But the rest of Sylas's words and the obvious agreement from my other mates reassures me. They're not casting me aside.

Tears well up anyway, all the emotions that've been churning inside me spilling over. August hugs me to him and grabs a folded blanket they had ready, tucking it around me.

"You've been through a lot," he says. "And you met it with as much courage as I could expect from any of our warriors. Get some rest. You're not on your own anymore."

I'm tired enough that I manage to sleep cuddled up against him for the rest of the brisk flight home. When we reach the Heart, I wake up just enough to walk groggily to my bedroom in the border castle. The last thing I remember is August lowering me onto the bed.

When I wake up next, I'm alone in the room, unsure

how much time has passed. My head still feels muddled, my chest heavy, but I can't bear to doze any longer.

I push myself onto my feet and limp through the halls to a room on the summer side with a balcony. As I step out, fresh sweet air tickles over my skin. I breathe it in deeply, savoring it, but it doesn't release much of the tension inside me.

In the distance, my pack-kin are moving around the pack village and the castle of Hearth-by-the-Heart. I turn toward the true Heart itself. The glowing white mass, like a ball of pure sunlight, pulses in its steady rhythm just south of the balcony.

The ripples of its energy flow over me with the warm breeze, momentarily soothing. But do they feel quite as strong as they used to?

I frown, stepping all the way to that side of the balcony. It's hard to remember exactly how big the Heart of the Mists was before, exactly how potent its magic. Maybe I'm imagining things. Still, cold fingers close around my gut inside of the summer heat.

This Heart may have embraced me. My mates may have happily welcomed me back. But Orion is still out there with the Heart of his own making, and I'm connected to him too whether I like it or not.

The one thing I know for sure is that he'll stop at nothing to use me to destroy everyone and everything here I care about.

ABOUT THE AUTHOR

Eva Chase lives in Canada with her family. She loves stories both swoony and supernatural, and strong women and the men who appreciate them. Along with the Bound to the Fae series, she is the author of the Flirting with Monsters series, the Cursed Studies trilogy, the Royals of Villain Academy series, the Moriarty's Men series, the Looking Glass Curse trilogy, the Their Dark Valkyrie series, the Witch's Consorts series, the Dragon Shifter's Mates series, the Demons of Fame Romance series, the Legends Reborn trilogy, and the Alpha Project Psychic Romance series.

Connect with Eva online:
www.evachase.com
eva@evachase.com